The First Advance Comment on Tom Sharpe:

"Tom Sharpe's comedy is exuberantly—I don't suppose 'gloriously' can be the right word—base-hearted. His characters, quite by their own lights, get into relentlessly magnetic, intricately horrible fixes that no one but his characters could deserve or come out of. America has deserved Sharpe for some time, and now at last we have him. At his best…he is far more satisfying than Kingsley Amis or any other nasty Brit novelist since Evelyn Waugh."—Roy Blount, Jr.

Wilt

Tom Sharpe

Vintage Books
A Division of Random House
New York

First Vintage Books Edition, April 1984
Copyright © 1976 by Tom Sharpe
All rights reserved under International and Pan-American
Copyright Conventions. Published in the United States by
Random House, Inc., New York. Originally published in Great
Britain by Martin Secker & Warburg Ltd., London, in 1976.
First American Edition.

Library of Congress Cataloging in Publication Data
Sharpe, Tom.
Wilt.
I. Title.
[PR6069.H345W49 1984]   823'.914   83-40336
ISBN 0-394-72418-6 (pbk.)

Manufactured in the United States of America

for Meat One

1

Whenever Henry Wilt took the dog for a walk, or, to be more accurate, when the dog took him, or, to be exact, when Mrs Wilt told them both to go and take themselves out of the house so that she could do her yoga exercises, he always took the same route. In fact the dog followed the route and Wilt followed the dog. They went down past the Post Office, across the playground, under the railway bridge and out on to the footpath by the river. A mile along the river and then under the railway line again and back through streets where the houses were bigger than Wilt's semi and where there were large trees and gardens and the cars were all Rovers and Mercedes. It was here that Clem, a pedigree Labrador, evidently feeling more at home, did his business while Wilt stood looking around rather uneasily, conscious that this was not his sort of neighbourhood and wishing it was. It was about the only time during their walk that he was at all aware of his surroundings. For the rest of the way Wilt's walk was an interior one and followed an itinerary completely at variance with his own appearance and that of his route. It was in fact a journey of wishful thinking, a pilgrimage along trails of remote possibility involving the irrevocable disappearance of Mrs Wilt, the sudden acquisition of wealth, power, what he would do if he was appointed Minister of Education or, better still, Prime Minister. It was partly concocted of a series of desperate expedients and partly in an unspoken dialogue so that anyone noticing Wilt (and most people didn't) might have seen his lips move occasionally and his mouth curl into what he fondly imagined was a sardonic smile as he dealt with questions or parried arguments with devastating repartee. It was on one of these walks taken in the rain after a particularly trying day at the Tech that Wilt first conceived the notion that he would only be able to fulfil his latent promise and call his life his own if some not entirely fortuitous disaster overtook his wife.

Like everything else in Henry Wilt's life it was not a sudden decision. He was not a decisive man. Ten years as an Assistant

Lecturer (Grade Two) at the Fenland College of Arts and Technology was proof of that. For ten years he had remained in the Liberal Studies Department teaching classes of Gasfitters, Plasterers, Bricklayers and Plumbers. Or keeping them quiet. And for ten long years he had spent his days going from classroom to classroom with two dozen copies of *Sons and Lovers* or Orwell's *Essays* or *Candide* or *The Lord of the Flies* and had done his damnedest to extend the sensibilities of Day-Release Apprentices with notable lack of success.

'Exposure to Culture', Mr Morris, the Head of Liberal Studies, called it but from Wilt's point of view it looked more like his own exposure to barbarism, and certainly the experience had undermined the ideals and illusions which had sustained him in his younger days. So had twelve years of marriage to Eva.

If Gasfitters could go through life wholly impervious to the emotional significance of the interpersonal relationships portrayed in *Sons and Lovers*, and coarsely amused by D. H. Lawrence's profound insight into the sexual nature of existence, Eva Wilt was incapable of such detachment. She hurled herself into cultural activities and self-improvement with an enthusiasm that tormented Wilt. Worse still, her notion of culture varied from week to week, sometimes embracing Barbara Cartland and Anya Seton, sometimes Ouspensky, sometimes Kenneth Clark, but more often the instructor at the Pottery Class on Tuesdays or the lecturer on Transcendental Meditation on Thursdays, so that Wilt never knew what he was coming home to except a hastily cooked supper, some forcibly expressed opinions about his lack of ambition, and a half-baked intellectual eclecticism that left him disoriented.

To escape from the memory of Gasfitters as putative human beings and of Eva in the lotus position, Wilt walked by the river thinking dark thoughts, made darker still by the knowledge that for the fifth year running his application to be promoted to Senior Lecturer was almost certain to be turned down and that unless he did something soon he would be doomed to Gasfitters Three and Plasterers Two – and to Eva – for the rest of his life. It was not a prospect to be borne. He

8

would act decisively. Above his head a train thundered by. Wilt stood watching its dwindling lights and thought about accidents involving level crossings.

'He's in such a funny state these days,' said Eva Wilt, 'I don't know what to make of him.'

'I've given up trying with Patrick,' said Mavis Mottram studying Eva's vase critically. 'I think I'll put the lupin just a fraction of an inch to the left. Then it will help to emphasize the oratorical qualities of the rose. Now the iris over here. One must try to achieve an almost *audible* effect of contrasting colours. Contrapuntal, one might say.'

Eva nodded and sighed. 'He used to be so energetic,' she said, 'but now he just sits about the house watching telly. It's as much as I can do to get him to take the dog for a walk.'

'He probably misses the children,' said Mavis. 'I know Patrick does.'

'That's because he has some to miss,' said Eva Wilt bitterly. 'Henry can't even whip up the energy to have any.'

'I'm so sorry, Eva. I forgot,' said Mavis, adjusting the lupin so that it clashed more significantly with a geranium.

'There's no need to be sorry,' said Eva, who didn't number self-pity among her failings, 'I suppose I should be grateful. I mean, imagine having children like Henry. He's so uncreative, and besides children are so tiresome. They take up all one's creative energy.'

Mavis Mottram moved away to help someone else to achieve a contrapuntal effect, this time with nasturtiums and hollyhocks in a cerise bowl. Eva fiddled with her rose. Mavis was so lucky. She had Patrick, and Patrick Mottram was such an energetic man. Eva, in spite of her size, placed great emphasis on energy, energy and creativity, so that even quite sensible people who were not unduly impressionable found themselves exhausted after ten minutes in her company. In the lotus position at her yoga class she managed to exude energy, and her attempts at Transcendental Meditation had been likened to a pressure-cooker on simmer. And with creative energy there came enthusiasm, the febrile enthusiasms of the evidently unfulfilled woman for whom each new idea heralds the dawn of a new day and vice versa. Since the ideas she espoused were either trite or incomprehensible to her, her attachment to them was correspondingly brief and did nothing to fill the gap left in her life by Henry Wilt's lack of attainment. While he lived a violent life in his imagination, Eva, lacking any imagination at all, lived violently in fact. She threw herself into things, situations, new friends, groups and happenings with a reckless abandon that concealed the fact that she lacked the emotional stamina to stay for more than a moment. Now, as she backed away from her vase, she bumped into someone behind her.

'I beg your pardon,' she said and turned to find herself looking into a pair of dark eyes.

'No need to apologize,' said the woman in an American accent. She was slight and dressed with a simple scruffiness that was beyond Eva Wilt's moderate income.

'I'm Eva Wilt,' said Eva, who had once attended a class on Getting to Know People at the Oakrington Village College. 'My husband lectures at the Tech and we live at 34 Parkview Avenue.'

'Sally Pringsheim,' said the woman with a smile. 'We're in Rossiter Grove. We're over on a sabbatical. Gaskell's a biochemist.'

Eva Wilt accepted the distinctions and congratulated herself on her perspicacity about the blue jeans and the sweater. People who lived in Rossiter Grove were a cut above Parkview Avenue and husbands who were biochemists on sabbatical were also in the University. Eva Wilt's world was made up of such nuances.

'You know, I'm not at all that sure I could live with an oratorical rose,' said Sally Pringsheim. 'Symphonies are OK in auditoriums but I can do without them in vases.'

Eva stared at her with a mixture of astonishment and admiration. To be openly critical of Mavis Mottram's flower arrangements was to utter blasphemy in Parkview Avenue. 'You know, I've always wanted to say that,' she said with a sudden surge of warmth, 'but I've never had the courage.'

Sally Pringsheim smiled. 'I think one should always say what one thinks. Truth is so essential in any really meaningful relationship. I always tell G baby exactly what I'm thinking.'

'Gee baby?' said Eva Wilt.

'Gaskell's my husband,' said Sally. 'Not that he's really a husband. It's just that we've got this open-ended arrangement for living together. Sure, we're legal and all that, but I think it's important sexually to keep one's options open, don't you?'

By the time Eva got home her vocabulary had come to include several new words. She found Wilt in bed pretending to be asleep and woke him up and told him about Sally Pringsheim. Wilt turned over and tried to go back to sleep wishing to God she had stuck to her contrapuntal flower arrangements. Sexually open-ended freewheeling options were the last thing he wanted just now, and, coming from the wife of a biochemist who could afford to live in Rossiter Grove, didn't augur well for the future. Eva Wilt was too easily influenced by wealth, intellectual status and new acquaintances to be allowed out with a woman who believed that clitoral stimulation oralwise was a concomitant part of a fully emancipated relationship and that unisex was here to stay. Wilt had enough troubles with his own virility without having Eva demand that her conjugal rights be supplemented oralwise. He spent a restless night thinking dark thoughts about accidental deaths involving fast trains, level crossings, their Ford Escort and Eva's seat belt, and got up early and made himself breakfast. He was just going off to a nine o'clock lecture to Motor Mechanics Three when Eva came downstairs with a dreamy look on her face.

'I've just remembered something I wanted to ask you last night,' she said. 'What does "transexual diversification" mean?'

'Writing poems about queers,' said Wilt hastily and went out to the car. He drove down Parkview Avenue and got stuck in a traffic jam at the roundabout. He sat and cursed silently. He was thirty-four and his talents were being dissipated on MM 3 and a woman who was clearly educationally subnormal. Worst

11

of all, he had to recognize the truth of Eva's constant criticism that he wasn't a man. 'If you were a proper man,' she was always saying, 'you would show more initiative. You've got to assert yourself.'

Wilt asserted himself at the roundabout and got into an altercation with a man in a mini-bus. As usual, he came off second best.

'The problem with Wilt as I see it is that he lacks drive,' said the Head of English, himself a nerveless man with a tendency to see and solve problems with a degree of equivocation that made good his natural lack of authority.

The Promotions Committee nodded its joint head for the fifth year running.

'He may lack drive but he *is* committed,' said Mr Morris, fighting his annual rearguard on Wilt's behalf.

'Committed?' said the Head of Catering with a snort. 'Committed to what? Abortion, Marxism or promiscuity? It's bound to be one of the three. I've yet to come across a Liberal Studies lecturer who wasn't a crank, a pervert or a red-hot revolutionary and a good many have been all three.'

'Hear, hear,' said the Head of Mechanical Engineering, on whose lathes a demented student had once turned out several pipe bombs.

Mr Morris bristled. 'I grant you that one or two lecturers have been ... er ... a little overzealous politically but I resent the imputation that ...'

'Let's leave generalities aside and get back to Wilt,' said the Vice-Principal. 'You were saying that he is committed.'

'He needs encouragement,' said Mr Morris. 'Damn it, the man has been with us ten years and he's still only Grade Two.'

'That's precisely what I mean about his lacking drive,' said the Head of English. 'If he had been worth promoting he'd have been a Senior Lecturer by now.'

'I must say I agree,' said the Head of Geography. 'Any man who is content to spend ten years taking Gasfitters and Plumbers is clearly unfit to hold an administrative post.'

'Do we always have to promote solely for administrative

reasons?' Mr Morris asked wearily. 'Wilt happens to be a good teacher.'

'If I may just make a point,' said Dr Mayfield, the Head of Sociology, 'at this moment in time it is vital we bear in mind that, in the light of the forthcoming introduction of the Joint Honours degree in Urban Studies and Medieval Poetry, provisional approval for which degree by the Council of National Academic Awards I am happy to announce at least in principle, that we maintain a viable staff position in regard to Senior Lectureships by allocating places for candidates with specialist knowledge in particular spheres of academic achievement rather than—'

'If I may just interrupt for a moment, in or out of time,' said Dr Board, Head of Modern Languages, 'are you saying we should have Senior Lectureships for highly qualified specialists who can't teach rather than promote Assistant Lecturers without doctorates who can?'

'If Dr Board had allowed me to continue,' said Dr Mayfield, 'he would have understood that I was saying . . .'

'I doubt it,' said Dr Board, 'quite apart from your syntax . . .'

And so for the fifth year running Wilt's promotion was forgotten. The Fenland College of Arts and Technology was expanding. New degree courses proliferated and more students with fewer qualifications poured in to be taught by more staff with higher qualifications until one day the Tech would cease to be a mere Tech and rise in status to become a Poly. It was the dream of every Head of Department and in the process Wilt's self-esteem and the hopes of Eva Wilt were ignored.

Wilt heard the news before lunch in the canteen.

'I'm sorry, Henry,' said Mr Morris as they lined up with their trays, 'it's this wretched economic squeeze. Even Modern Languages had to take a cut. They only got two promotions through.'

Wilt nodded. It was what he had come to expect. He was in the wrong department, in the wrong marriage and in the wrong life. He took his fish fingers across to a table in the corner and ate by himself. Around him other members of staff sat discussing A-level prospects and who was going to sit on the course board next term. They taught Maths or Economics or English, subjects that counted and where promotion was easy. Liberal Studies didn't count and promotion was out of the question. It was as simple as that. Wilt finished his lunch and went up to the reference library to look up Insulin in the Pharmacopoeia. He had an idea it was the one untraceable poison.

At five to two, none the wiser, he went down to Room 752 to extend the sensibilities of fifteen apprentice butchers, designated on the timetable as Meat One. As usual they were late and drunk.

'We've been drinking Bill's health,' they told him when they drifted in at ten past two.

'Really?' said Wilt, handing out copies of *The Lord of the Flies*. 'And how is he?'

'Bloody awful,' said a large youth with 'Stuff Off' painted across the back of his leather jacket. 'He's puking his guts out. It's his birthday and he had four Vodkas and a Babycham . . .'

'We'd got to the part where Piggy is in the forest,' said Wilt, heading them off a discussion of what Bill had drunk for his birthday. He reached for a board duster and rubbed a drawing of a Dutch Cap off the blackboard.

'That's Mr Sedgwick's trademark,' said one of the butchers, 'he's always going on about contraceptives and things. He's got a thing about them.'

'A thing about them?' said Wilt loyally.

'You know, birth control. Well, he used to be a Catholic, didn't he? And now he's not, he's making up for lost time,' said a small pale-faced youth unwrapping a Mars Bar.

'Someone should tell him about the pill,' said another youth lifting his head somnolently from the desk. 'You can't feel a thing with a Frenchie. You get more thrill with the pill.'

'I suppose you do,' said Wilt, 'but I understood there were side-effects.'

'Depends which side you want it,' said a lad with sideburns.

Wilt turned back to *The Lord of the Flies* reluctantly. He had read the thing two hundred times already.

'Now Piggy goes into the forest ...' he began, only to be stopped by another butcher, who evidently shared his distaste for the misfortunes of Piggy.

'You only get bad effects with the pill if you use ones that are high in oestrogen.'

'That's very interesting,' said Wilt. 'Oestrogen? You seem to know a lot about it.'

'Old girl down our street got a bloodclot in her leg ...'

'Silly old clot,' said the Mars Bar.

'Listen,' said Wilt. 'Either we hear what Peter has to tell us about the effects of the pill or we get on and read about Piggy.'

'Fuck Piggy,' said the sideburns.

'Right,' said Wilt heartily, 'then keep quiet.'

'Well,' said Peter, 'this old girl, well she wasn't all that old, maybe thirty, she was on the pill and she got this bloodclot and the doctor told my auntie it was the oestrogen and she'd better take a different sort of pill just in case and the old girl down the street, her old man had to go and have a vasectomy so's she wouldn't have another bloodclot.'

'Buggered if anyone's going to get me to have a vasectomy,' said the Mars Bar, 'I want to know I'm all there.'

'We all have ambitions,' said Wilt.

'Nobody's going to hack away at my knackers with a bloody great knife,' said the sideburns.

'Nobody'd want to,' said someone else.

'What about the bloke whose missus you banged,' said the Mars Bar. 'I bet he wouldn't mind having a go.'

Wilt applied the sanction of Piggy again and got them back on to vasectomy.

'Anyway, it's not irreversible any more,' said Peter. 'They can put a tiny little gold tap in and you can turn it on when you want a nipper.'

'Go on! That's not true.'

'Well, not on the National Health you can't, but if you pay they can. I read about it in a magazine. They've been doing experiments in America.'

'What happens if the washer goes wrong?' asked the Mars Bar.

'I suppose they call a plumber in.'

Wilt sat and listened while Meat One ranged far and wide about vasectomy and the coil and Indians getting free transistors and the plane that landed at Audley End with a lot of illegal immigrants and what somebody's brother who was a policeman in Brixton said about blacks and how the Irish were just as bad and bombs and back to Catholics and birth control and who'd want to live in Ireland where you couldn't even buy French letters and so back to the Pill. And all the time his mind filled itself obsessively with ways and means of getting rid of Eva. A diet of birth-control pills high on oestrogen? If he ground them up and mixed them with the Ovaltine she took at bedtime there was a chance she'd develop bloodclots all over the place in no time at all. Wilt put the notion out of his head. Eva with bloodclots was too awful to stomach, and anyway it might not work. No, it would have to be something quick, certain and painless. Preferably an accident.

At the end of the hour Wilt collected the books and made his way back to the Staff Room. He had a free period. On the way he passed the site of the new Administration block. The ground had been cleared and the builders had moved in and were boring pile holes for the foundations. Wilt stopped and watched as the drilling machine wound slowly down into the ground. They were making wide holes. Very wide. Big enough for a body.

'How deep are you going?' he asked one of the workmen.

'Thirty feet.'

'Thirty feet?' said Wilt. 'When's the concrete going in?'

'Monday, with any luck,' said the man.

Wilt passed on. A new and quite horrible idea had just occurred to him.

2

It was one of Eva Wilt's better days. She had days, better days, and one of those days. Days were just days when nothing went wrong and she got the washing-up done and the front room vacuumed and the windows washed and the beds made and the bath Vimmed and the lavatory pan Harpicked and went round to the Harmony Community Centre and helped with Xeroxing or sorted old clothes for the Jumble Sale and generally made herself useful and came home for lunch and went to the library and had tea with Mavis or Susan or Jean and talked about life and how seldom Henry made love to her even perfunctorily nowadays and how she had missed her opportunity by refusing a bank clerk who was a manager now and came home and made Henry's supper and went out to Yoga or Flower Arrangement or Meditation or Pottery and finally climbed into bed with the feeling that she had got something done.

On one of those days nothing went right. The activities were exactly the same but each episode was tainted with some minor disaster like the fuse blowing on the vacuum-cleaner or the drain in the sink getting blocked with a piece of carrot so that by the time Henry came home he was either greeted by silence or subjected to a quite unwarranted exposé of all his faults and shortcomings. On one of those days Wilt usually took the dog for an extended walk via the Ferry Path Inn and spent a restless night getting up and going to the bathroom, thus nullifying the cleansing qualities of the Harpic Eva had puffed round the pan and providing her with a good excuse to point out his faults once again in the morning.

'What the hell am I supposed to do?' he had asked after one of those nights. 'If I pull the chain you grumble because I've woken you up and if I don't you say it looks nasty in the morning.'

'Well, it does, and in any case you don't have to wash all the Harpic off the sides. And don't say you don't. I've seen you. You aim it all the way round so that it all gets taken off. You do it quite deliberately.'

'If I pulled the chain it would all get flushed off anyway and you'd get woken up into the bargain,' Wilt told her, conscious that he did make a habit of aiming at the Harpic. He had a grudge against the stuff.

'Why can't you just wait until the morning? And anyway it serves you right,' she continued, forestalling his obvious answer, 'for drinking all that beer. You're supposed to be taking Clem for a walk, not swilling ale in that horrid pub.'

'To pee or not to pee, that is the question,' said Wilt helping himself to All-Bran. 'What do you expect me to do? Tie a knot in the damned thing?'

'It wouldn't make any difference to me if you did,' said Eva bitterly.

'It would make a hell of a lot of difference to me, thank you very much.'

'I was talking about our sex life and you know it.'

'Oh, that,' said Wilt.

But that was on one of those days.

On one of her better days something unexpected happened to inject the daily round with a new meaning and to awake in her those dormant expectations that somehow everything would suddenly change for the better and stay that way. It was on such expectations that her faith in life was based. They were the spiritual equivalent of the trivial activities that kept her busy and Henry subdued. On one of her better days the sun shone brighter, the floor in the hall gleamed brighter and Eva Wilt was brighter herself and hummed 'Some day my prince will come' while Hoovering the stairs. On one of her better days Eva went forth to meet the world with a disarming goodheartedness and awoke in others the very same expectations that so thrilled her in herself. And on one of her better days Henry had to get his own supper and if he was wise kept out of the house as long as possible. Eva Wilt's expectations demanded something a sight more invigorating than Henry Wilt after a day at the Tech. It was on the evenings of such days that he came nearest to genuinely deciding to murder her and to hell with the consequences.

*

On this particular day she was on her way to the Community Centre when she ran into Sally Pringsheim. It was one of those entirely fortuitous meetings that resulted from Eva making her way on foot instead of by bicycle and going through Rossiter Grove instead of straight down Parkview Avenue which was half a mile shorter. Sally was just driving out of the gate in a Mercedes with a P registration which meant it was brand new. Eva noted the fact and smiled accordingly.

'How funny me running into you like this,' she said brightly as Sally stopped the car and unlocked the door.

'Can I give you a lift? I'm going into town to look for something casual to wear tonight. Gaskell's got some Swedish professor coming over from Heidelberg and we're taking him to Ma Tante's.'

Eva Wilt climbed in happily, her mind computing the cost of the car and the house and the significance of wearing something casual at Ma Tante's (where she had heard that starters like Prawn Cocktails cost 95p) and the fact that Dr Pringsheim entertained Swedish professors when they came to Ipford.

'I was going to walk to town,' she lied. 'Henry's taken the car and it's such a lovely day.'

'Gaskell's bought a bicycle. He says it's quicker and it keeps him fit,' said Sally, thus condemning Henry Wilt to yet another misfortune. Eva made a note to see that he bought a bike at the police auction and cycled to work in rain or snow. 'I was thinking of trying Felicity Fashions for a shantung poncho. I don't know what they're like but I've been told they're good. Professor Grant's wife goes there and she says they have the best selection.'

'I'm sure they must have,' said Eva Wilt, whose patronage of Felicity Fashions had consisted of looking in the window and wondering who on earth could afford dresses at forty pounds. Now she knew. They drove into town and parked in the multi-storey car park. By that time Eva had stored a lot more information about the Pringsheims in her memory. They came from California. Sally had met Gaskell while hitch-hiking through Arizona. She had been to Kansas State but had dropped out to live on a commune. There had been other men in her life. Gaskell loathed cats. They gave him hay fever. Women's Lib meant more than burning your bra. It meant total commitment to the programme of women's superiority over men. Love was great if you didn't let it get to you. Compost was in and colour TV out. Gaskell's father had owned a chain of stores which was sordid. Money was handy and Rossiter Grove was a bore. Above all, fucking had to be, just *had* to be fun whichever way you looked at it.

Eva Wilt received this information with a jolt. In her circle 'fuck' was a word husbands used when they hit their thumbs with hammers. When Eva used it she did so in the isolation of the bathroom and with a wistfulness that robbed it of its crudity and imbued it with a splendid virility so that a good fuck became the most distant and abstract of all her expectations and quite removed from Henry's occasional early morning fumblings. And if 'fuck' was reserved for the bathroom, fucking was even more remote. It suggested an almost continuous activity, a familiar occurrence that was both casual and satisfying and added a new dimension to life. Eva Wilt stumbled out of the car and followed Sally to Felicity Fashions in a state of shock.

If fucking was fun, shopping with Sally Pringsheim was a revelation. It was marked by a decisiveness that was truly breathtaking. Where Eva would have hummed and haaed, Sally selected and having selected moved on down the racks, discarded things she didn't like leaving them hanging over chairs, seized others, glanced at them and said she supposed they would do with a bored acceptance that was infectious, and left the shop with a pile of boxes containing two hundred pounds' worth of shantung ponchos, silk summer coats, scarves and blouses. Eva Wilt had spent seventy on a pair of yellow lounging pyjamas and a raincoat with lapels and a belt that Sally said was pure Gatsby.

'Now all you need is the hat and you'll be it,' she said as they loaded the boxes into the car. They bought the hat, a trilby, and then had coffee at the Mombasa Coffee House where Sally leant across the table intensely, smoking a long thin cigar, and talking about body contact in a loud voice so that Eva was conscious that the women at several nearby tables had stopped talking and were listening rather disapprovingly.

'Gaskell's nipples drive me wild,' Sally said. 'They drive him wild too when I suck them.'

Eva drank her coffee and wondered what Henry would do if she took it into her head to suck his nipples. Drive him wild was hardly the word and besides she was beginning to regret having spent seventy pounds. That would drive him wild too. Henry didn't approve of credit cards. But she was enjoying herself too much to let the thought of his reaction spoil her day.

'I think teats are so important,' Sally went on. Two women at the next table paid their bill and walked out.

'I suppose they must be,' said Eva Wilt uneasily. 'I've never had much use for mine.'

'Haven't you?' said Sally. 'We'll have to do something about that.'

'I don't see that there is much anyone can do about it,' said Eva. 'Henry never takes his pyjamas off and my nightie gets in the way.'

'Don't tell me you wear things in bed. Oh you poor thing. And nighties, God, how humiliating for you! I mean it's typical of a male-dominated society, all this costume differentiation. You must be suffering from touch deprivation. Gaskell says it's as bad as vitamin deficiency.'

'Well, Henry is always tired when he gets home,' Eva told her. 'And I go out a lot.'

'I'm not surprised,' said Sally, 'Gaskell says male fatigue is a symptom of penile insecurity. Is Henry's big or small?'

'Well it depends,' said Eva hoarsely. 'Sometimes it's big and sometimes it isn't.'

'I much prefer men with small ones,' said Sally, 'they try so much harder.'

They finished their coffee and went back to the car discussing Gaskell's penis and his theory that in a sexually undifferentiated society nipple stimulation would play an increasingly important role in developing the husband's sense of his hermaphroditic nature.

'He's written an article on it,' Sally said as they drove home. 'It's called "The Man As Mother". It was published in *Suck* last year.'

'Suck?' said Eva.

'Yes, it's a journal published by the Society for Undifferentiated Sexual Studies in Kansas. G's done a lot of work for them on animal behaviour. He did his thesis on Role Play in Rats there.'

'That sounds very interesting,' said Eva uncertainly. Roll or role? Whichever it was it was impressive and certainly Henry's occasional pieces on Day Release Apprentices and Literature in the *Liberal Studies Quarterly* hardly measured up to Dr Pringsheim's monographs.

'Oh I don't know. It's all so obvious really. If you put two male rats together in a cage long enough one of them is simply bound to develop active tendencies and the other passive ones,' said Sally wearily. 'But Gaskell was absolutely furious. He thought they ought to alternate. That's G all over. I told him how silly he was being. I said, "G honey, rats are practically undifferentiated anyway. I mean how can you expect them to be able to make an existential choice?" and you know what he said? He said, "Pubic baby, rats are the paradigm. Just remember that and you won't go far wrong. Rats are the paradigm." What do you think of that?'

'I think rats are rather horrid,' said Eva without thinking. Sally laughed and put her hand on her knee.

'Oh Eva, darling,' she murmured, 'you're so adorably down to earth. No, I'm not taking you back to Parkview Avenue. You're coming home with me for a drink and lunch. I'm simply dying to see you in those lemon loungers.'

They turned into Rossiter Grove.

If rats were a paradigm for Dr Pringsheim, Printers Three were a paradigm for Henry Wilt, though of a rather different sort. They represented all that was most difficult, insensitive and downright bloodyminded about Day Release Classes and to make matters worse the sods thought they were literate because they could actually read and Voltaire was an idiot because he made everything go wrong for Candide. Coming after Nursery Nurses and during his Stand-In period, Printers Three brought out the worst in him. They had obviously brought out the worst in Cecil Williams who should have been taking them.

'It's the second week he's been off sick,' they told Wilt.

'I'm not at all surprised,' said Wilt. 'You lot are enough to make anyone sick.'

'We had one bloke went and gassed himself. Pinkerton his name was. He took us for a term and made us read this book *Jude the Obscure*. That wasn't half a depressing book. All about this twit Jude.'

'I had an idea it was,' said Wilt.

'Next term old Pinky didn't come back. He went down by the river and stuck a pipe up the exhaust and gassed himself.'

'I can't say I blame him,' said Wilt.

'Well I like that. He was supposed to set us an example.'

Wilt looked at the class grimly.

'I'm sure he had that in mind when he gassed himself,' he said. 'And now if you'll just get on and read quietly, eat quietly and smoke so that no one can see you from the Admin block, I've got work to do.'

'Work? You lot don't know what work is. All you do is sit at a desk all day and read. Call that work? Buggered if I do and they pay you to do it . . .'

'Shut up,' said Wilt with startling violence. 'Shut your stupid trap.'

'Who's going to make me?' said the Printer.

Wilt tried to control his temper and for once found it impossible. There was something incredibly arrogant about Printers Three.

'I am,' he shouted.

'You and who else? You couldn't make a mouse shut its trap, not if you tried all day.'

Wilt stood up. 'You fucking little shit,' he shouted. 'You dirty snivelling . . .'

'I must say, Henry, I'd have expected you to show more restraint,' said the Head of Liberal Studies an hour later when Wilt's nose had stopped bleeding and the Tech Sister had put a Band-Aid on his eyebrow.

'Well it wasn't my class and they got my goat by gloating about Pinkerton's suicide. If Williams hadn't been off sick it wouldn't have happened,' Wilt explained. 'He's always sick when he has to take Printers Three.'

Mr Morris shook his head dispiritedly. 'I don't care who they were. You simply can't go around assaulting students ...'

'Assaulting students? I never touched ...'

'All right, but you did use offensive language. Bob Fenwick was in the next classroom and he heard you call this Allison fellow a fucking little shit and an evil-minded moron. Now, is it any wonder he took a poke at you?'

'I suppose not,' said Wilt. 'I shouldn't have lost my temper. I'm sorry.'

'In that case we'll just forget it happened,' said Mr Morris. 'But just remember if I'm to get you a Senior Lectureship I can't have you blotting your copybook having punch-ups with students.'

'I didn't have a punch-up,' said Wilt, 'he punched me.'

'Well, let's just hope he doesn't go to the police and charge you with assault. That's the last sort of publicity we want.'

'Just take me off Printers Three,' said Wilt, 'I've had my fill of the brutes.'

He went down the corridor and collected his coat and brief-case from the Staff Room. His nose felt twice its normal size and his eyebrow hurt abominably. On his way out to the car park he passed several other members of staff but no one stopped to ask him what had happened. Henry Wilt passed unnoticed out of the Tech and got into his car. He shut the door and sat for several minutes watching the piledrivers at work on the new block. Up, down, up, down. Nails in a coffin. And one day, one inevitable day he would be in his coffin, still unnoticed, still an Assistant Lecturer (Grade Two) and quite forgotten by everyone except some lout in Printers Three who would always remember the day he had punched a

Liberal Studies lecturer on the nose and got away with it. He'd probably boast about it to his grandchildren.

Wilt started the car and drove out on to the main road filled with loathing for Printers Three, the Tech, life in general and himself in particular. He understood now why terrorists were prepared to sacrifice themselves for the good of some cause. Given a bomb and a cause he would cheerfully have blown himself and any innocent bystanders to Kingdom Come just to prove for one glorious if brief moment that he was an effective force. But he had neither bomb nor cause. Instead he drove home recklessly and parked outside 34 Parkview Avenue. Then he unlocked the front door and went inside.

There was a strange smell in the hall. Some sort of perfume. Musky and sweet. He put his brief-case down and looked into the living-room. Eva was evidently out. He went into the kitchen and put the kettle on and felt his nose. He would have a good look at it in the bathroom mirror. He was halfway upstairs and conscious that there was a positively miasmic quality about the perfume when he was brought to a halt. Eva Wilt stood in the bedroom doorway in a pair of astonishingly yellow pyjamas with enormously flared trousers. She looked quite hideous, and to make matters worse she was smoking a long thin cigarette in a long thin holder and her mouth was a brilliant red.

'Penis baby,' she murmured hoarsely and swayed. 'Come in here. I'm going to suck your nipples till you come me oralwise.'

Wilt turned and fled downstairs. The bitch was drunk. It was one of her better days. Without waiting to turn the kettle off, Henry Wilt went out of the front door and got back into the car. He wasn't staying around to have her suck his nipples. He'd had all he could take for one day.

3

Eva Wilt went downstairs and looked for penis baby half-heartedly. For one thing she didn't want to find him and for another she didn't feel like sucking his nipples and for a third she knew she shouldn't have spent seventy pounds on a raincoat and a pair of beach pyjamas she could have got for thirty at Blowdens. She didn't need them and she couldn't see herself walking down Parkview Avenue looking like The Great Gatsby. Besides, she felt a bit sick.

Still, he had left the kettle on so he must be somewhere. It wasn't like Henry to go out and leave the kettle on. She looked in the lounge. It had been the sitting-room until lunchtime when Sally called her sitting-room a lounge. She looked in the dining-room, now the diner, and even in the garden but Henry had vanished, taking with him the car, and her hopes that nipple-sucking would bring new meaning to their marriage and put an end to her body contact deprivation. Finally she gave up the search and made herself a nice pot of tea and sat in the kitchen wondering what on earth had induced her to marry a male chauvinist pig like Henry Wilt who wouldn't have known a good fuck if he had been handed one on a plate and whose idea of a sophisticated evening was a boneless chicken curry at the New Delhi and a performance of *King Lear* at the Guild-hall. Why couldn't she have married someone like Gaskell Pringsheim who entertained Swedish professors at Ma Tante and who understood the importance of clitoral stimulation as a necessary con-something-or-other of a truly satisfying interpersonal penetration? Other people still found her attractive. Patrick Mottram did and so did John Frost who taught her pottery, and Sally had said she was lovely. Eva sat staring into space, the space between the washing-up rack and the Kenwood mixer Henry had given her for Christmas, and thought about Sally and how she had looked at her so strangely when she was changing into her lemon loungers. Sally had stood in the doorway of the Pringsheims' bedroom, smoking a cigar and watching her movements with a sensual calculation that had made Eva blush.

'Darling, you have such a lovely body,' she had said as Eva turned hurriedly and scrambled into the trousers to avoid revealing the hole in her panties. 'You mustn't let it go to waste.'

'Do you really think they suit me?'

But Sally had been staring at her breasts intently. 'Booby baby,' she murmured. Eva Wilt's breasts were prominent and Henry, in one of his many off moments, had once said something about the dugs of hell going dingalingaling for you but not for me. Sally was more appreciative, and had insisted that Eva remove her bra and burn it. They had gone down to the kitchen and had drunk Tequila and had put the bra on a dish with a sprig of holly on it and Sally had poured brandy over it and had set it alight. They had to carry the dish out into the garden because it smelt so horrible and smoked so much and they had lain on the grass laughing as it smouldered. Looking back on the episode Eva regretted her action. It had been a good bra with double-stretch panels designed to give confidence where a woman needs it, as the TV adverts put it. Still, Sally had said she owed it to herself as a free woman and with two drinks inside her Eva was in no mood to argue.

'You've got to feel free,' Sally had said. 'Free to be. Free to be.'

'Free to be what?' said Eva.

'Yourself, darling,' Sally whispered, 'your secret self,' and had touched her tenderly where Eva Wilt, had she been sober and less elated, would staunchly have denied having a self. They had gone back into the house and had lunch, a mixture of more Tequila, salad and Ryvita and cottage cheese which Eva, whose appetite for food was almost as omnivorous as her enthusiasm for new experiences, found unsatisfying. She had hinted as much but Sally had poohpoohed the idea of three good meals a day.

'It's not good caloriewise to have a high starch intake,' she said, 'and besides it's not how much you put into yourself but what. Sex and food, honey, are much the same. A little a lot is better than a lot a little.' She had poured Eva another Tequila, insisted she take a bite of lemon before knocking it back and had helped her upstairs to the big bedroom with the big bed and the big mirror in the ceiling.

'It's time for TT,' she said adjusting the slats of the Venetian blinds.

'Tea tea,' Eva mumbled, 'but we've just had din din.'

'Touch Therapy, darling,' said Sally and pushed her gently back on to the bed. Eva Wilt stared up at her reflection in the mirror; a large woman, two large women in yellow pyjamas lying on a large bed, a large crimson bed; two large women without yellow pyjamas on a large crimson bed; four women naked on a large crimson bed.

'Oh Sally, no Sally.'

'Darling,' said Sally and silenced her protest oralwise. It had been a startlingly new experience though only partly remembered. Eva had fallen asleep before the Touch Therapy had got well under way and had woken an hour later to find Sally fully dressed standing by the bed with a cup of black coffee.

'Oh I do feel bad,' Eva said, referring as much to her moral condition as to her physical.

'Drink this and you'll feel better.'

Eva had drunk the coffee and got dressed while Sally explained that post-contact inhibitory depression was a perfectly natural reaction to Touch Therapy at first.

'You'll find it comes naturally after the first few sessions. You'll probably break down and cry and scream and then feel tremendously liberated and relieved.'

'Do you think so? I'm sure I don't know.'

Sally had driven her home. 'You and Henry must come to our barbecue Thursday night,' she said. 'I know G baby will want to meet you. You'll like him. He's a breast baby. He'll go crazy about you.'

'I tell you she was pissed,' said Wilt as he sat in the Braintrees' kitchen while Peter Braintree opened a bottle of beer for him. 'Pissed and wearing some godawful yellow pyjamas and smoking a cigarette in a long bloody holder.'

'What did she say?'

'Well if you must know, she said, "Come here ..." No, it's too much. I have a perfectly foul day at the Tech. Morris tells me I haven't got my senior lectureship. Williams is off sick again so I lose a free period. I get punched in the face by a great lout in Printers Three and I come home to a drunk wife who calls me penis baby.'

'She called you what?' said Peter Braintree, staring at him.

'You heard me.'

'Eva called you penis baby? I don't believe it.'

'Well you go round there and see what she calls you,' said Wilt bitterly, 'and don't blame me if she sucks your nipples off oralwise while she's about it.'

'Good Lord. Is that what she threatened to do?'

'That and more,' said Wilt.

'It doesn't sound like Eva. It really doesn't.'

'It didn't fucking look like her either, come to that. She was all dolled up in yellow beach pyjamas. You should have seen the colour. It would have made a buttercup look drab. And she'd got some ghastly scarlet lipstick smeared round her mouth and she was smoking ... She hasn't smoked for six years and then all this penis baby nipple-sucking stuff. And oralwise.'

Peter Braintree shook his head. 'That's a filthy word,' he said.

'It's a perfectly filthy act too, if you ask me,' said Wilt.

'Well, I must say it all sounds pretty peculiar,' said Braintree, 'God knows what I'd do if Susan came home and started insisting on sucking my teats.'

'Do what I did. Get out of the house,' said Wilt. 'And anyway it isn't just nipples either. Damn it, we've been married twelve long years. It's a bit late in the day to start arsing about oralwise. The thing is she's on this sexual liberation kick. She came home last night from Mavis Mottram's flower arrangement do jabbering about clitoral stimulation and open-ended freewheeling sexual options.'

'Freewheeling what?'

'Sexual options. Perhaps I've got it wrong. I know sexual options came into it somewhere. I was half asleep at the time.'

'Where the hell did she get all this from?' asked Braintree.

'Some bloody Yank called Sally Pringsheim,' said Wilt. 'You know what Eva's like. I mean she can smell intellectual clap-trap a mile off and homes in on it like a bloody dung-beetle heading for an open sewer. You've no idea how many phoney "latest ideas" I've had to put up with. Well, most of them I can manage to live with. I just let her get on with it and go my own quiet way, but when it comes to participating oralwise while she blathers on about Women's Lib, well you can count me out.'

'What I don't understand about Sexual Freedom and Women's Lib is why you have to go back to the nursery to be liberated,' said Braintree. 'There seems to be this loony idea that you have to be passionately in love all the time.'

'Apes,' said Wilt morosely.

'Apes? What about apes?'

'It's all this business about the animal model. If animals do it then humans must. Territorial Imperative and the Naked Ape. You stand everything on its head and instead of aspiring you retrogress a million years. Hitch your wagon to an orang-outang. The egalitarianism of the lowest common denominator.'

'I don't quite see what that has to do with sex,' said Braintree.

'Nor do I,' said Wilt. They went down to the Pig In A Poke and got drunk.

It was midnight before Wilt got home and Eva was asleep. Wilt climbed surreptitiously into bed and lay in the darkness thinking about high levels of oestrogen.

In Rossiter Grove the Pringsheims came back from Ma Tante's tired and bored.

'Swedes are the bottom,' said Sally as she undressed.

Gaskell sat down and took off his shoes. 'Ungstrom's all right. His wife has just left him for a low-temperature physicist at Cambridge. He's not usually so depressed.'

'You could have fooled me. And talking about wives, I've met the most unliberated woman you've ever set eyes on. Name of Eva Wilt. She's got boobs like cantaloupes.'

'Don't,' said Dr Pringsheim, 'if there's one thing I don't need right now it's unliberated wives with breasts.' He climbed into bed and took his glasses off.

'I had her round here today.'

'Had her?'

Sally smiled, 'Gaskell, honey, you've got a toadsome mind.'

Gaskell Pringsheim smiled myopically at himself in the mirror above. He was proud of his mind. 'I just know you, lover,' he said, 'I know your funny little habits. And while we're on the subject of habits what are all those boxes in the guest room? You haven't been spending money again? You know our budget this month ...'

Sally flounced into bed. 'Budget fudget,' she said, 'I'm sending them all back tomorrow.'

'All?'

'Well, not all, but most. I had to impress booby baby somehow.'

'You didn't have to buy half a shop just to ...'

'Gaskell, honey, if you would just let me finish,' said Sally, 'she's a manic, a lovely, beautiful, obsessive compulsive manic. She can't sit still for half a minute without tidying and cleaning and polishing and washing up.'

'That's all we need, a manic compulsive woman around the house all the time. Who needs two?'

'Two? I'm not manic.'

'You're manic enough for me,' said Gaskell.

'But this one's got boobs, baby, boobs. Anyway I've invited them over on Thursday for the barbecue.'

'What the hell for?'

'Well, if you won't buy me a dishwasher like I've asked you a hundred times, I'm going out to get me one. A nice manic compulsive dishwasher with boobs on.'

'Jesus,' sighed Gaskell, 'are you a bitch.'

'Henry Wilt, you are a sod,' Eva said next morning. Wilt sat up in bed. He felt terrible. His nose was even more painful than the day before, his head ached and he had spent much of the night expunging the Harpic from the bowl in the bathroom.

He was in no mood to be woken and told he was a sod. He looked at the clock. It was eight o'clock and he had Bricklayers Two at nine. He got out of bed and made for the bathroom.

'Did you hear what I said?' Eva demanded, getting out of bed herself.

'I heard,' said Wilt, and saw that she was naked. Eva Wilt naked at eight o'clock in the morning was almost as startling a sight as Eva Wilt drunk, smoking and dressed in lemon yellow pyjamas at six o'clock at night. And even less enticing. 'What the hell are you going about like that for?'

'If it comes to that, what's wrong with your nose? I suppose you got drunk and fell down. It looks all red and swollen.'

'It *is* all red and swollen. And if you must know I didn't fall down. Now for goodness sake get out of the way. I've got a lecture at nine.'

He pushed past her and went into the bathroom and looked at his nose. It looked awful. Eva followed him in. 'If you didn't fall on it what did happen?' she demanded.

Wilt squeezed foam from an aerosol and patted it gingerly on his chin.

'Well?' said Eva.

Wilt picked up his razor and put it under the hot tap. 'I had an accident,' he muttered.

'With a lamp-post, I suppose. I knew you'd been drinking.'

'With a Printer,' said Wilt indistinctly and started to shave.

'With a Printer?'

'To be precise, I got punched in the face by a particularly pugnacious apprentice printer.'

Eva stared at him in the mirror. 'You mean to say a student hit you in the classroom?'

Wilt nodded.

'I hope you hit him back.'

Wilt cut himself.

'No I bloody didn't,' he said, dabbing his chin with a finger. 'Now look what you've made me do.'

Eva ignored his complaint. 'Well you should have. You're not a man. You should have hit him back.'

Wilt put down the razor. 'And got the sack. Got hauled up in court for assaulting a student. Now that's what I call a brilliant idea.' He reached for the sponge and washed his face.

Eva retreated to the bedroom satisfied. There would be no mention of her lemon loungers now. She had taken his mind off her own little extravagance and given him a sense of grievance that would keep him occupied for the time being. By the time she had finished dressing, Wilt had eaten a bowl of All-Bran, drunk half a cup of coffee and was snarled up in a traffic jam at the roundabout. Eva went downstairs and had her own breakfast and began the daily round of washing up and Hoovering and cleaning the bath and ...

'Commitment,' said Dr Mayfield, 'to an integrated approach is an essential element in ...'

The Joint Committee for the Further Development of Liberal Studies was in session. Wilt squirmed in his chair and wished to hell it wasn't. Dr Mayfield's paper 'Cerebral Content and the Non-Academic Syllabus' held no interest for him, and besides, it was delivered in such convoluted sentences and with so much monotonous fervour that Wilt found it difficult to stay awake. He stared out of the window at the machines boring away on the site of the new Admin block. There was a reality about the work going on down there that was in marked contrast to the impractical theories Dr Mayfield was expounding. If the man really thought he could instil Cerebral Content, whatever that was, into Gasfitters Three he was out of his mind. Worse still, his blasted paper was bound to provoke an argument at question time. Wilt looked round the room. The various factions were all there, the New Left, the Left, the Old Left, the Indifferent Centre, the Cultural Right and the Reactionary Right.

Wilt classed himself with the Indifferents. In earlier years he had belonged to the Left politically and to the Right culturally. In other words he had banned the bomb, supported abortion and the abolition of private education and had been against capital punishment, thus earning himself something of a reputation as a radical while at the same time advocating a

33

return to the craft of the wheelwright, the blacksmith and the handloom weaver which had done much to undermine the efforts of the Technical staff to instil in their students an appreciation of the opportunities provided by modern technology. Time and the intransigent coarseness of Plasterers had changed all that. Wilt's ideals had vanished, to be replaced by the conviction that the man who said the pen was mightier than the sword ought to have tried reading *The Mill on the Floss* to Motor Mechanics Three before he opened his big mouth. In Wilt's view, the sword had much to recommend it.

As Dr Mayfield droned on, as question time with its ideological arguments followed, Wilt studied the pile hole on the building site. It would make an ideal depository for a body and there would be something immensely satisfying in knowing that Eva, who in her lifetime had been so unbearable, was in death supporting the weight of a multi-storey concrete building. Besides it would make her discovery an extremely remote possibility and her identification out of the question. Not even Eva, who boasted a strong constitution and a stronger will, could maintain an identity at the bottom of a pile shaft. The difficulty would be in getting her to go down the hole in the first place. Sleeping pills seemed a sensible preliminary but Eva was a sound sleeper and didn't believe in pills of any sort. 'I can't imagine why not,' Wilt thought grimly, 'she's prepared to believe in just about everything else.'

His reverie was interrupted by Mr Morris who was bringing the meeting to a close. 'Before you all go,' he said, 'there is one more subject I want to mention. We have been asked by the Head of Engineering to conduct a series of one-hour lectures to Sandwich-Course Trainee Firemen. The theme this year will be Problems of Contemporary Society. I have drawn up a list of topics and the lecturers who will give them.'

Mr Morris handed out subjects at random. Major Millfield got Media, Communications and Participatory Democracy about which he knew nothing and cared less. Peter Braintree was given The New Brutalism in Architecture, Its Origins and Social Attributes, and Wilt ended up with Violence and the Break-Up of Family Life. On the whole he thought he had done rather well. The subject fitted in with his present preoccupations. Mr Morris evidently agreed.

'I thought you might like to have a go at it after yesterday's little episode with Printers Three,' he said, as they went out. Wilt smiled wanly and went off to take Fitters and Turners Two. He gave them *Shane* to read and spent the hour jotting down notes for his lecture. In the distance he could hear the pile-boring machines grinding away. Wilt could imagine Eva lying at the bottom as they poured the concrete in. In her lemon pyjamas. It was a nice thought, and helped him with his notes. He wrote down a heading, Crime in the family, subheading (A) Murder of Spouse, decline in since divorce laws.

Yes, he should be able to talk about that to Trainee Firemen.

4

'I loathe parties,' said Wilt on Thursday night, 'and if there's one thing worse than parties it's university parties and bottle parties are worst of all. You take along a bottle of decent burgundy and end up drinking someone else's rotgut.'

'It isn't a party,' said Eva, 'it's a barbecue.'

'It says here "Come and Touch and Come with Sally and Gaskell 9PM Thursday. Bring your own ambrosia or take pot luck with the Pringsheim punch." If ambrosia doesn't mean Algerian bilgewater I'd like to know what it does mean.'

'I thought it was that stuff people take to get a hard-on,' said Eva.

Wilt looked at her with disgust. 'You've picked up some choice phrases since you've met these bloody people. A hard-on. I don't know what's got into you.'

'You haven't. That's for sure,' said Eva, and went through to the bathroom. Wilt sat on the bed and looked at the card. The beastly thing was shaped like a ... What the hell was it shaped like? Anyway it was pink and opened out and inside were all these ambiguous words. Come and Touch and Come.

Anyone touched him and they'd get an earful. And what about pot luck? A lot of trendy dons smoking joints and talking about set-theoretic data-manipulation systems or the significance of pre-Popper Hegelianism in the contemporary dialectical scene, or something equally unintelligible, and using fuck and cunt every now and then to show that they were still human.

'And what do you do?' they would ask him.

'Well, actually I teach at the Tech.'

'At the Tech? How frightfully interesting,' looking over his shoulder towards more stimulating horizons, and he would end the evening with some ghastly woman who felt strongly that Techs fulfilled a real function and that intellectual achievement was vastly overrated and that people should be oriented in a way that would make them community co-ordinated and that's what Techs were doing, weren't they? Wilt knew what Techs were doing. Paying people like him £3500 a year to keep Gasfitters quiet for an hour.

And Pringsheim Punch. Planters Punch. Printers Punch. He'd had enough punches recently.

'What the hell am I to wear?' he asked.

'There's that Mexican shirt you bought on the Costa del Sol last year,' Eva called from the bathroom. 'You haven't had a chance to wear it since.'

'And I don't intend to now,' muttered Wilt, rummaging through a drawer in search of something nondescript that would demonstrate his independence. In the end he put on a striped shirt with blue jeans.

'You're surely not going like that?' Eva told him emerging from the bathroom largely naked. Her face was plastered with white powder and her lips were carmine.

'Jesus wept,' said Wilt, 'Mardi Gras with pernicious anaemia.'

Eva pushed passed him. 'I'm going as The Great Gatsby,' she announced, 'and if you had any imagination you'd think of something better than a business shirt with blue jeans.'

'The Great Gatsby happened to be a man,' said Wilt.

'Bully for him,' said Eva, and put on her lemon loungers.

Wilt shut his eyes and took off his shirt. By the time they left the house he was wearing a red shirt with jeans while Eva, in spite of the hot night, insisted on putting on her new raincoat and trilby.

'We might as well walk,' said Wilt.

They took the car. Eva wasn't yet prepared to walk down Parkview Avenue in a trilby, a belted raincoat and lemon loungers. On the way they stopped at an off-licence where Wilt bought a bottle of Cyprus red.

'Don't think I'm going to touch the muck,' he said, 'and you had better take the car keys now. If it's as bad as I think it will be, I'm walking home early.'

It was. Worse. In his red shirt and blue jeans Wilt looked out of place.

'Darling Eva,' said Sally, when they finally found her talking to a man in a loincloth made out of a kitchen towel advertising Irish cheeses, 'you look great. The twenties suit you. And so this is Henry.' Henry didn't feel Henry at all. 'In period costume too. Henry meet Raphael.'

The man in the loincloth studied Wilt's jeans. 'The fifties are back,' he said languidly, 'I suppose it was bound to happen.'

Wilt looked pointedly at a Connemara Cheddar and tried to smile.

'Help yourself, Henry,' said Sally, and took Eva off to meet the freest but the most liberated woman who was simply dying to meet booby baby. Wilt went into the garden and put his bottle on the table and looked for a corkscrew. There wasn't one. In the end he looked into a large bucket with a ladle in it. Half an orange and segments of bruised peach floated in a purple liquid. He poured himself a paper cup and tried it. As he had anticipated, it tasted like cider with wood alcohol and orange squash. Wilt looked round the garden. In one corner a man in a chef's hat and a jockstrap was cooking, was *burning* sausages over a charcoal grill. In another corner a dozen people were lying in a circle listening to the Watergate tapes. There was a sprinkling of couples talking earnestly and a number of individuals standing by themselves looking supercilious and remote. Wilt recognized himself among them and selected the least attractive girl on the theory that he might just as well jump in the deep end and get it over with. He'd end up with her anyway.

'Hi,' he said, conscious that already he was slipping into the Americanese that Eva had succumbed to. The girl looked at him blankly and moved away.

'Charming,' said Wilt, and finished his drink. Ten minutes and two drinks later he was discussing Rapid Reading with a small round man who seemed deeply interested in the subject.

In the kitchen Eva was cutting up French bread while Sally stood with a drink and talked about Lévi-Strauss with an Ethiopian who had just got back from New Guinea.

'I've always felt that L-S was all wrong on the woman's front,' she said, languidly studying Eva's rear, 'I mean he disregards the essential similarity ...' She stopped and stared out of the window. 'Excuse me a moment,' she said, and went out to rescue Dr Scheimacher from the clutches of Henry Wilt. 'Ernst is such a sweetie,' she said, when she came back, 'you'd never guess he got the Nobel prize for spermatology.'

Wilt stood in the middle of the garden and finished his third drink. He poured himself a fourth and went to listen to the Watergate tapes. He got there in time to hear the end.

'You get a much clearer insight into Tricky Dick's character quadraphonically,' someone said as the group broke up.

'With the highly gifted child one has to develop a special relationship. Roger and I find that Tonio responds best to a constructional approach.'

'It's a load of bull. Take what he says about quasars for example ...'

'I can't honestly see what's wrong with buggery ...'

'I don't care what Marcuse thinks about tolerance. What I'm saying is ...'

'At minus two-fifty nitrogen ...'

'Bach does have his moments I suppose but he has his limitations ...'

'We've got this place at St Trop ...'

'I still think Kaldor had the answer ...'

Wilt finished his fourth drink and went to look for Eva. He'd had enough. He was halted by a yell from the man in the chef's hat.

'Burgers up. Come and get it.'

Wilt staggered off and got it. Two sausages, a burnt beefburger and a slosh of coleslaw on a paper plate. There didn't seem to be any knives or forks.

'Poor Henry's looking so forlorn,' said Sally, 'I'll go and transfuse him.'

She went out and took Wilt's arm.

'You're so lucky to have Eva. She's the babiest baby.'

'She's thirty-five,' said Wilt drunkenly, 'thirty-five if she's a day.'

'It's marvellous to meet a man who says what he means,' said Sally, and took a piece of beefburger from his plate. 'Gaskell just never says anything straightforwardly. I love down-to-earth people.' She sat down on the grass and pulled Wilt down with her. 'I think it's terribly important for two people to tell one another the truth,' she went on, breaking off another piece of beefburger and popping it into Wilt's mouth. She licked her fingers slowly and looked at him with wide eyes. Wilt chewed the bit uneasily and finally swallowed it. It tasted like burnt mincemeat with a soupçon of Lancôme. Or a bouquet.

'Why two?' he asked, rinsing his mouth out with coleslaw.

'Why two what?'

'Why two people,' said Wilt. 'Why is it so important for two people to tell the truth?'

'Well, I mean ...'

'Why not three? Or four? Or a hundred?'

'A hundred people can't have a relationship. Not an intimate one,' said Sally, 'not a meaningful one.'

'I don't know many twos who can either,' said Wilt. Sally dabbed her finger in his coleslaw.

'Oh but you do. You and Eva have this real thing going between you.'

'Not very often,' said Wilt. Sally laughed.

'Oh baby, you're a truth baby,' she said, and got up and fetched two more drinks. Wilt looked down into his paper cup doubtfully. He was getting very drunk.

'If I'm a truth baby, what sort of baby are you, baby?' he asked, endeavouring to instil the last baby with more than a soupcon of contempt. Sally snuggled up to him and whispered in his ear.

'I'm a body baby,' she said.

'I can see that,' said Wilt. 'You've got a very nice body.'

'That's the nicest thing anybody has ever said to me,' said Sally.

'In that case,' said Wilt, picking up a blackened sausage, 'you must have had a deprived childhood.'

'As a matter of fact I did,' Sally said and plucked the sausage from his fingers. 'That's why I need so much loving now.' She put most of the sausage in her mouth, drew it slowly out and nibbled the end. Wilt finished off the coleslaw and washed it down with Pringsheim Punch.

'Aren't they all awful?' said Sally, as shouts and laughter came from the corner of the garden by the grill.

Wilt looked up.

'As a matter of fact they are,' he said. 'Who's the clown in the jockstrap?'

'That's Gaskell. He's so arrested. He loves playing at things. In the States he just loves to ride footplate on a locomotive and he goes to rodeos and last Christmas he insisted on dressing up as Santa Claus and going down to Watts and giving out presents to the black kids at an orphanage. Of course they wouldn't let him.'

'If he went in a jockstrap I'm not in the least surprised,' said Wilt. Sally laughed.

'You must be an Aries,' she said, 'you don't mind what you say.' She got to her feet and pulled Wilt up. 'I'm going to show you his toy room. It's ever so droll.'

Wilt put his plate down and they went into the house. In the kitchen Eva was peeling oranges for a fruit salad and talking about circumcision rites with the Ethiopian, who was slicing bananas for her. In the lounge several couples were dancing back to back very vigorously to an LP of Beethoven's Fifth played at 78.

'Christ,' said Wilt, as Sally collected a bottle of Vodka from a cupboard. They went upstairs and down a passage to a small bedroom filled with toys. There was a model train set on the floor, a punchbag, an enormous Teddy Bear, a rocking horse, a fireman's helmet and a lifesize inflated doll that looked like a real woman.

'That's Judy,' said Sally, 'she's got a real cunt. Gaskell is a plastic freak.' Wilt winced. 'And here are Gaskell's toys. Puberty baby.'

Wilt looked round the room at the mess and shook his head. 'Looks as though he's making up for a lost childhood,' he said.

'Oh, Henry, you're so perceptive,' said Sally, and unscrewed the top of the Vodka bottle.

'I'm not. It's just bloody obvious.'

'Oh you are. You're just terribly modest, is all. Modest and shy and manly.' She swigged from the bottle and gave it to Wilt. He took a mouthful inadvisedly and had trouble swallowing it. Sally locked the door and sat down on the bed. She reached up a hand and pulled Wilt towards her.

'Screw me, Henry baby,' she said and lifted her skirt, 'fuck me, honey. Screw the pants off me.'

'That,' said Wilt, 'would be a bit difficult.'

'Oh. Why?'

'Well for one thing you don't appear to be wearing any and anyway why should I?'

'You want a reason? A reason for screwing?'

'Yes,' said Wilt. 'Yes I do.'

'Reason's treason. Feel free.' She pulled him down and kissed him. Wilt didn't feel at all free. 'Don't be shy, baby.'

'Shy?' said Wilt lurching to one side. 'Me shy?'

'Sure you're shy. OK, you're small. Eva told me ...'

'Small? What do you mean I'm small?' shouted Wilt furiously.

Sally smiled up at him. 'It doesn't matter. It doesn't matter. Nothing matters. Just you and me and ...'

'It bloody well does matter,' snarled Wilt. 'My wife said I was small. I'll soon show the silly bitch who's small. I'll show ...'

'Show me, Henry baby, show me. I like them small. Prick me to the quick.'

'It's not true,' Wilt mumbled.

'Prove it, lover,' said Sally squirming against him.

'I won't,' said Wilt, and stood up.

Sally stopped squirming and looked at him. 'You're just afraid,' she said. 'You're afraid to be free.'

'Free? Free?' shouted Wilt, trying to open the door. 'Locked in a room with another man's wife is freedom? You've got to be joking.'

Sally pulled down her skirt and sat up.

'You won't?'

'No,' said Wilt.

'Are you a bondage baby? You can tell me. I'm used to bondage babies. Gaskell is real ...'

'Certainly not,' said Wilt. 'I don't care what Gaskell is.'

'You want a blow job, is that it? You want for me to give you a blow job?' She got off the bed and came towards him. Wilt looked at her wildly.

'Don't you touch me,' he shouted, his mind alive with images of burning paint. 'I don't want anything from you.'

Sally stopped and stared at him. She wasn't smiling any more.

'Why not? Because you're small? Is that why?'

Wilt backed against the door.

'No, it isn't.'

'Because you haven't the courage of your instincts? Because you're a psychic virgin? Because you're not a man? Because you can't take a woman who thinks?'

'Thinks?' yelled Wilt, stung into action by the accusation that he wasn't a man. 'Thinks? You think? You know something? I'd rather have it off with that plastic mechanical doll than you. It's got more sex appeal in its little finger than you have in your whole rotten body. When I want a whore I'll buy one.'

42

'Why you little shit,' said Sally, and lunged at him. Wilt scuttled sideways and collided with the punchbag. The next moment he had stepped on a model engine and was hurtling across the room. As he slumped down the wall on to the floor Sally picked up the doll and leant over him.

In the kitchen Eva had finished the fruit salad and had made coffee. It was a lovely party. Mr Osewa had told her all about his job as underdevelopment officer in Cultural Affairs to UNESCO and how rewarding he found it. She had been kissed twice on the back of the neck by Dr Scheimacher in passing and the man in the Irish Cheese loincloth had pressed himself against her rather more firmly than was absolutely necessary to reach the tomato ketchup. And all around her terribly clever people were being so outspoken. It was all so sophisticated. She helped herself to another drink and looked around for Henry. He was nowhere to be seen.

'Have you seen Henry?' she asked when Sally came into the kitchen holding a bottle of Vodka and looking rather flushed.

'The last I saw of him he was sitting with some dolly bird,' said Sally, helping herself to a spoonful of fruit salad. 'Oh, Eva darling, you're absolutely Cordon Bleu baby.' Eva blushed.

'I do hope he's enjoying himself. Henry's not awfully good at parties.'

'Eva baby, be honest. Henry's not awfully good period.'

'It's just that he ...' Eva began but Sally kissed her.

'You're far too good for him,' she said, 'we've got to find you someone really beautiful.' While Eva sipped her drink, Sally found a young man with a frond of hair falling across his forehead who was lying on a couch with a girl, smoking and staring at the ceiling.

'Christopher precious,' she said, 'I'm going to steal you for a moment. I want you to do someone for me. Go into the kitchen and sweeten the woman with the boobies and the awful yellow pyjamas.'

'Oh God. Why me?'

'My sweet, you know you're utterly irresistible. But the sexiest. For me, baby, for me.'

Christopher got off the couch and went into the kitchen and Sally stretched out beside the girl.

'Christopher is a dreamboy,' she said.

'He's a gigolo,' said the girl. 'A male prostitute.'

'Darling,' said Sally, 'it's about time we women had them.'

In the kitchen Eva stopped pouring coffee. She was feeling delightfully tipsy.

'You mustn't,' she said hastily.

'Why not?'

'I'm married.'

'I like it. I like it.'

'Yes but ...'

'No buts, lover.'

'Oh.'

Upstairs in the toy room Wilt, recovering slowly from the combined assaults on his system of Pringsheim Punch, Vodka, his nymphomaniac hostess and the corner of the cupboard against which he had fallen, had the feeling that something was terribly wrong. It wasn't simply that the room was oscillating, that he had a lump on the back of his head or that he was naked. It was rather the sensation that something with all the less attractive qualities of a mousetrap, or a vice, or a starving clam, had attached itself implacably to what he had up till now always considered to be the most private of his parts. Wilt opened his eyes and found himself staring into a smiling if slightly swollen face. He shut his eyes again, hoped against hope, opened them again, found the face still there and made an effort to sit up.

It was an unwise move. Judy, the plastic doll, inflated beyond her normal pressure, resisted. With a squawk Wilt fell back on to the floor. Judy followed. Her nose bounced on his face and her breasts on his chest. With a curse Wilt rolled on to his side and considered the problem. Sitting up was out of the question. That way led to castration. He would have to try something else. He rolled the doll over further and climbed on top only to decide that his weight on it was increasing the pressure on what remained of his penis and that if he wanted to get gangrene that was the way to go about getting it. Wilt rolled off precipitately and groped for a valve. There must be one somewhere if he could only find it. But if there was a valve it was well hidden and by the feel of things he hadn't got time to waste finding it. He felt round on the floor for something to use as a dagger, something sharp, and finally broke off a piece of railway track and plunged it into his assailant's back. There was a squeak of plastic but Judy's swollen smile remained unchanged and her unwanted attentions as implacable as ever. Again and again he stabbed her but to no avail. Wilt dropped his makeshift dagger and considered other means. He was getting frantic, conscious of a new threat. It was no longer that he was the subject of her high air pressure. His own internal pressures were mounting. The Pringsheim Punch and the Vodka were making their presence felt. With a desperate thought that if he didn't get out of her soon he would burst, Wilt seized Judy's head, bent it sideways and sank his teeth into her neck. Or would have had her pounds per square inch permitted. Instead he bounced off and spent the next two minutes trying to find his false tooth which had been dislodged in the exchange.

By the time he had got it back in place, panic had set in. He had to get out of the doll. He just had to. There would be a razor in the bathroom or a pair of scissors. But where on earth was the bathroom? Never mind about that. He'd find the damned thing. Carefully, very carefully he rolled the doll on to her back and followed her over. Then he inched his knees up until he was straddling the thing. All he needed now was something to hold on to while he got to his feet. Wilt leant over and grasped the edge of a chair with one hand while lifting Judy's head off the floor with the other. A moment later he was on his feet. Holding the doll to him he shuffled towards the door and opened it. He peered out into the passage. What if someone saw him? To hell with that. Wilt no longer cared what people thought about him. But which way was the bathroom? Wilt turned right, and peering frantically over Judy's shoulder, shuffled off down the passage.

·

Downstairs, Eva was having a wonderful time. First Christopher, then the man in the Irish Cheese loincloth and finally Dr Scheimacher, had all made advances to her and been rebuffed. It was such a change from Henry's lack of interest. It showed she was still attractive. Dr Scheimacher had said that she was an interesting example of latent steatopygia, Christopher tried to kiss her breasts and the man in the loincloth had made the most extraordinary suggestion to her. And through it all, Eva had remained entirely virtuous. Her massive skittishness, her insistence on dancing and, most effective of all, her habit of saying in a loud and not wholly cultivated voice, 'Oh, you are awful' at moments of their greatest ardour, had had a markedly deterrent effect. Now she sat on the floor in the living-room, while Sally and Gaskell and the bearded man from the Institute of Ecological Research argued about sexually interchangeable role-playing in a population-restrictive society. She felt strangely elated. Parkview Avenue and Mavis Mottram and her work at the Harmony Community Centre seemed to belong to another world. She had been accepted by people who flew to California or Tokyo to conferences and Think Tanks as casually as she took the bus to town. Dr Scheimacher had mentioned that he was flying to New Delhi in the morning, and Christopher had just come back from a photographic assignment in Trinidad. Above all, there was an aura of importance about what they were doing, a glamour that was wholly lacking in Henry's job at the Tech. If only she could get him to do something interesting and adventurous. But Henry was such a stick-in-the-mud. She had made a mistake in marrying him. She really had. All he was interested in was books, but life wasn't to be found in books. Like Sally said, life was for living. Life was people and experiences and fun. Henry would never see that.

In the bathroom Wilt could see very little. He certainly couldn't see any way of getting out of the doll. His attempt to slit the beastly thing's throat with a razor had failed, thanks largely to the fact that the razor in question was a Wilkinson bonded blade. Having failed with the razor he had tried

46

shampoo as a lubricant but apart from working up a lather which even to his jaundiced eye looked as though he had aroused the doll to positively frenzied heights of sexual expectation the shampoo had achieved nothing. Finally he had reverted to a quest for the valve. The damned thing had one somewhere if only he could find it. In this endeavour he peered into the mirror on the door of the medicine cabinet but the mirror was too small. There was a large one over the washbasin. Wilt pulled down the lid of the toilet and climbed on to it. This way he would be able to get a clear view of the doll's back. He was just inching his way round when there were footsteps in the passage. Wilt stopped inching and stood rigid on the toilet lid. Someone tried the door and found it locked. The footsteps retreated and Wilt breathed a sigh of relief. Now then, just let him find that valve.

And at that moment disaster struck. Wilt's left foot stepped in the shampoo that had dripped on to the toilet seat, slid sideways off the edge and Wilt, the doll and the door of the medicine cabinet with which he had attempted to save himself were momentarily airborne. As they hurtled into the bath, as the shower curtain and fitting followed, as the contents of the medicine cabinet cascaded on to the washbasin, Wilt gave a last despairing scream. There was a pop reminiscent of champagne corks and Judy, finally responding to the pressure of Wilt's eleven stone dropping from several feet into the bath, ejected him. But Wilt no longer cared. He had in every sense passed out. He was only dimly aware of shouts in the corridor, of someone breaking the door down, of faces peering at him and of hysterical laughter. When he came to he was lying on the bed in the toy room. He got up and put on his clothes and crept downstairs and out of the front door. It was 3AM.

5

Eva sat on the edge of the bed crying.

'How could he? How could he do a thing like that?' she said, 'in front of all these people.'

'Eva baby, men are like that. Believe me,' said Sally.

'But with a doll . . . .'

'That's symbolic of the male chauvinist pig attitude to women. We're just fuck artefacts to them. Objectification. So now you know how Henry feels about you.'

'It's horrible,' said Eva.

'Sure it's horrible. Male domination debases us to the level of objects.'

'But Henry's never done anything like that before,' Eva wailed.

'Well, he's done it now.'

'I'm not going back to him. I couldn't face it. I feel so ashamed.'

'Honey, you just forget about it. You don't have to go anywhere. Sally will look after you. You just lie down and get some sleep.'

Eva lay back, but sleep was impossible. The image of Henry lying naked in the bath on top of that horrible doll was fixed in her mind. They had to break the door down and Dr Scheimacher had cut his hand on a broken bottle trying to get Henry out of the bath . . . Oh, it was all too awful. She would never be able to look people in the face again. The story was bound to get about and she would be known as the woman whose husband went around . . . With a fresh paroxysm of embarrassment Eva buried her head in the pillow and wept.

'Well that sure made the party go with a bang,' said Gaskell. 'Guy screws a doll in the bathroom and everyone goes berserk.' He looked round the living-room at the mess. 'If anyone thinks I'm going to start clearing this lot up now they'd better think again. I'm going to bed.'

'Just don't wake Eva up. She's hysterical,' said Sally.

'Oh great. Now we've got a manic obsessive compulsive woman with hysteria in the house.'

'And tomorrow she's coming with us on the boat.'

'She's what?'

'You heard me. She's coming with us on the boat.'

'Now wait a bit ...'

'I'm not arguing with you, G. I'm telling you. She's coming with us.'

'Why, for Chrissake?'

'Because I'm not having her go back to that creep of a husband of hers. Because you won't get me a cleaning-woman and because I like her.'

'Because I won't get you a cleaning-woman. Now I've heard it all.'

'Oh no you haven't,' said Sally, 'you haven't heard the half of it. You may not know it but you married a liberated woman. No male pig is going to put one over on me ...'

'I'm not trying to put one over on you,' said Gaskell. 'All I'm saying is that I don't want to have to ...'

'I'm not talking about you. I'm talking about that creep Wilt. You think he got into that doll by himself? Think again, G baby, think again.'

Gaskell sat down on the sofa and stared at her.

'You must be out of your mind. What the hell did you want to do a thing like that for?'

'Because when I liberate someone I liberate them. No mistake.'

'Liberate someone by ...' he shook his head. 'It doesn't make sense.'

Sally poured herself a drink. 'The trouble with you, G, is that you talk big but you don't do. It's yakkity yak with you. "My wife is a liberated woman. My wife's free." Nice-sounding talk but come the time your liberated wife takes it into her head to do something, you don't want to know.'

'Yeah, and when you take it into your goddam head to do something who takes the can back? I do. Where's petticoats then? Who got you out of that mess in Omaha? Who paid the fuzz in Houston that time ...'

'So you did. So why did you marry me? Just why?'

Gaskell polished his glasses with the edge of the chef's hat. 'I don't know,' he said, 'so help me I don't know.'

'For kicks, baby, for kicks. Without me you'd have died of boredom. With me you get excitement. With me you get kicks.'

'In the teeth.'

Gaskell got up wearily and headed for the stairs. It was at times like these that he wondered why he had married.

Wilt walked home in agony. His pain was no longer physical. It was the agony of humiliation, hatred and self-contempt. He had been made to look a fool, a pervert and an idiot in front of people he despised. The Pringsheims and their set were everything he loathed, false, phoney, pretentious, a circus of intellectual clowns whose antics had not even the merit of his own, which had at least been real. Theirs were merely a parody of enjoyment. They laughed to hear themselves laughing and paraded a sensuality that had nothing to do with feelings or even instincts but was dredged up from shallow imaginations to mimic lust. *Copulo ergo sum.* And that bitch, Sally, had taunted him with not having the courage of his instincts as if instinct consisted of ejaculating into the chemically sterilized body of a woman he had first met twenty minutes before. And Wilt had reacted instinctively, shying away from a concupiscence that had to do with power and arrogance and an intolerable contempt for him which presupposed that what he was, what little he was, was a mere extension of his penis and that the ultimate expression of his thoughts, feelings, hopes and ambitions was to be attained between the legs of a trendy slut. And *that* was being liberated.

'Feel free,' she had said and had knotted him into that fucking doll. Wilt ground his teeth underneath a streetlamp.

And what about Eva? What sort of hell was she going to make for him now? If life had been intolerable with her before this, it was going to be unadulterated misery now. She wouldn't believe that he hadn't been screwing that doll, that he hadn't got into it of his own accord, that he had been put into it by Sally. Not in a month of Sundays. And even if by some miracle she accepted his story, a fat lot of difference that would make.

'What sort of man do you think you are, letting a woman do a thing like that to you?' she would ask. There was absolutely no reply to the question. What sort of man was he? Wilt had no idea. An insignificant little man to whom things happened and for whom life was a chapter of indignities. Printers punched him in the face and he was blamed for it. His wife bullied him and other people's wives made a laughing-stock out of him. Wilt wandered on along suburban streets past semi-detached houses and little gardens with a mounting sense of determination. He had had enough of being the butt of circumstance. From now on things would happen because he wanted them to. He would change from being the recipient of misfortune. He would be the instigator. Just let Eva try anything now. He would knock the bitch down.

Wilt stopped. It was all very well to talk. The bloody woman had a weapon she wouldn't hesitate to use. Knock her down, my eye. If anyone went down it would be Wilt, and in addition she would parade his affair with the doll to everyone they knew. It wouldn't be long before the story reached the Tech. In the darkness of Parkview Avenue Wilt shuddered at the thought. It would be the end of his career. He went through the gate of Number 34 and unlocked the front door with the feeling that unless he took some drastic action in the immediate future he was doomed.

In bed an hour later he was still awake, wide awake and wrestling with the problem of Eva, his own character and how to change it into something he could respect. And what did he respect? Under the blankets Wilt clenched his fist.

'Decisiveness,' he murmured. 'The ability to act without hesitation. Courage.' A strange litany of ancient virtues. But how to acquire them now? How had they turned men like him into Commandos and professional killers during the war? By training them. Wilt lay in the darkness and considered ways in which he could train himself to become what he was clearly not. By the time he fell asleep he had determined to attempt the impossible.

At seven the alarm went. Wilt got up and went into the bathroom and stared at himself in the mirror. He was a hard man, a man without feelings. Hard, methodical, cold-blooded and logical. A man who made no mistakes. He went downstairs and ate his All-Bran and drank his cup of coffee. So Eva wasn't home. She had stayed the night at the Pringsheims. Well that was something. It made things easier for him. Except that she still had the car and the keys. He certainly wasn't going to go round and get the car. He walked down to the roundabout and caught the bus to the Tech. He had Bricklayers One in Room 456. When he arrived they were talking about grad-bashing.

'There was this student all dressed up like a waiter see. "Do you mind?" he says, "Do you mind getting out of my way." Just like that and all I was doing was looking in the window at the books . . .'

'At the books?' said Wilt sceptically. 'At eleven o'clock at night you were looking at books? I don't believe it.'

'Magazines and cowboy books,' said the bricklayer. 'They're in a junk shop in Finch Street.'

'They've got girlie mags,' someone else explained. Wilt nodded. That sounded more like it.

'So I says "Mind what?" ' continued the bricklayer, 'and he says, "Mind out of my way." His way. Like he owned the bloody street.'

'So what did you say?' asked Wilt.

'Say? I didn't say anything. I wasn't wasting words on him.'

'What did you do then?'

'Well, I put the boot in and duffed him up. Gave him a good going-over and no mistake. Then I pushed off. There's one bloody grad who won't be telling people to get out of his way for a bit.'

The class nodded approvingly.

'They're all the bloody same, students,' said another bricklayer. 'Think because they've got money and go to college they can order you about. They could all do with a going-over. Do them a power of good.'

Wilt considered the implications of mugging as part of an intellectual's education. After his experience the previous night he was inclined to think there was something to be said for it. He would have liked to have duffed up half the people at the Pringsheims' party.

'So none of you feel there's anything wrong with beating a student up if he gets in your way?' he asked.

'Wrong?' said the bricklayers in unison. 'What's wrong with a good punch-up? It's not as if a grad is an old woman or something. He can always hit back, can't he?'

They spent the rest of the hour discussing violence in the modern world. On the whole, the bricklayers seemed to think it was a good thing.

'I mean what's the point of going out on a Saturday night and getting pissed if you can't have a bit of a barney at the same time? Got to get rid of your aggression somehow,' said an unusually articulate bricklayer, 'I mean it's natural isn't it?'

'So you think man is a naturally aggressive animal,' said Wilt.

'Course he is. That's history for you, all them wars and things. It's only bloody poofters don't like violence.'

Wilt took this view of things along to the Staff Room for his free period and collected a cup of coffee from the vending machine. He was joined by Peter Braintree.

'How did the party go?' Braintree asked.

'It didn't,' said Wilt morosely.

'Eva enjoy it?'

'I wouldn't know. She hadn't come home by the time I got up this morning.'

'Hadn't come home?'

'That's what I said,' said Wilt.

'Well did you ring up and find out what had happened to her?'

'No,' said Wilt.

'Why not?'

'Because I'd look a bit of a twit ringing up and being told

she was shacked up with the Abyssinian ambassador, wouldn't I?'

'The Abyssinian ambassador? Was he there?'

'I don't know and I don't want to know. The last I saw of her she was being chatted up by this big black bloke from Ethiopia. Something to do with the United Nations. She was making fruit salad and he was chopping bananas for her.'

'Doesn't sound a very compromising sort of activity to me,' said Braintree.

'No, I daresay it doesn't. Only you weren't there and don't know what sort of party it was,' said Wilt rapidly coming to the conclusion that an edited version of the night's events was called for. 'A whole lot of middle-aged with-it kids doing their withered thing.'

'It sounds bloody awful. And you think Eva ...'

'I think Eva got pissed and somebody gave her a joint and she passed out,' said Wilt, 'that's what I think. She's probably sleeping it off in the downstairs loo.'

'Doesn't sound like Eva to me,' said Braintree. Wilt drank his coffee and considered his strategy. If the story of his involvement with that fucking doll was going to come out, perhaps it would be better if he told it his way first. On the other hand ...

'What were you doing while all this was going on?' Braintree asked.

'Well,' said Wilt, 'as a matter of fact ...' He hesitated. On second thoughts it might be better not to mention the doll at all. If Eva kept her trap shut ... 'I got a bit slewed myself.'

'That sounds more like it,' said Braintree, 'I suppose you made a pass at another woman too.'

'If you must know,' said Wilt, 'another woman made a pass at me. Mrs Pringsheim.'

'Mrs Pringsheim made a pass at you?'

'Well, we went upstairs to look at her husband's toys....'

'His toys? I thought you told me he was a biochemist.'

'He is a biochemist. He just happens to like playing with toys. Model trains and Teddy Bears and things. She says he's a case of arrested development. She would, though. She's that sort of loyal wife.'

'What happened then?'

'Apart from her locking the door and lying on the bed with her legs wide open and asking me to screw her and threatening me with a blow job, nothing happened,' said Wilt.

Peter Braintree looked at him sceptically. 'Nothing?' he said finally. 'Nothing? I mean what did you do?'

'Equivocated,' said Wilt.

'That's a new word for it,' said Braintree. 'You go upstairs with Mrs Pringsheim and equivocate while she lies on a bed with her legs open and you want to know why Eva hasn't come home? She's probably round at some lawyer's office filing a petition for divorce right now.'

'But I tell you I didn't screw the bitch,' said Wilt. 'I told her to hawk her pearly somewhere else.'

'And you call that equivocating? Hawk her pearly? Where the hell did you get that expression from?'

'Meat One,' said Wilt and got up and fetched himself another cup of coffee.

By the time he came back to his seat he had decided on his version.

'I don't know what happened after that,' he said when Braintree insisted on hearing the next episode. 'I passed out. It must have been the vodka.'

'You just passed out in a locked room with a naked woman? Is that what happened?' said Braintree. He didn't sound as if he believed a word of the story.

'Precisely,' said Wilt.

'And when you came to?'

'I was walking home,' said Wilt. 'I've no idea what happened in between.'

'Oh well, I daresay we'll hear about that from Eva,' said Braintree. 'She's bound to know.'

He got up and went off and Wilt was left alone to consider his next move. The first thing to do was to make sure that Eva didn't say anything. He went through to the telephone in the corridor and dialled his home number. There was no reply. Wilt went along to Room 187 and spent an hour with Turners and Fitters. Several times during the day he tried to telephone Eva but there was no answer.

'She's probably spent the day round at Mavis Mottram's weeping on her shoulder and telling all and sundry what a pig I am,' he thought. 'She's bound to be waiting for me when I get home tonight.'

But she wasn't. Instead there was a note on the kitchen table and a package. Wilt opened the note.

'I'm going away with Sally and Gaskell to think things over. What you did last night was horrible. I won't ever forgive you. Don't forget to buy some dog food. Eva. P.S. Sally says next time you want a blow job get Judy to give you one.'

Wilt looked at the package. He knew without opening it what it contained. That infernal doll. In a sudden paroxysm of rage Wilt picked it up and hurled it across the kitchen at the sink. Two plates and a saucer bounced off the washing-up rack and broke on the floor.

'Bugger the bitch,' said Wilt inclusively, Eva, Judy, and Sally Pringsheim all coming within the ambit of his fury. Then he sat down at the table and looked at the note again. 'Going away to think things over.' Like hell she was. Think? The stupid cow wasn't capable of thought. She'd emote, drool over his deficiencies and work herself into an ecstasy of self-pity. Wilt could hear her now blathering on about that blasted bank manager and how she should have married him instead of saddling herself with a man who couldn't even get promotion at the Tech and who went around fucking inflatable dolls in other people's bathrooms. And there was that filthy slut, Sally Pringsheim, egging her on. Wilt looked at the post-script: 'Sally says next time you want a blow job ...' Christ. As if he'd wanted a blow job the last time. But there it was, a new myth in the making, like the business of his being in love with Betty Crabtree when all he had done was give her a lift home one night after an Evening Class. Wilt's home life was punctuated by such myths, weapons in Eva's armoury to be brought out when the occasion demanded and brandished above his head. And now Eva had the ultimate deterrent at her disposal, the doll and Sally Pringsheim and a blow job. The balance of recrimination which had been the sustaining factor in their relationship had shifted dramatically. It would take an act of desperate invention on Wilt's part to restore it.

'Don't forget to buy some dog food.' Well at least she had left him the car. It was standing in the carport. Wilt went out and drove round to the supermarket and bought three tins of dog food, a boil-in-the-bag curry and a bottle of gin. He was going to get pissed. Then he went home and sat in the kitchen watching Clem gulp his Bonzo while the bag boiled. He poured himself a stiff gin, topped it up with lime and wandered about. And all the time he was conscious of the package lying there on the draining board waiting for him to open it. And inevitably he would open it. Out of sheer curiosity. He knew it and they knew it wherever they were, and on Sunday night Eva would come home and the first thing she would do would be to ask about the doll and if he had had a nice time with it. Wilt helped himself to some more gin and considered the doll's utility. There must be some way of using the thing to turn the tables on Eva.

By the time he had finished his second gin he had begun to formulate a plan. It involved the doll, a pile hole and a nice test of his own strength of character. It was one thing to have fantasies about murdering your wife. It was quite another to put them into effect and between the two there lay an area of uncertainty. By the end of his third gin Wilt was determined to put the plan into effect. If it did nothing else it would prove he was capable of executing a murder.

Wilt got up and unwrapped the doll. In his interior dialogue Eva was telling him what would happen if Mavis Mottram got to hear about his disgusting behaviour at the Pringsheim's. 'You'd be the laughing stock of the neighbourhood,' she said, 'you'd never live it down.'

Wouldn't he though? Wilt smiled drunkenly to himself and went upstairs. For once Eva was mistaken. He might not live it down but Mrs Eva Wilt wouldn't be around to gloat. She wouldn't live at all.

Upstairs in the bedroom he closed the curtains and laid the doll on the bed and looked for the valve which had eluded him the previous night. He found it and fetched a footpump from the garage. Five minutes later Judy was in good shape. She lay on the bed and smiled up at him. Wilt half closed his eyes and squinted at her. In the half darkness he had to admit that she was hideously lifelike. Plastic Eva with the mastic boobs. All that remained was to dress it up. He rummaged around in several drawers in search of a bra and blouse, decided she didn't need a bra, and picked out an old skirt and a pair of tights. In a cardboard box in the wardrobe he found one of Eva's wigs. She had had a phase of wigs. Finally a pair of shoes. By the time he had finished, Eva Wilt's replica lay on the bed smiling fixedly at the ceiling.

'That's my girl,' said Wilt and went down to the kitchen to see how the boil-in-the-bag was coming along. It was burnt-in-the-bag. Wilt turned the stove off and went into the lavatory under the stairs and sat thinking about his next move. He would use the doll for dummy runs so that if and when it came to the day he would be accustomed to the whole process of murder and would act without feeling like an automaton. Killing by conditioned reflex. Murder by habit. Then again he would know how to time the whole affair. And Eva's going off with the Pringsheims for the weekend would help too. It would establish a pattern of sudden disappearances. He would provoke her somehow to do it again and again and again. And then the visit to the doctor.

'It's just that I can't sleep, doctor. My wife keeps on going off and leaving me and I just can't get used to sleeping on my own.' A prescription for sleeping tablets. Then on the night. 'I'll make the Ovaltine tonight, dear. You're looking tired. I'll bring it up to you in bed.' Gratitude followed by snores. Down to the car ... fairly early would be best ... around ten thirty ... over to the Tech and down the hole. Perhaps inside a plastic bag ... no, not a plastic bag. 'I understand you bought a large plastic bag recently, sir. I wonder if you would mind showing it to us.' No, better just to leave her down the hole they were going to fill with concrete next morning. And finally a bewildered Wilt. He would go round to the Pringsheims'. 'Where's Eva? Yes, you do.' 'No, we don't.' 'Don't lie to me. She's always coming round here.' 'We're not lying.

We haven't seen her.' After that he would go to the police.

Motiveless, clueless and indiscoverable. And proof that he was a man who could act. Or wasn't. What if he broke down under the strain and confessed? That would be some sort of vindication too. He would know what sort of man he was one way or another and at least he would have acted for once in his life. And fifteen years in prison would be almost identical to fifteen, more, twenty years at the Tech confronting louts who despised him and talking about Piggy and the Lord of the Flies. Besides he could always plead the book as a mitigating circumstance at his trial.

'Me lud, members of the Jury, I ask you to put yourself in the defendant's place. For twelve years he has been confronted by the appalling prospect of reading this dreadful book to classes of bored and hostile youths. He has had to endure agonies of repetition, of nausea and disgust at Mr Golding's revoltingly romantic view of human nature. Ah, but I hear you say that Mr Golding is not a romantic, that his view of human nature as expressed in his portrait of a group of young boys marooned on a desert island is the very opposite of romanticism and that the sentimentality of which I accuse him and to which my client's appearance in this court attests is to be found not in *The Lord of the Flies* but in its predecessor, *Coral Island*. But, me lud, gentlemen of the Jury, there is such a thing as inverted romanticism, the romanticism of disillusionment, of pessimism and of nihilism. Let us suppose for one moment that my client had spent twelve years reading not Mr Golding's work but *Coral Island* to groups of apprentices; is it reasonable to imagine that he would have been driven to the desperate remedy of murdering his wife? No. A hundred times no. Mr Ballantyne's book would have given him the inspiration, the self-discipline, the optimism and the belief in man's ability to rescue himself from the most desperate situation by his own ingenuity ...'

It might not be such a good idea to pursue that line of argument too far. The defendant Wilt had after all exercised a good deal of ingenuity in rescuing himself from a desperate situation. Still, it was a nice thought. Wilt finished his business in the lavatory and looked around for the toilet paper. There wasn't any. The bloody roll had run out. He reached in his pocket and found Eva's note and put it to good use. Then he flushed it down the U-bend, puffed some Harpic after it to express his opinion of it and her and went out to the kitchen and helped himself to another gin.

He spent the rest of the evening sitting in front of the TV with a piece of bread and cheese and a tin of peaches until it was time to try his first dummy run. He went out to the front door and looked up and down the street. It was almost dark now and there was no one in sight. Leaving the front door open he went upstairs and fetched the doll and put it in the back seat of the car. He had to push and squeeze a bit to get it in but finally the door shut. Wilt climbed in and backed the car out into Parkview Avenue and drove down to the round-about. By the time he reached the car park at the back of the Tech it was half past ten exactly. He stopped and sat in the car looking around. Not a soul in sight and no lights on. There wouldn't be. The Tech closed at nine.

6

Sally lay naked on the deck of the cabin cruiser, her tight breasts pointing to the sky and her legs apart. Beside her Eva lay on her stomach and looked downriver.

'Oh God, this is divine,' Sally murmured. 'I have this deep thing about the countryside.'

'You've got this deep thing period,' said Gaskell steering the cruiser erratically towards a lock. He was wearing a Captain's cap and sunglasses.

'Cliché baby,' said Sally.

'We're coming to a lock,' said Eva anxiously. 'There are some men there.'

'Men? Forget men, darling. There's just you and me and G and G's not a man, are you G baby?'

'I have my moments,' said Gaskell.

'But so seldom, so awfully seldom,' Sally said. 'Anyway what does it matter? We're here idyllicstyle, cruising down the river in the good old summertime.'

'Shouldn't we have cleared the house up before we left?' Eva asked.

'The secret of parties is not to clear up afterward but to clear off. We can do all that when we get back.'

Eva got up and went below. They were quite near the lock and she wasn't going to be stared at in the nude by the two old men sitting on the bench beside it.

'Jesus, Sally, can't you do something about soulmate? She's getting on my teats,' said Gaskell.

'Oh G baby, she's never. If she did you'd Cheshire cat.'

'Cheshire cat?'

'Disappear with a smile, honey chil', foetus first. She's but positively gargantuanly uterine.'

'She's but positively gargantuanly boring.'

'Time, lover, time. You've got to accentuate the liberated, eliminate the negative and not mess with Mister-in-between.'

'Not mess with Missus-in-between. Operative word missus,' said Gaskell bumping the boat into the lock.

'But that's the whole point.'

'What is?' said Gaskell.

'Messing with Missus-in-between. I mean it's all ways with Eva and us. She does the housework. Gaskell baby can play ship's captain and teatfeast on boobs and Sally sweetie can minotaur her labyrinthine mind.'

'Mind?' said Gaskell. 'Polyunsaturated hasn't got a mind. And talking of cretins, what about Mister-in-between?'

'He's got Judy to mess with. He's probably screwing her now and tomorrow night he'll sit up and watch *Kojak* with her. Who knows, he may even send her off to Mavis Contracuntal Mottram's Flower Arrangement evening. I mean they're suited. You can't say he wasn't hooked on her last night.'

'You can say that again,' said Gaskell and closed the lock gates.

As the cruiser floated downwards the two old men sitting on

the bench stared at Sally. She took off her sunglasses and glared at them.

'Don't blow your prostates, senior citizens,' she said rudely. 'Haven't you seen a fanny before?'

'You talking to me?' said one of the men.

'I wouldn't be talking to myself.'

'Then I'll tell you,' said the man, 'I've seen one like yours before. Once.'

'Once is about right,' said Sally. 'Where?'

'On an old cow as had just dropped her calf,' said the man and spat into a neat bed of geraniums.

In the cabin Eva sat and wondered what they were talking about. She listened to the lapping of the water and the throb of the engine and thought about Henry. It wasn't like him to do a thing like that. It really wasn't. And in front of all those people. He must have been drunk. It was so humiliating. Well, he could suffer. Sally said men ought to be made to suffer. It was part of the process of liberating yourself from them. You had to show them that you didn't need them and violence was the only thing the male psyche understood. That was why she was so harsh with Gaskell. Men were like animals. You had to show them who was master.

Eva went through to the galley and polished the stainless-steel sink. Henry would have to learn how important she was by missing her and doing the housework and cooking for himself and when she got back she would give him such a telling-off about that doll. I mean, it wasn't natural. Perhaps Henry ought to go and see a psychiatrist. Sally said that he had made the most horrible suggestion to her too. It only went to show that you couldn't trust anyone. And Henry of all people. She would never have imagined Henry would think of doing anything like that. But Sally had been so sweet and understanding. She knew how women felt and she hadn't even been angry with Henry.

'It's just that he's a sphincter baby,' she had said. 'It's symptomatic of a male-dominated chauvinist pig society. I've never known an MCP who didn't say "Bugger you" and mean it.'

'Henry's always saying "Bugger",' Eva had admitted. 'It's bugger this, and bugger that.'

'There you are, Eva baby. What did I tell you? It's semantic degradation analwise.'

'It's bloody disgusting,' said Eva, and so it was.

She went on polishing and cleaning until they were clear of the lock and steering downriver towards the open water of the Broads. Then she went up on deck and sat looking out over the flat empty landscape at the sunset. It was all so romantic and exciting, so different from everything she had known before. This was life as she had always dreamt it might be, rich and gay and fulfilling. Eva Wilt sighed. In spite of everything she was at peace with the world.

In the car park at the back of the Tech Henry Wilt wasn't at peace with anything. On the contrary, he was at war with Eva's replica. As he stumbled drunkenly round the car and struggled with Judy he was conscious that even an inflatable doll had a will of its own when it came to being dragged out of small cars. Judy's arms and legs got caught in things. If Eva behaved in the same way on the night of her disposal he would have the devil's own job getting her out of the car. He would have to tie her up in a neat bundle. That would be the best thing to do. Finally, by tugging at the doll's legs, he hauled her out and laid her on the ground. Then he got back into the car to look for her wig. He found it under the seat and after rearranging Judy's skirt so that it wasn't quite so revealing, he put the wig on her head. He looked round the car park at the terrapin huts and the main building but there was no one to be seen. All clear. He picked the doll up and carrying it under his arm set off towards the building site. Halfway there he realized that he wasn't doing it properly. Eva drugged and sleeping would be far too heavy to carry under his arm. He would have to use a fireman's lift. Wilt stopped and hoisted the doll on to his back, and set off again weaving erratically, partly because, thanks to the gin, he couldn't help it, and partly because it added verisimilitude to the undertaking. With Eva over his shoulder he would be bound to weave a bit. He reached the fence and dropped the doll over. In the process the wig fell off again. Wilt groped around in the mud and found it. Then he went round to the gate. It was locked. It would be. He would have to remember that. Details like that were important. He tried to climb over but couldn't. He needed something to give him a leg up. A bicycle. There were usually some in the racks by the main gate. Stuffing the wig into his pocket Wilt made his way round the terrapin huts and past the canteen and was just crossing the grass by the Language Lab when a figure appeared out of the darkness and a torch shone in his face. It was the caretaker.

'Here, where do you think you're going?' the caretaker asked. Wilt halted.

'I've ... I've just come back to get some notes from the Staff Room.'

'Oh it's you, Mr Wilt,' said the caretaker. 'You should know by now that you can't get in at this time of night. We lock up at nine thirty.'

'I'm sorry. I forgot,' said Wilt.

The caretaker sighed. 'Well, since it's you and it's just this once ...' he said, and unlocked the door to the General Studies building. 'You'll have to walk up. The lifts don't work at this time of night. I'll wait for you down here.'

Wilt staggered slowly up five flights of stairs to the Staff Room and went to his locker. He took out a handful of papers and a copy of *Bleak House* he'd been meaning to take home for some months and hadn't. He stuffed the notes into his pocket and found the wig. While he was about it he might as well pick up an elastic band. That would keep the wig on Judy's head. He found some in a box in the stationery cupboard, stuffed the notes into his other pocket and went downstairs.

'Thanks very much,' he told the caretaker. 'Sorry to have bothered you.' He wove off round the corner to the bike sheds.

'Pissed as a newt,' said the caretaker, and went back into his office.

Wilt watched him light his pipe and then turned his attention to the bicycles. The bloody things were all locked. He would just have to carry one round. He put *Bleak House* in the basket, picked the bike up and carried it all the way round to the fence. Then he climbed up and over and groped around in the darkness for the doll. In the end he found it and spent five minutes trying to keep the wig on while he fastened the elastic band under her chin. It kept on jumping off. 'Well, at least that's one problem I won't have with Eva,' he muttered to himself when the wig was secured. Having satisfied himself that it wouldn't come off he moved cautiously forward skirting mounds of gravel, machines, sacks and reinforcing rods when it suddenly occurred to him that he was running a considerable risk of disappearing down one of the pile holes himself. He put the doll down and fumbled in his pocket for the torch and shone it on the ground. Some yards ahead there was a large square of thick plywood. Wilt moved forward and lifted it. Underneath was the hole, a nice big hole. Just the right size. She would fit in there perfectly. He shone the torch down. Must be thirty feet deep. He pushed the plywood to one side and went back for the doll. The wig had fallen off again.

'Fuck,' said Wilt, and reached in his pocket for another elastic band. Five minutes later Judy's wig was firmly in place with four elastic bands fastened under her chin. That should do it. Now all he had to do was to drag the replica to the hole and make sure it fitted. At this point Wilt hesitated. He was beginning to have doubts about the soundness of the scheme. Too many unexpected contingencies had arisen for his liking. On the other hand there was a sense of exhilaration about being alone on the building site in the middle of the night. Perhaps it would be better if he went home now. No, he had to see the thing through. He would put the doll into the hole to make quite sure that it fitted. Then he would deflate it and go home and repeat the process until he had trained himself to kill by proxy. He would keep the doll in the boot of the car. Eva never looked there. And in future he would only blow her up when he reached the car park. That way Eva would have no idea what was going on. Definitely not. Wilt smiled to himself at the simplicity of the scheme. Then he picked Judy up and pushed her towards the hole feet first. She slid in easily while Wilt leant forward. Perfect. And at that moment he slipped on the muddy ground. With a desperate effort which necessitated letting go of the doll he hurled himself to one side and grabbed at the plywood. He got to his feet cautiously and cursed. His trousers were covered with mud and his hands were shaking.

'Damned near went down myself,' he muttered, and looked around for Judy. But Judy had disappeared. Wilt reached for his torch and shone it down the hole. Halfway down the doll was wedged lightly against the sides and for once the wig was still on. Wilt stared desperately down at the thing and wondered what the hell to do. It – or she – must be at least twenty feet down. Fifteen. Anyway a long way down and certainly too far for him to reach. But still too near the top not to be clearly visible to the workmen in the morning. Wilt switched off the torch and pulled the plywood square so that it covered the hole. That way he wouldn't be in danger of joining the doll. Then he stood up and tried to think of ways of getting it out.

Rope with a hook on the end of it? He hadn't a rope or a hook. He might be able to find a rope but hooks were another matter. Get a rope and tie it to something and climb down it and bring the doll up? Certainly not. It would be bad enough climbing down the rope with two hands but to think of climbing back up with one hand holding the doll in the other was sheer lunacy. That way he would end up at the bottom of the hole himself and if one thing was clear in his mind it was that he didn't intend to be discovered at the bottom of a thirty-foot pile hole on Monday morning clutching a plastic fucking doll with a cunt dressed in his wife's clothes. That way lay disaster. Wilt visualized the scene in the Principal's office as he tried to explain how he came to be ... And anyway they might not find him or hear his yells. Those damned cement lorries made a hell of a din and he bloody well wasn't going to risk being buried under ... Shit. Talk about poetic justice. No, the only thing to do was to get that fucking doll down to the bottom of the hole and hope to hell that no one spotted it before they poured the concrete in. Well, at least that way he would learn if it was a sensible method of getting rid of Eva. There was that to be said for it. Every cloud had ...

Wilt left the hole and looked around for something to move Judy down to the bottom. He tried a handful of gravel but she merely wobbled a bit and stayed put. Something weightier was needed. He went across to a pile of sand and scooped some into a plastic sack and poured it down the hole, but apart from adding an extra dimension of macabre realism to Mrs Wilt's wig the sand did nothing. Perhaps if he dropped a brick on the doll it would burst. Wilt looked around for a brick and ended up with a large lump of clay. That would have to do. He dropped it down the hole. There was a thump, a rattle of gravel and another thump. Wilt shone his torch down. Judy had reached the bottom of the hole and had settled into a grotesque position with her legs crumpled up in front of her and one arm outstretched towards him as if in supplication. Wilt fetched another lump of clay and hurled it down. This time the wig slid sideways and her head lolled. Wilt gave up. There was nothing more he could do. He pulled the plywood back over the hole and went back to the fence.

Here he ran into more trouble. The bicycle was on the other side. He fetched a plank, leant it against the fence and climbed over. Now to carry the bike back to the shed. Oh bugger the bicycle. It could stay where it was. He was fed up with the whole business. He couldn't even dispose of a plastic doll properly. It was ludicrous to think that he could plan, commit and carry through a real murder with any hope of success. He must have been mad to think of it. It was all that blasted gin.

'That's right, blame the gin,' Wilt muttered to himself, as he trudged back to his car. 'You had this idea months ago.' He climbed into the car and sat there in the darkness wondering what on earth had ever possessed him to have fantasies of murdering Eva. It was insane, utterly insane, and just as mad to imagine that he could train himself to become a cold-blooded killer. Where had the idea originated from? What was it all about? All right, Eva was a stupid cow who made his life a misery by nagging at him and by indulging a taste for Eastern mysticism with a frenetic enthusiasm calculated to derange the soberest of husbands, but why his obsession with murder? Why the need to prove his manliness by violence? Where had he got that from? In the middle of the car park, Henry Wilt, suddenly sober and clear-headed, realized the extraordinary effect that ten years of Liberal Studies had had upon him. For ten long years Plasterers Two and Meat One had been exposed to culture in the shape of Wilt and *The Lord of the Flies*, and for as many years Wilt himself had been exposed to the barbarity, the unhesitating readiness to commit violence of Plasterers Two and Meat One. That was the genesis of it all. That and the unreality of the literature he had been forced to absorb. For ten years Wilt had been the duct along which travelled creatures of imagination, Nostromo, Jack and Piggy, Shane, creatures who acted and whose actions effected something. And all the time he saw himself, mirrored in their eyes, an ineffectual passive person responding solely to the dictates of circumstance. Wilt shook his head. And out of all that and the traumas of the past two days had been born this *acte gratuit*, this semi-crime, the symbolic murder of Eva Wilt.

He started the car and drove out of the car park. He would go and see the Braintrees. They would still be up and glad to see him and besides he needed to talk to someone. Behind him on the building site his notes on Violence and the Break-Up of Family Life drifted about in the night wind and stuck in the mud.

7

'Nature is so libidinous,' said Sally, shining a torch through the porthole at the reeds. 'I mean take bullrushes. I mean they're positively archetypally phallus. Don't you think so, G?'

'Bullrushes?' said Gaskell, gazing helplessly at a chart. 'Bullrushes do nothing for me.'

'Maps neither, by the look of it.'

'Charts, baby, charts.'

'What's in a name?'

'Right now, a hell of a lot. We're either in Frogwater Reach or Fen Broad. No telling which.'

'Give me Fen Broad every time. I just adore broads. Eva sweetheart, how's about another pot of coffee? I want to stay awake all night and watch the dawn come up over the bullrushes.'

'Yes, well I don't,' said Gaskell. 'Last night was enough for me. That crazy guy with the doll in the bath and Schei cutting himself. That's enough for one day. I'm going to hit the sack.'

'The deck,' said Sally, 'hit the deck, G. Eva and I are sleeping down here. Three's a crowd.'

'Three? With boobs around it's five at the least. OK, so I sleep on deck. We've got to be up early if we're to get off this damned sandbank.'

'Has Captain Pringsheim stranded us, baby?'

'It's these charts. If only they would give an exact indication of depth.'

'If you knew where we were, you'd probably find they do. It's no use knowing it's three feet—'

'Fathoms, honey, fathoms.'

'Three fathoms in Frogwater Reach if we're really in Fen Broad.'

'Well, wherever we are, you'd better start hoping there's a tide that will rise and float us off,' said Gaskell.

'And if there isn't?'

'Then we'll have to think of something else. Maybe someone will come along and tow us off.'

'Oh God, G, you're the skilfullest,' said Sally. 'I mean why couldn't we have just stayed out in the middle? But no, you had to come steaming up this creek wham into a mudbank and all because of what? Ducks, goddamned ducks.'

'Waders, baby, waders. Not just ducks.'

'OK, so they're waders. You want to photograph them so now we're stuck where no one in their right minds would come in a boat. Who do you think is going to come up here? Jonathan Seagull?'

In the galley Eva made coffee. She was wearing the bright red plastic bikini Sally had lent her. It was rather too small for her so that she bulged round it uncomfortably and it was revealingly tight but at least it was better than going around naked even though Sally said nudity was being liberated and look at the Amazonian Indians. She should have brought her own things but Sally had insisted on hurrying and now all she had were the lemon loungers and the bikini. Honestly Sally was so authora ... authorasomething ... well, bossy then.

'Dual-purpose plastic, baby, apronwise,' she had said, 'and G has this thing about plastic, haven't you, G?'

'Bio-degradably yes.'

'Bio-degradably?' asked Eva, hoping to be initiated into some new aspect of women's liberation.

'Plastic bottles that disintegrate instead of lying around making an ecological swamp,' said Sally, opening a porthole and dropping an empty cigar packet over the side, 'that's G's lifework. That and recyclability. Infinite recyclability.'

'Right,' said Gaskell. 'We've got in-built obsolescence in the automotive field where it's outmoded. So what we need now is in-built bio-degradable deliquescence in ephemera.'

Eva listened uncomprehendingly but with the feeling that she was somehow at the centre of an intellectual world far surpassing that of Henry and his friends who talked about new degree courses and their students so boringly.

'We've got a compost heap at the bottom of the garden,' she said when she finally understood what they were talking about. 'I put the potato peelings and odds and ends on it.'

Gaskell raised his eyes to the cabin roof. Correction. Deckhead.

'Talking of odds and ends,' said Sally, running a fond hand over Eva's bottom, 'I wonder how Henry is getting along with Judy.'

Eva shuddered. The thought of Henry and the doll lying in the bath still haunted her.

'I can't think what had got into him,' she said, and looked disapprovingly at Gaskell when he sniggered. 'I mean it's not as if he has ever been unfaithful or anything like that. And lots of husbands are. Patrick Mottram is always going off and having affairs with other women but Henry's been very good in that respect. He may be quiet and not very pushing but no one could call him a gadabout.'

'Oh sure,' said Gaskell, 'so he's got a hang-up about sex. My heart bleeds for him.'

'I don't see why you should say he's got something wrong with him because he's faithful,' said Eva.

'G didn't mean that, did you, G?' said Sally. 'He meant that there has to be true freedom in a marriage. No dominance, no jealousy, no possession. Right, G?'

'Right,' said Gaskell.

'The test of true love is when you can watch your wife having it off with someone else and still love her,' Sally went on.

'I could never watch Henry . . .' said Eva. 'Never.'

'So you don't love him. You're insecure. You don't trust him.'

'Trust him?' said Eva. 'If Henry went to bed with another woman I don't see how I could trust him. I mean if that's what he wants to do why did he marry me?'

'That,' said Gaskell, 'is the sixty-four-thousand dollar question.' He picked up his sleeping bag and went out on deck. Behind him Eva had begun to cry.

'There, there,' said Sally, putting her arm round her. 'G was just kidding. He didn't mean anything.'

'It's not that,' said Eva, 'it's just that I don't understand anything any more. It's all so complicated.'

'Christ, you look bloody awful,' said Peter Braintree as Wilt stood on the doorstep.

'I feel bloody awful,' said Wilt. 'It's all this gin.'

'You mean Eva's not back?' said Braintree, leading the way down the passage to the kitchen.

'She wasn't there when I got home. Just a note saying she was going away with the Pringsheims to think things over.'

'To think things over? Eva? What things?'

'Well . . .' Wilt began and thought better of it, 'that business with Sally I suppose. She says she won't ever forgive me.'

'But you didn't do anything with Sally. That's what you told me.'

'I know I didn't. That's the whole point. If I had done what that nymphomaniac bitch wanted there wouldn't have been all this bloody trouble.'

'I don't see that, Henry. I mean if you had done what she wanted Eva would have had something to grumble about. I don't see why she should be up in the air because you didn't.'

'Sally must have told her that I did do something,' said Wilt, determined not to mention the incident in the bathroom with the doll.

'You mean the blow job?'

'I don't know what I mean. What is a blow job anyway?'

Peter Braintree looked puzzled.

'I'm not too sure,' he said, 'but it's obviously something you don't want your husband to do. If I came home and told Betty I'd done a blow job she'd think I'd been robbing a bank.'

'I wasn't going to do it anyway,' said Wilt. 'She was going to do it to me.'

'Perhaps it's a suck off,' said Braintree, putting a kettle on the stove. 'That's what it sounds like to me.'

'Well it didn't sound like that to me,' said Wilt with a shudder. 'She made it sound like a paint-peeling exercise with a blow lamp. You should have seen the look on her face.'

He sat down at the kitchen table despondently.

Braintree eyed him curiously. 'You certainly seem to have been in the wars,' he said.

Wilt looked down at his trousers. They were covered with mud and there were round patches caked to his knees. 'Yes . . . well . . . well I had a puncture on the way here,' he explained with lack of conviction. 'I had to change a tyre and I knelt down. I was a bit pissed.'

Peter Braintree grunted doubtfully. It didn't sound very convincing to him. Poor old Henry was obviously a bit under the weather. 'You can wash up in the sink,' he said.

Presently Betty Braintree came downstairs. 'I couldn't help hearing what you said about Eva,' she said. 'I'm so sorry, Henry. I wouldn't worry. She's bound to come back.'

'I wouldn't be too sure,' said Wilt, gloomily, 'and anyway I'm not so sure I want her back.'

'Oh, Eva's all right,' Betty said. 'She gets these sudden urges and enthusiasms but they don't last long. It's just the way she's made. It's easy come and easy go with Eva.'

'I think that's what's worrying Henry,' said Braintree, 'the easy come bit.'

'Oh surely not. Eva isn't that sort at all.'

Wilt sat at the kitchen table and sipped his coffee. 'I wouldn't put anything past her in the company she's keeping now,' he muttered lugubriously. 'Remember what happened when she went through that macrobiotic diet phase? Dr Mannix told me I was the nearest thing to a case of scurvy he'd seen since the Burma railway. And then there was that episode with the trampoline. She went to a Keep Fit Class at Bulham Village College and bought herself a fucking trampoline. You know she put old Mrs Portway in hospital with that contraption.'

'I knew there was some sort of accident but Eva never told me what actually happened,' said Betty.

'She wouldn't. It was a ruddy miracle we didn't get sued,' said Wilt. 'It threw Mrs Portway clean through the greenhouse roof. There was glass all over the lawn and it wasn't even as though Mrs Portway was a healthy woman at the best of times.'

'Wasn't she the woman with the rheumatoid arthritis?'

Wilt nodded dismally. 'And the duelling scars on her face,' he said. 'That was our greenhouse, that was.'

'I must say I can think of better places for trampolines than greenhouses,' said Braintree. 'It wasn't a very big greenhouse was it?'

'It wasn't a very big trampoline either, thank God,' said Wilt, 'she'd have been in orbit otherwise.'

'Well it all goes to prove one thing,' said Betty, looking on the bright side, 'Eva may do crazy things but she soon gets over them.'

'Mrs Portway didn't,' said Wilt, not to be comforted. 'She was in hospital for six weeks and the skin grafts didn't take. She hasn't been near our house since.'

'You'll see. Eva will get fed up with these Pringsheim people in a week or two. They're just another fad.'

'A fad with a lot of advantages if you ask me,' said Wilt. 'Money, status and sexual promiscuity. All the things I couldn't give her and all dressed up in a lot of intellectual claptrap about Women's Lib and violence and the intolerance of tolerance and the revolution of the sexes and you're not fully mature unless you're ambisextrous. It's enough to make you vomit and it's just the sort of crap Eva would fall for. I mean she'd buy rotten herrings if some clown up the social scale told her they were the sophisticated things to eat. Talk about being gullible!'

'The thing is that Eva's got too much energy,' said Betty. 'You should try and persuade her to get a full-time job.'

'Full-time job?' said Wilt. 'She's had more full-time jobs than I've had hot dinners. Mind you, that's not saying much these days. All I ever get is a cold supper and a note saying she's gone to Pottery or Transcendental Meditation or something equally half-baked. And anyway Eva's idea of a job is to take over the factory. Remember Potters, that engineering firm that went broke after a strike a couple of years ago? Well, if you ask me that was Eva's fault. She got this job with a consultancy firm doing time and motion study and they sent her out to the factory and the next thing anyone knew they had a strike on their hands ...'

They went on talking for another hour until the Braintrees asked him to stay the night. But Wilt wouldn't. 'I've got things to do tomorrow.'

'Such as?'

'Feed the dog for one thing.'

'You can always drive over and do that. Clem won't starve overnight.'

But Wilt was too immersed in self-pity to be persuaded and besides he was still worried about that doll. He might have another go at getting the thing out of that hole. He drove home and went to bed in a tangle of sheets and blankets. He hadn't made it in the morning.

'Poor old Henry,' said Betty as she and Peter went upstairs. 'He did look pretty awful.'

'He said he'd had a puncture and had to change the wheel.'

'I wasn't thinking of his clothes. It was the look on his face that worried me. You don't think he's on the verge of a breakdown?'

Peter Braintree shook his head. 'You'd look like that if you had Gasfitters Three and Plasterers Two every day of your life for ten years and then your wife ran away,' he told her.

'Why don't they give him something better to teach?'

'Why? Because the Tech wants to become a Poly and they keep starting new degree courses and hiring people with PhDs to teach them and then the students don't enrol and they're lumbered with specialists like Dr Fitzpatrick who knows all there is to know about child labour in four cotton mills in Manchester in 1837 and damn all about anything else. Put him in front of a class of Day Release Apprentices and all hell would break loose. As it is I have to go into his A-level classes once a week and tell them to shut up. On the other hand Henry looks meek but he can cope with rowdies. He's too good at his job. That's his trouble and besides he's not a bumsucker and that's the kiss of death at the Tech. If you don't lick arses you get nowhere.'

'You know,' said Betty, 'teaching at that place has done horrible things to your language.'

'It's done horrible things to my outlook on life, never mind my language,' said Braintree. 'It's enough to drive a man to drink.'

'It certainly seems to have done that to Henry. His breath reeked of gin.'

'He'll get over it.'

But Wilt didn't. He woke in the morning with the feeling that something was missing quite apart from Eva. That bloody doll. He lay in bed trying to think of some way of retrieving the thing before the workmen arrived on the site on Monday morning but apart from pouring a can of petrol down the hole and lighting it, which seemed on reflection the best way of drawing attention to the fact that he had stuffed a plastic doll dressed in his wife's clothes down there, he could think of nothing practical. He would just have to trust to luck.

When the Sunday papers came he got out of bed and went down to read them over his All-Bran. Then he fed the dog and mooched about the house in his pyjamas, walked down to the Ferry Path Inn for lunch, slept in the afternoon and watched the box all evening. Then he made the bed and got into it and spent a restless night wondering where Eva was, what she was doing, and why, since he had occupied so many fruitless hours speculating on ways of getting rid of her homicidally, he should be in the least concerned now that she had gone of her own accord.

'I mean if I didn't want this to happen why did I keep thinking up ways of killing her,' he thought at two o'clock. 'Sane people don't go for walks with a Labrador and devise schemes for murdering their wives when they can just as easily divorce them.' There was probably some foul psychological reason for it. Wilt could think of several himself, rather too many in fact to be able to decide which was the most likely one. In any case a psychological explanation demanded a degree of self-knowledge which Wilt, who wasn't at all sure he had a self to know, felt was denied him. Ten years of Plasterers Two and Exposure to Barbarism had at least given him the insight to know that there was an answer for every question and it didn't much matter what answer you gave so long as you gave it convincingly. In the fourteenth century they would have said the devil put such thoughts into his head, now in a post-Freudian world it had to be a complex or, to be really up-to-date, a chemical imbalance. In a hundred years they would have come up with some completely different explanation. With the comforting thought that the truths of one age were the absurdities of another and that it didn't much matter what you thought so long as you did the right thing, and in his view he did, Wilt finally fell asleep.

At seven he was woken by the alarm clock and by half past eight had parked his car in the parking lot behind the Tech.

He walked past the building site where the workmen were already at work. Then he went up to the Staff Room and looked out of the window. The square of plywood was still in place covering the hole but the pile-boring machine had been backed away. They had evidently finished with it.

At five to nine he collected twenty-five copies of *Shane* from the cupboard and took them across to Motor Mechanics Three. *Shane* was the ideal soporific. It would keep the brutes quiet while he sat and watched what happened down below. Room 593 in the Engineering block gave him a grandstand view. Wilt filled in the register and handed out copies of *Shane* and told the class to get on with it. He said it with a good deal more vigour than was usual even for a Monday morning and the class settled down to consider the plight of the home-steaders while Wilt stared out of the window, absorbed in a more immediate drama.

A lorry with a revolving drum filled with liquid concrete had arrived on the site and was backing slowly towards the plywood square. It stopped and there was an agonizing wait while the driver climbed down from the cab and lit a cigarette. Another man, evidently the foreman, came out of a wooden hut and wandered across to the lorry and presently a little group was gathered round the hole. Wilt got up from his desk and went over to the window. Why the hell didn't they get a move on? Finally the driver got back into his cab and two men re-moved the plywood. The foreman signalled to the driver. The chute for the concrete was swung into position. Another sig-nal. The drum began to tilt. The concrete was coming. Wilt watched as it began to pour down the chute and just at that moment the foreman looked down the hole. So did one of the workmen. The next instant all hell had broken loose. There were frantic signals and shouts from the foreman. Through the window Wilt watched the open mouths and the gesticula-tions but still the concrete came. Wilt shut his eyes and shuddered. They had found that fucking doll.

Outside on the building site the air was thick with misunder-standing.

'What's that? I'm pouring as fast as I can,' shouted the

driver, misconstruing the frenzied signals of the foreman. He pulled the lever still further and the concrete flood increased. The next moment he was aware that he had made some sort of mistake. The foreman was wrenching at the door of the cab and screaming blue murder.

'Stop, for God's sake stop,' he shouted. 'There's a woman down that hole!'

'A what?' said the driver, and switched off the engine.

'A fucking woman and look what you've been and fucking done. I told you to stop. I told you to stop pouring and you went on. You've been and poured twenty tons of liquid concrete on her.'

The driver climbed down from his cab and went round to the chute where the last trickles of cement were still sliding hesitantly into the hole.

'A woman?' he said. 'What? Down that hole? What's she doing down there?'

The foreman stared at him demonically. 'Doing?' he bellowed, 'what do you think she's doing? What would you be doing if you'd just had twenty tons of liquid concrete dumped on top of you? Fucking drowning, that's what.'

The driver scratched his head. 'Well I didn't know she was down there. How was I to know? You should have told me.'

'Told you?' shrieked the foreman. 'I told you. I told you to stop. You weren't listening.'

'I thought you wanted me to pour faster. I couldn't hear what you were saying.'

'Well, every other bugger could,' yelled the foreman. Certainly Wilt in Room 593 could. He stared wild-eyed out of the window as the panic spread. Beside him Motor Mechanics Three had lost all interest in *Shane*. They clustered at the window and watched.

'Are you quite sure?' asked the driver.

'Sure? Course I'm sure,' yelled the foreman. 'Ask Barney.'

The other workman, evidently Barney, nodded. 'She was down there all right. I'll vouch for that. All crumpled up she was. She had one hand up in the air and her legs was ...'

'Jesus,' said the driver, visibly shaken. 'What the hell are we going to do now?'

It was a question that had been bothering Wilt. Call the Police, presumably. The foreman confirmed his opinion. 'Get the cops. Get an ambulance. Get the Fire Brigade and get a pump. For God's sake get a pump.'

'Pump's no good,' said the driver, 'you'll never pump that concrete out of there, not in a month of Sundays. Anyway it wouldn't do any good. She'll be dead by now. Crushed to death. Wouldn't drown with twenty tons on her. Why didn't she say something?'

'Would it have made any difference if she had?' asked the foreman hoarsely. 'You'd have still gone on pouring.'

'Well, how did she get down there in the first place?' said the driver, to change the subject.

'How the fuck would I know. She must have fallen . . .'

'And pulled that plywood sheet over her, I suppose,' said Barney, who clearly had a practical turn of mind. 'She was bloody murdered.'

'We all know that,' squawked the foreman. 'By Chris here. I told him to stop pouring. You heard me. Everyone for half a mile must have heard me but not Chris. Oh, no, he has to go on—'

'She was murdered before she was put down the hole,' said Barney. 'That wooden cover wouldn't have been there if she had fallen down herself.'

The foreman wiped his face with a handkerchief and looked at the square of plywood. 'There is that to it,' he muttered. 'No one can say we didn't take proper safety precautions. You're right. She must have been murdered. Oh, my God!'

'Sex crime, like as not,' said Barney. 'Raped and strangled her. That or someone's missus. You mark my words. She was all crumpled up and that hand . . . I'll never forget that hand, not if I live to be a hundred.'

The foreman stared at him lividly. He seemed incapable of expressing his feelings. So was Wilt. He went back to his desk and sat with his head in his hands while the class gaped out of the window and tried to catch what was being said. Presently sirens sounded in the distance and grew louder. A police car arrived, four fire engines hurtled into the car park and an ambulance followed. As more and more uniformed men gathered around what had once been a hole in the ground it became apparent that getting the doll down there had been a damned sight easier than getting it out.

'That concrete starts setting in twenty minutes,' the driver explained when a pump was suggested for the umpteenth time. An Inspector of Police and the Fire Chief stared down at the hole.

'Are you sure you saw a woman's body down there?' the Inspector asked. 'You're positive about it?'

'Positive?' squeaked the foreman. 'Course I'm positive. You don't think ... Tell them, Barney. He saw her too.'

Barney told the Inspector even more graphically than before. 'She had this hair see and her hand was reaching up like it was asking for help and there were these fingers ... I tell you it was horrible. It didn't look natural.'

'No, well, it wouldn't,' said the Inspector sympathetically. 'And you say there was a board on top of the hole when you arrived this morning.'

The foreman gesticulated silently and Barney showed them the board. 'I was standing on it at one time,' he said. 'It was here all right so help me God.'

'The thing is, how are we to get her out?' said the Fire Chief. It was a point that was put to the manager of the construction company when he finally arrived on the scene. 'God alone knows,' he said. 'There's no easy way of getting that concrete out now. We'd have to use drills to get down thirty feet.'

At the end of the hour they were no nearer a solution to the problem. As the Motor Mechanics dragged themselves away from this fascinating situation to go to Technical Drawing, Wilt collected the unread copies of *Shane* and walked across to the Staff Room in a state of shock. The only consolation he could think of was that it would take them at least two or three days to dig down and discover that what had all the appearances of being the body of a murdered woman was in fact an inflatable doll. Or had been once. Wilt rather doubted if it would be inflated now. There had been something horribly intractable about that liquid concrete.

8

There was something horribly intractable about the mud-bank on which the cabin cruiser had grounded. To add to their troubles the engine had gone wrong. Gaskell said it was a broken con rod.

'Is that serious?' asked Sally.

'It just means we'll have to be towed to a boatyard.'

'By what?'

'By a passing cruiser I guess,' said Gaskell.

Sally looked over the side at the bullrushes.

'Passing?' she said. 'We've been here all night and half the morning and nothing has passed so far and if it did we wouldn't be able to see it for all these fucking bullrushes.'

'I thought bullrushes did something for you.'

'That was yesterday,' snapped Sally. 'Today they just mean we're invisible to anyone more than fifty feet away. And now you've screwed the motor. I told you not to rev it like that.'

'So how was I to know it would bust a con rod,' said Gaskell. 'I was just trying to get us off this mudbank. You just tell me how I'm supposed to do it without revving the goddam motor.'

'You could get out and push.'

Gaskell peered over the side. 'I could get out and drown,' he said.

'So the boat would be lighter,' said Sally. 'We've all got to make sacrifices and you said the tide would float us off.'

'Well I was mistaken. That's fresh water down there and means the tide doesn't reach this far.'

'Now he tells me. First we're in Frogwater Beach ...'

'Reach,' said Gaskell.

'Frogwater wherever. Then we're in Fen Broad. Now where are we for God's sake?'

'On a mudbank,' said Gaskell.

In the cabin Eva bustled about. There wasn't much space for

bustling but what there was she put to good use. She made the bunks and put the bedding away in the lockers underneath and she plumped the cushions and emptied the ashtrays. She swept the floor and polished the table and wiped the windows and dusted the shelves and generally made everything as neat and tidy as it was possible to make it. And all the time her thoughts got untidier and more muddled so that by the time she was finished and every object in sight was in its right place and the whole cabin properly arranged she was quite confused and in two minds about nearly everything.

The Pringsheims were ever so sophisticated and rich and intellectual and said clever things all the time but they were always quarrelling and getting at one another about something and to be honest they were quite impractical and didn't know the first thing about hygiene. Gaskell went to the lavatory and didn't wash his hands afterwards and goodness only knew when he had last had a shave. And look at the way they had walked out of the house in Rossiter Grove without clearing up after the party and the living-room all over cups and things. Eva had been quite shocked. She would never have left her house in that sort of mess. She had said as much to Sally but Sally had said how nonspontaneous could you get and anyway they were only renting the house for the summer and that it was typical of a male-oriented social system to expect a woman to enter a contractual relationship based upon female domestic servitude. Eva tried to follow her and was left feeling guilty because she couldn't and because it was evidently infra dig to be houseproud and she was.

And then there was what Henry had been doing with that doll. It was so unlike Henry to do anything like that and the more she thought about it the more unlike Henry it became. He must have been drunk but even so ... without his clothes on? And where had he found the doll? She had asked Sally and had been horrified to learn that Gaskell was mad about plastic and just adored playing games with Judy and men were like that and so to the only meaningful relationships being between women because women didn't need to prove their virility by any overt act of extrasexual violence did they? By which time Eva was lost in a maze of words she didn't understand but which sounded important and they had had another session of Touch Therapy.

And that was another thing she was in two minds about. Touch Therapy. Sally had said she was still inhibited and being inhibited was a sign of emotional and sensational immaturity. Eva battled with her mixed feelings about the matter. On the one hand she didn't want to be emotionally and sensationally immature and if the revulsion she felt lying naked in the arms of another woman was anything to go by and in Eva's view the nastier a medicine tasted the more likely it was to do you good, then she was certainly improving her psycho-sexual behaviour pattern by leaps and bounds. On the other hand she wasn't altogether convinced that Touch Therapy was quite nice. It was only by the application of considerable will-power that she overcame her objections to it and even so there was an undertow of doubt about the propriety of being touched quite so sensationally. It was all very puzzling and to cap it all she was on the Pill. Eva had objected very strongly and had pointed out that Henry and she had always wanted babies and she'd never had any but Sally had insisted.

'Eva baby,' she had said, 'with Gaskell one just never knows. Sometimes he goes for months without so much as a twitch and then, bam, he comes all over the place. He's totally undiscriminating.'

'But I thought you said you had this big thing between you,' Eva said.

'Oh, sure. In a blue moon. Scientists sublimate and G just lives for plastic. And we wouldn't want you to go back to Henry with G's genes in your ovum, now would we?'

'Certainly not,' said Eva horrified at the thought and had taken the pill after breakfast before going through to the tiny galley to wash up. It was all so different from Trascendental Meditation and Pottery.

On deck Sally and Gaskell were still wrangling.

'What the hell are you giving brainless boobs?' Gaskell asked.

'TT, Body Contact, Tactile Liberation,' said Sally. 'She's sensually deprived.'

'She's mentally deprived too. I've met some dummies in my time but this one is the dimwittiest. Anyway, I meant those pills she takes at breakfast.'

Sally smiled. 'Oh those,' she said.

'Yes those. You blowing what little mind she's got or something?' said Gaskell. 'We've got enough troubles without Moby Dick taking a trip.'

'Oral contraceptives, baby, just the plain old Pill.'

'Oral contraceptives? What the hell for? I wouldn't touch her with a sterilized stirring rod.'

'Gaskell, honey, you're so naïve. For authenticity, pure authenticity. It makes my relationship with her so much more real, don't you think. Like wearing a rubber on a dildo.'

Gaskell gaped at her. 'Jesus, you don't mean you've . . .'

'Not yet. Long John Silver is still in his bag but one of these days when she's a little more emancipated. . . .' She smiled wistfully over the bullrushes. 'Perhaps it doesn't matter all that much us being stuck here. It gives us time, so much lovely time and you can look at your ducks . . .'

'Waders,' said Gaskell, 'and we're going to run up one hell of a bill at the Marina if we don't get this boat back in time.'

'Bill?' said Sally. 'You're crazy. You don't think we're paying for this hulk?'

'But you hired her from the boatyard. I mean you're not going to tell me you just took the boat,' said Gaskell. 'For Chrissake, that's theft!'

Sally laughed. 'Honestly, G, you're so moral. I mean you're inconsistent. You steal books from the library and chemicals from the lab but when it comes to boats you're all up in the air.'

'Books are different,' said Gaskell hotly.

'Yes,' said Sally, 'books you don't go to jail for. That's what's different. So you want to think I stole the boat, you go on thinking that.'

Gaskell took out a handkerchief and wiped his glasses. 'Are you telling me you didn't?' he asked finally.

'I borrowed it.'

'Borrowed it? Who from?'

'Schei.'

'Scheimacher?'

'That's right. He said we could have it whenever we wanted it so we've got it.'

'Does he know we've got it?'

Sally sighed. 'Look, he's in India isn't he, currying sperm? So what does it matter what he knows? By the time he gets back we'll be in the Land of the Free.'

'Shit,' said Gaskell wearily, 'one of these days you're going to land us in it up to the eyeballs.'

'Gaskell honey, sometimes you bore me with your worrying so.'

'Let me tell you something. You worry me with your goddam attitude to other people's property.'

'Property is theft.'

'Oh sure. You just get the cops to see it that way when they catch up with you. The fuzz don't go a ball on stealing in this country.'

The fuzz weren't going much of a ball on the well-nourished body of a woman apparently murdered and buried under thirty feet and twenty tons of rapidly setting concrete. Barney had supplied the well-nourished bit. 'She had big breasts too,' he explained, in the seventh version of what he had seen. 'And this hand reaching up—'

'Yes, well we know all about the hand,' said Inspector Flint. 'We've been into all that before but this is the first time you've mentioned breasts.'

'It was the hand that got me,' said Barney. 'I mean you don't think of breasts in a situation like that.'

The Inspector turned to the foreman. 'Did you notice the deceased's breasts?' he enquired. But the foreman just shook his head. He was past speech.

'So we've got a well-nourished woman ... What age would you say?'

Barney scratched his chin reflectively. 'Not old,' he said finally. 'Definitely not old.'

'In her twenties?'

'Could have been.'

'In her thirties?'

Barney shrugged. There was something he was trying to recall. Something that had seemed odd at the time.

'But definitely not in her forties?'

'No,' said Barney. 'Younger than that.' He said it rather hesitantly.

'You're not being very specific,' said Inspector Flint.

'I can't help it,' said Barney plaintively. 'You see a woman down a dirty great hole with concrete sloshing down on top of her you don't ask her her age.'

'Quite. I realize that but if you could just think. Was there anything peculiar about her . . .'

'Peculiar? Well, there was this hand see . . .'

Inspector Flint sighed. 'I mean anything out of the ordinary about her appearance. Her hair for instance. What colour was it?'

Barney got it. 'I knew there was something,' he said, triumphantly. 'Her hair. It was crooked.'

'Well, it would be, wouldn't it. You don't dump a woman down a thirty-foot pile shaft without mussing up her hair in the process.'

'No, it wasn't like that. It was on sideways and flattened. Like she'd been hit.'

'She probably had been hit. If what you say about the wooden cover being in place is true, she didn't go down there of her own volition. But you still can't give any precise indication of her age?'

'Well,' said Barney, 'bits of her looked young and bits didn't. That's all I know.'

'Which bits?' asked the Inspector, hoping to hell Barney wasn't going to start on that hand again.

'Well, her legs didn't look right for her teats if you see what I mean.' Inspector Flint didn't. 'They were all thin and crumpled-up like.'

'Which were? Her legs or her teats?'

'Her legs, of course,' said Barney. 'I've told you she had these lovely great . . .'

'We're treating this as a case of murder,' Inspector Flint told the Principal ten minutes later. The Principal sat behind his desk and thought despairingly about adverse publicity.

'You're quite convinced it couldn't have been an accident?'

'The evidence to date certainly doesn't suggest accidental death,' said the Inspector. 'However, we'll only be absolutely certain on that point when we manage to reach the body and I'm afraid that is going to take some time.'

'Time?' said the Principal. 'Do you mean to say you can't get her out this morning?'

Inspector Flint shook his head. 'Out of the question, sir,' he said. 'We are considering two methods of reaching the body and they'll both take several days. One is to drill down through the concrete and the other is to sink another shaft next to the original hole and try and get at her from the side.'

'Good Lord,' said the Principal, looking at his calendar, 'but that means you're going to be digging away out there for several days.'

'I'm afraid it can't be helped. Whoever put her down there make a good job of it. Still, we'll try to be as unobtrusive as possible.'

Out of the window the Principal could see four police cars, a fire engine and a big blue van. 'This is really most unfortunate,' he murmured.

'Murder always is,' said the Inspector, and got to his feet. 'It's in the nature of the thing. In the meantime we are sealing off the site and we'd be grateful for your cooperation.'

'Anything you require,' said the Principal, with a sigh.

In the Staff Room the presence of so many uniformed men peering down a pile hole provoked mixed reactions. So did the dozen policemen scouring the building site, stopping now and then to put things carefully into envelopes, but it was the arrival of the dark blue caravan that finally clinched matters.

'That's a Mobile Murder Headquarters,' Peter Fenwick explained. 'Apparently some maniac has buried a woman at the bottom of one of the piles.'

The New Left, who had been clustered in a corner discussing the likely implications of so many paramilitary Fascist pigs, heaved a sigh of unmartyred regret but continued to express doubts.

'No, seriously,' said Fenwick, 'I asked one of them what they were doing. I thought it was some sort of bomb scare.'

Dr Cox, Head of Science, confirmed it. His office looked directly on to the hole. 'It's too dreadful to contemplate,' he murmured. 'Every time I look up I think what she must have suffered.'

'What do you suppose they are putting into those en-velopes?' asked Dr Mayfield.

'Clues,' said Dr Board, with evident satisfaction. 'Hairs. Bits of skin and bloodstains. The usual trivial detritus of violent crime.'

Dr Cox hurried from the room and Dr Mayfield looked disgusted. 'How revolting,' he said. 'Isn't it possible that there has been some mistake? I mean why should anyone want to murder a woman here?'

Dr Board sipped his coffee and looked wistfully at him. 'I can think of any number of reasons,' he said happily. 'There are at least a dozen women in my Evening Class whom I would cheerfully beat to death and drop down holes. Sylvia Swansbeck for one.'

'Whoever did it must have known they were going to pour concrete down today,' said Fenwick. 'It looks like an inside job to me.'

'One of our less community-conscious students perhaps,' suggested Dr Board, 'I don't suppose they've had time to check if any of the staff are missing.'

'You'll probably find it had nothing to do with the Tech,' said Dr Mayfield. 'Some maniac ...'

'Come now, give credit where credit is due,' interrupted Dr Board. 'There was obviously an element of premeditation in-volved. Whoever the murderer was ... is, he planned it pretty carefully. What puzzles me is why he didn't shovel earth down on top of the wretched woman so that she couldn't be seen. Probably intended to but was disturbed before he could get around to it. One of those little accidents of fate.'

In the corner of the Staff Room Wilt sat and drank his

coffee, conscious that he was the only person not staring out of the window. What the hell was he to do? The sensible thing would be to go to the police and explain that he had been trying to get rid of an inflatable doll that someone had given him. But would they believe him? If that was all that had happened why had he dressed it up in a wig and clothes? And why had he left it inflated? Why hadn't he just thrown the thing away? He was just rehearsing the pros and cons of the argument when the Head of Engineering came in and announced that the police intended boring another hole next to the first one instead of digging down through the concrete.

'They'll probably be able to see bits of her sticking out the side,' he explained. 'Apparently she had one arm up in the air and with all that concrete coming down on top of her there's a chance that arm will have been pressed against the side of the hole. Much quicker that way.'

'I must say I can't see the need for haste,' said Dr Board. 'I should have thought she'd be pretty well preserved in all that concrete. Mummified I daresay.'

In his corner Wilt rather doubted it. With twenty tons of concrete on top of her even Judy who had been an extremely resilient doll was hardly likely to have withstood the pressure. She would have burst as sure as eggs were eggs in which case all the police would find was the empty plastic arm of a doll. They would hardly bother to dig a burst plastic doll out.

'And another thing,' continued the Head of Engineering, 'if the arm is sticking out they'll be able to take fingerprints straight away.'

Wilt smiled to himself. That was one thing they weren't going to find on Judy, fingerprints. He finished his coffee more cheerfully and went off to a class of Senior Secretaries. He found them agog with news of the murder.

'Do you think it was a sex killing?' a small blonde girl in the front row asked as Wilt handed out copies of *This Island Now*. He had always found the chapter on the Vicissitudes of Adolescence appealed to Senior Secs. It dealt with sex and violence and was twelve years out of date but then so were the Senior Secretaries. Today there was no need for the book.

'I don't think it was any sort of killing,' said Wilt taking his place behind the desk.

'Oh but it was. They saw a woman's body down there,' the small blonde insisted.

'They thought they saw something down there that looked like a body,' said Wilt. 'That doesn't mean it was one. People's imaginations play tricks with them.'

'The police don't think so,' said a large girl whose father was something in the City. 'They must be certain to go to all that trouble. We had a murder on our golf course and all they found were bits of body cut up and put in the water hazard on the fifteenth. They'd been there six months. Someone sliced a ball on the dogleg twelfth and it went into the pond. They fished out a foot first. It was all puffy and green ...' A pale girl from Wilstanton fainted in the third row. By the time Wilt had revived her and taken her to the Sick Room, the class had got on to Crippen, Haigh and Christie. Wilt returned to find them discussing acid baths.

'... and all they found were her false teeth and gallstones.'

'You seem to know a lot about murder,' Wilt said to the large girl.

'Daddy plays bridge with the Chief Constable,' she explained. 'He comes to dinner and tells super stories. He says they ought to bring back hanging.'

'I'm sure he does,' said Wilt grimly. It was typical of Senior Secs that they knew Chief Constables who wanted to bring back hanging. It was all mummy and daddy and horses with Senior Secretaries.

'Anyway, hanging doesn't hurt,' said the large girl. 'Sir Frank says a good hangman can have a man out of the condemned cell and on to the trap with a noose around his neck and pull the lever in twenty seconds.'

'Why confine the privilege to men?' asked Wilt bitterly. The class looked at him wth reproachful eyes.

'The last woman they hanged was Ruth Ellis,' said the blonde in the front row.

'Anyway with women it's different,' said the large girl.

'Why?' said Wilt inadvisedly.

'Well it's slower.'

'Slower?'

'They had to tie Mrs Thomson to a chair,' volunteered the blonde. 'She behaved disgracefully.'

'I must say I find your judgements peculiar,' said Wilt. 'A woman murdering her husband is doubtless disgraceful. The fact that she puts up a fight when they come to execute her doesn't strike me as disgraceful at all. I find that ...'

'It's not just that,' interrupted the large girl, who wasn't to be diverted.

'What isn't?' said Wilt.

'It's being slower with women. They have to make them wear waterproof pants.'

Wilt gaped at her in disgust. 'Waterproof what?' he asked without thinking.

'Waterproof pants,' said the large girl.

'Dear God,' said Wilt.

'You see, when they get to the bottom of the rope their insides drop out,' continued the large girl, administering the *coup de grâce*. Wilt stared at her wildly and stumbled from the room.

'What's the matter with him?' said the girl. 'Anyone would think I had said something beastly.'

In the corridor Wilt leant against the wall and felt sick. Those fucking girls were worse than Gasfitters. At least Gasfitters didn't go in for such disgusting anatomical details and besides Senior Secs all came from so-called respectable families. By the time he felt strong enough to face them again the hour had ended. Wilt went back into the classroom sheepishly and collected the books.

'Name of Wilt mean anything to you? Henry Wilt?' asked the Inspector.

'Wilt?' said the Vice-Principal, who had been left to cope with the police while the Principal spent his time more profitably trying to offset the adverse publicity caused by the whole appalling business. 'Well, yes it does. He's one of our Liberal Studies lecturers. Why? Is there ...'

'If you don't mind, sir, I'd just like a word with him. In private.'

'But Wilt's a most inoffensive man,' said the Vice-Principal. 'I'm sure he couldn't help you at all.'

'Possibly not but all the same ...'

'You're not suggesting for one moment that Henry Wilt had anything to do with ...' the Vice-Principal stopped and studied the expression on the Inspector's face. It was ominously neutral.

'I'd rather not go into details,' said Inspector Flint, 'and it's best if we don't jump to conclusions.'

The Vice-Principal picked up the phone. 'Do you wan: him to come across to that ... er ... caravan?' he asked.

Inspector Flint shook his head. 'We like to be as inconspicuous as possible. If I could just have the use of an empty office.'

'There's an office next door. You can use that.'

Wilt was in the canteen having lunch with Peter Braintree when the Vice-Principal's secretary came down with a message.

'Can't it wait?' asked Wilt.

'He said it was most urgent.'

'It's probably your Senior Lectureship come through at last,' said Braintree brightly. Wilt swallowed the rest of his Scotch egg and got up.

'I doubt that,' he said and went wanly out of the canteen and up the stairs. He had a horrid suspicion that promotion was the last thing the Vice-Principal wanted to see him about.

'Now, sir,' said the Inspector when they were seated in the office, 'my name is Flint, Inspector Flint, CID, and you're Mr Wilt? Mr Henry Wilt?'

'Yes,' said Wilt.

'Now, Mr Wilt, as you may have gathered we are investigating the suspected murder of a woman whose body is believed to have been deposited at the bottom of one of the foundation holes for the new building. I daresay you know about it.' Wilt nodded. 'And naturally we are interested in anything that might be of assistance. I wonder if you would mind having a look at these notes.'

He handed Wilt a piece of paper. It was headed 'Notes on Violence and the Break-Up of Family Life', and underneath were a number of sub-headings.

1 Increasing use of violence in public life to attain political ends.
a Bombing b Hijacking c Kidnapping d Assassination
2 Ineffectuality of Police Methods in combating Violence.
a Negative approach. Police able only to react to crime after it has taken place.
b Use of violence by police themselves.
c Low level of intelligence of average policeman.
d Increasing use of sophisticated methods such as diversionary tactics by criminals.
3 Influence of media. TV brings crime techniques into the home.

There was more. Much more. Wilt looked down the list with a sense of doom.

'You recognize the handwriting?' asked the Inspector.

'I do,' said Wilt, adopting rather prematurely the elliptical language of the witness box.

'You admit that you wrote those notes?' The Inspector reached out a hand and took the notes back.

'Yes.'

'They express your opinion of police methods?'

Wilt pulled himself together. 'They were jottings I was making for a lecture to Sandwich-Course Trainee Firemen,' he explained. 'They were simply rough ideas. They need amplifying of course . . .'

'But you don't deny you wrote them?'

'Of course I don't. I've just said I did, haven't I?'

The Inspector nodded and picked up a book. 'And this is yours too?'

Wilt looked at *Bleak House*. 'It says so, doesn't it?'

Inspector Flint opened the cover. 'So it does,' he said with a show of astonishment, 'so it does.'

Wilt stared at him. There was no point in maintaining the pretence any longer. The best thing to do was to get it over quickly. They had found that bloody book in the basket of the bicycle and the notes must have fallen out of his pocket on the building site.

'Look, Inspector,' he said, 'I can explain everything. It's really quite simple. I did go into that building site ...'

The Inspector stood up. 'Mr Wilt, if you're prepared to make a statement I think I should warn you ...'

Wilt went down to the Murder Headquarters and made a statement in the presence of a police stenographer. His progress to the blue caravan and his failure to come out again were noted with interest by members of the staff teaching in the Science block, by students in the canteen and by twenty-five fellow lecturers gaping through the windows of the Staff Room.

9

'Goddam the thing,' said Gaskell as he knelt greasily beside the engine of the cruiser, 'you'd think that even in this pre-technological monarchy they'd fit a decent motor. This contraption must have been made for the Ark.'

'Ark Ark the Lark,' said Sally, 'and cut the crowned heads foolery. Eva's a reginaphile.'

'A what?'

'Reginaphile. Monarchist. Get it. She's the Queen's Bee so don't be anti-British. We don't want her to stop working as well as the motor. Maybe it isn't the con rod.'

'If I could only get the head off I could tell,' said Gaskell.

'And what good would that do? Buy you another?' said Sally and went into the cabin where Eva was wondering what they were going to have for supper. 'Tarbaby is still tinkering with the motor. He says it's the con rod.'

'Con rod?' said Eva.

'Only connect, baby, only connect.'

'With what?'

'The thigh bone's connected to the knee bone. The con rod's connected to the piston and as everyone knows pistons are penis symbols. The mechanized male's substitute for sex. The Outboard Motor Syndrome. Only this happens to be inboard like his balls never dropped. Honestly, Gaskell is so regressive.'

'I'm sure I don't know,' said Eva.

Sally lay back on the bunk and lit a cigar. 'That's what I love about you, Eva. You don't know. Ignorance is blissful, baby. I lost mine when I was fourteen.'

Eva shook her head. 'Men,' she said disapprovingly.

'He was old enough to be my grandfather,' said Sally. 'He *was* my grandfather.'

'Oh no. How awful.'

'Not really,' said Sally laughing, 'he was an artist. With a beard. And the smell of paint on his smock and there was this studio and he wanted to paint me in the nude. I was so pure in those days. He made me lie on this couch and he arranged my legs. He was always arranging my legs and then standing back to look at me and painting. And then one day when I was lying there he came over and bent my legs back and kissed me and then he was on top of me and his smock was up and . . .'

Eva sat and listened, fascinated. She could visualize it all so clearly, even the smell of paint in the studio and the brushes. Sally had had such an exciting life, so full of incident and so romantic in a dreadful sort of way. Eva tried to remember what she had been like at fourteen and not even going out with boys and there was Sally lying on a couch with a famous artist in his studio.

'But he raped you,' she said finally. 'Why didn't you tell the police?'

'The police? You don't understand. I was at this terribly exclusive school. They would have sent me home. It was progressive and all that but I shouldn't have been out being painted by this artist and my parents would never have forgiven me. They were so strict.' Sally sighed, overcome by the rigours of her wholly fictitious childhood. 'And now you can see why I'm so afraid of being hurt by men. When you've been raped you know what penile aggression means.'

'I suppose you do,' said Eva, in some doubt as to what penile aggression was.

'You see the world differently too. Like G says, nothing's good and nothing's bad. It just is.'

'I went to a lecture on Buddhism once,' said Eva, 'and that's what Mr Podgett said. He said—'

'Zen's all wrong. Like you just sit around waiting. That's passive. You've got to make things happen. You sit around waiting long enough, you're dead. Someone's trampled all over you. You've got to see things happen your way and no one else's.'

'That doesn't sound very sociable,' said Eva. 'I mean if we all did just what we wanted all the time it wouldn't be very nice for other people.'

'Other people are hell,' said Sally. 'That's Sartre and he should know. You do what you want is good and no moral kickback. Like G says, rats are the paradigm. You think rats go around thinking what's good for other people?'

'Well no, I don't suppose they do,' said Eva.

'Right. Rats aren't ethical. No way. They just do. They don't get screwed up thinking.'

'Do you think rats can think?' asked Eva, now thoroughly engaged in the problems of rodent psychology.

'Of course they can't. Rats just are. No *Schadenfreude* with rats.'

'What's *Schadenfreude*?'

'Second cousin to *Weltschmerz*,' said Sally, stubbing her cigar out in the ashtray. 'So we can all do what we want whenever we want to. That's the message. It's only people like G who've got the know bug who get balled up.'

'No bug?' said Eva.

'They've got to know how everything works. Scientists. Lawrence was right. It's all head and no body with G.'

'Henry's a bit like that,' said Eva. 'He's always reading or talking about books. I've told him he doesn't know what the real world is like.'

In the Mobile Murder Headquarters Wilt was learning. He

sat opposite Inspector Flint whose face was registering increasing incredulity.

'Now, we'll just go over that again,' said the Inspector. 'You say that what those men saw down that hole was in actual fact an inflatable plastic doll with a vagina.'

'The vagina is incidental,' said Wilt, calling forth reserves of inconsequence.

'That's as maybe,' said the Inspector. 'Most dolls don't have them but ... all right, we'll let that pass. The point I'm trying to get at is that you're quite positive there isn't a real live human being down there.'

'Positive,' said Wilt, 'and if there were it is doubtful if it would still be alive now.'

The Inspector studied him unpleasantly. 'I don't need you to point that out to me,' he said. 'If there was the faintest possibility of whatever it is down there being alive I wouldn't be sitting here, would I?'

'No,' said Wilt.

'Right. So now we come to the next point. How is it that what those men saw, they say a woman and you say a doll ... that this thing was wearing clothes, had hair and even more remarkably had its head bashed in and one hand stretched up in the air?'

'That was the way it fell,' said Wilt. 'I suppose the arm got caught up on the side and lifted up.'

'And its head was bashed in?'

'Well, I did drop a lump of mud on it,' Wilt admitted, 'that would account for that.'

'You dropped a lump of mud on its head?'

'That's what I said,' Wilt agreed.

'I know that's what you said. What I want to know is why you felt obliged to drop a lump of mud on the head of an inflatable doll that had, as far as I can gather, never done you any harm.'

Wilt hesitated. That damned doll had done him a great deal of harm one way and another but this didn't seem an opportune moment to go into that. 'I don't know really,' he said finally, 'I just thought it might help.'

'Help what?'

'Help . . . I don't know. I just did it, that's all. I was drunk at the time.'

'All right, we'll come back to that in a minute. There's still one question you haven't answered. If it was a doll, why was it wearing clothes?'

Wilt looked desperately round the caravan and met the eyes of the police stenographer. There was a look in them that didn't inspire confidence. Talk about lack of suspension of disbelief.

'You're not going to believe this,' Wilt said. The Inspector looked at him and lit a cigarette.

'Well?'

'As a matter of fact I had dressed it up,' Wilt said, squirming with embarrassment.

'You had dressed it up?'

'Yes,' said Wilt.

'And may one enquire what purpose you had in mind when you dressed it up?'

'I don't know exactly.'

The Inspector sighed significantly. 'Right. We go back to the beginning. We have a doll with a vagina which you dress up and bring down here in the dead of night and deposit at the bottom of a thirty-foot hole and drop lumps of mud on its head. Is that what you're saying?'

'Yes,' said Wilt.

'You wouldn't prefer to save everyone concerned a lot of time and bother by admitting here and now that what is at present resting, hopefully at peace, under twenty tons of concrete at the bottom of that pile is the body of a murdered woman?'

'No,' said Wilt, 'I most definitely wouldn't.'

Inspector Flint sighed again. 'You know, we're going to get to the bottom of this thing,' he said. 'It may take time and it may take expense and God knows it's taking patience but when we do get down there—'

'You're going to find an inflatable doll,' said Wilt.

'With a vagina?'

'With a vagina.'

In the Staff Room Peter Braintree staunchly defended Wilt's innocence. 'I tell you I've known Henry well for the past seven years and whatever has happened he had nothing to do with it.'

Mr Morris, the Head of Liberal Studies, looked out of the window sceptically. 'They've had him in there since ten past two. That's four hours,' he said. 'They wouldn't do that unless they thought he had some connection with the dead woman.'

'They can think what they like. I know Henry and even if the poor sod wanted to he's incapable of murdering anyone.'

'He did punch that Printer on Tuesday. That shows he's capable of irrational violence.'

'Wrong again. The Printer punched him,' said Braintree.

'Only after Wilt had called him a snivelling fucking moron,' Mr Morris pointed out. 'Anyone who goes into Printers Three and calls one of them that needs his head examined. They killed poor old Pinkerton, you know. He gassed himself in his car.'

'They had a damned good try at killing old Henry come to that.'

'Of course, that blow might have affected his brain,' said Mr Morris, with morose satisfaction. 'Concussion can do funny things to a man's character. Change him overnight from a nice quiet inoffensive little fellow like Wilt into a homicidal maniac who suddenly goes berserk. Stranger things have happened.'

'I daresay Henry would be the first to agree with you,' said Braintree. 'It can't be very pleasant sitting in that caravan being questioned by detectives. I wonder what they're doing to him.'

'Just asking questions. Things like "How have you been getting on with your wife?" and "Can you account for your movements on Saturday night?" They start off gently and then work up to the heavy stuff later on.'

Peter Braintree sat in silent horror. Eva. He'd forgotten all about her and as for Saturday night he knew exactly what Henry had said he had been doing before he turned up on the doorstep covered with mud and looking like death . . .

'All I'm saying,' said Mr Morris, 'is that it seems very strange to me that they find a dead body at the bottom of a shaft filled with concrete and the next thing you know they've got Wilt in that Murder HQ for questioning. Very strange indeed. I wouldn't like to be in his shoes.' He got up and left the room and Peter Braintree sat on wondering if there was anything he should do like phone a lawyer and ask him to come round and speak to Henry. It seemed a bit premature and presumably Henry could ask to see a lawyer himself if he wanted one.

Inspector Flint lit another cigarette with an air of insouciant menace. 'How well do you get on with your wife?' he asked.

Wilt hesitated. 'Well enough,' he said.

'Just well enough? No more than that?'

'We get along just fine,' said Wilt, conscious that he had made an error.

'I see. And I suppose she can substantiate your story about this inflatable doll.'

'Substantiate it?'

'The fact that you made a habit of dressing it up and carrying on with it.'

'I didn't make a habit of anything of the sort,' said Wilt indignantly.

'I'm only asking. You were the one who first raised the fact that it had a vagina. I didn't. You volunteered the information and naturally I assumed ...'

'What did you assume?' said Wilt. 'You've got no right ...'

'Mr Wilt,' said the Inspector, 'put yourself in my position. I am investigating a case of suspected murder and a man comes along and tells me that what two eye-witnesses describe as the body of a well-nourished woman in her early thirties ...'

'In her early thirties? Dolls don't have ages. If that bloody doll was more than six months old ...'

'Please, Mr Wilt, if you'll just let me continue. As I was saying we have a prima facie case of murder and you admit yourself to having put a doll with a vagina down that hole. Now if you were in my shoes what sort of inference would you draw from that?'

Wilt tried to think of some totally innocent interpretation and couldn't.

'Wouldn't you be the first to agree that it does look a bit peculiar?'

Wilt nodded. It looked horribly peculiar.

'Right,' continued the Inspector. 'Now if we put the nicest possible interpretation on your actions and particularly on your emphasis that this doll had a vagina—'

'I didn't emphasize it. I only mentioned the damned thing to indicate that it was extremely lifelike. I wasn't suggesting I made a habit of ...' He stopped and looked miserably at the floor.

'Go on, Mr Wilt, don't stop now. It often helps to talk.'

Wilt stared at him frantically. Talking to Inspector Flint wasn't helping him one iota. 'If you're implying that my sex life was confined to copulating with an inflatable fucking doll dressed in my wife's clothes ...'

'Hold it there,' said the Inspector, stubbing out his cigarette significantly. 'Ah, so we've taken another step forward. You admit then that whatever is down that hole is dressed in your wife's clothes? Yes or no.'

'Yes,' said Wilt miserably.

Inspector Flint stood up. 'I think it's about time we all went and had a little chat with Mrs Wilt,' he said. 'I want to hear what she has to say about your funny little habits.'

'I'm afraid that's going to be a little difficult,' said Wilt.

'Difficult?'

'Well you see the thing is she's gone away.'

'Gone away?' said the Inspector. 'Did I hear you say that Mrs Wilt has gone away?'

'Yes.'

'And where has Mrs Wilt gone to?'

'That's the trouble. I don't know.'

'You don't know?'

'No, I honestly don't know,' said Wilt.

'She didn't tell you where she was going?'

'No. She just wasn't there when I got home.'

'She didn't leave a note or anything like that?'

'Yes,' said Wilt, 'as a matter of fact she did.'

'Right, well let's just go up to your house and have a look at that note.'

'I'm afraid that's not possible,' said Wilt. 'I got rid of it.'

'You got rid of it?' said the Inspector. 'You got rid of it? How?'

Wilt looked pathetically across at the police stenographer. 'To tell the truth I wiped my bottom with it,' he said.

Inspector Flint gazed at him demonically. 'You did what?'

'Well, there was no toilet paper in the lavatory so I . . .' he stopped. The Inspector was lighting yet another cigarette. His hands were shaking and he had a distant look in his eyes that suggested he had just peered over some appalling abyss. 'Mr Wilt,' he said when he had managed to compose himself, 'I trust I am a reasonably tolerant man, a patient man and a humane man, but if you seriously expect me to believe one word of your utterly preposterous story you must be insane. First you tell me you put a doll down that hole. Then you admit that it was dressed in your wife's clothes. Now you say that she went away without telling you where she was going and finally to cap it all you have the temerity to sit there and tell me that you wiped your arse with the one piece of solid evidence that could substantiate your statement.'

'But I did,' said Wilt.

'Balls,' shouted the Inspector. 'You and I both know where Mrs Wilt has gone and there's no use pretending we don't. She's down at the bottom of that fucking hole and you put her there.'

'Are you arresting me?' Wilt asked as they walked in a tight group across the road to the police car.

'No,' said Inspector Flint, 'you're just helping the police with their enquiries. It will be on the news tonight.'

'My dear Braintree, of course we'll do all we can,' said the Vice-Principal. 'Wilt has always been a loyal member of staff and there has obviously been some dreadful mistake. I'm sure you needn't worry. The whole thing will right itself before long.'

'I hope you're right,' said Braintree, 'but there are complicating factors. For one thing there's Eva ...'

'Eva? Mrs Wilt? You're not suggesting ...'

'I'm not suggesting anything. All I'm saying is ... well, she's missing from home. She walked out on Henry last Friday.'

'Mrs Wilt walked ... well I hardly knew her, except by reputation of course. Wasn't she the woman who broke Mr Lockyer's collar-bone during a part-time Evening Class in Judo some years back?'

'That was Eva,' said Braintree.

'She hardly sounds the sort of woman who would allow Wilt to put her down ...'

'She isn't,' said Braintree hastily. 'If anyone was liable to be murdered in the Wilt household it was Henry. I think the police should be informed of that.'

They were interrupted by the Principal who came in with a copy of the evening paper. 'You've seen this I suppose,' he said, waving it distraughtly. 'It's absolutely appalling.' He put the paper down on the desk and indicated the headlines. MURDERED WOMAN BURIED IN CONCRETE AT TECH. LECTURER HELPING POLICE.

'Oh dear,' said the Vice-Principal. 'Oh dear. How very unfortunate. It couldn't have come at a worse moment.'

'It shouldn't have come at all,' snapped the Principal. 'And that's not all. I've already had half a dozen phone calls from parents wanting to know if we make a habit of employing murderers on the full-time staff. Who is this fellow Wilt anyway?'

'He's in Liberal Studies,' said the Vice-Principal. 'He's been with us ten years.'

'Liberal Studies. I might have guessed it. If they're not poets manqués they're Maoists or ... I don't know where the hell Morris gets them from. And now we've got a blasted murderer. God knows what I'm going to tell the Education Committee tonight. They've called an emergency meeting for eight.'

'I must say I resent Wilt being called a murderer,' said Braintree loyally. 'There is nothing to suggest that he has murdered anyone.'

The Principal studied him for a moment and then looked back at the headlines. 'Mr Braintree, when someone is helping the police with their enquiries into a murder it may not be proven that he is a murderer but the suggestion is there.'

'This certainly isn't going to help us get the new CNAA degree off the ground,' intervened the Vice-Principal tactfully. 'We've got a visit from the Inspection Committee scheduled for Friday.'

'From what the police tell me it isn't going to help get the new Administration block off the ground either,' said the Principal. 'They say it's going to take at least three days to bore down to the bottom of that pile and then they'll have to drill through the concrete to get the body out. That means they'll have to put a new pile down and we're already well behind schedule and our building budget has been halved. Why on earth couldn't he have chosen somewhere else to dispose of his damned wife?'

'I don't think ...' Braintree began.

'I don't care what you think,' said the Principal, 'I'm merely telling you what the police think.'

Braintree left them still wrangling and trying to figure out ways and means of counteracting the adverse publicity the case had already brought the Tech. He went down to the Liberal Studies office and found Mr Morris in a state of despair. He was trying to arrange stand-in lecturers for all Wilt's classes.

'But he'll probably be back in the morning,' Braintree said.

'Like hell he will,' said Mr Morris. 'When they take them in like that they keep them. Mark my words. The police may make mistakes, I'm not saying they don't, but when they act this swiftly they're on to a sure thing. Mind you, I always thought Wilt was a bit odd.'

'Odd? I've just come from the VP's office. You want to hear what the Principal's got to say about Liberal Studies staff.'

'Christ,' said Mr Morris, 'don't tell me.'

'Anyway what's so odd about Henry?'

'Too meek and mild for my liking. Look at the way he accepted remaining a Lecturer Grade Two all these years.'

'That was hardly his fault.'

'Of course it was his fault. All he had to do was threaten to resign and go somewhere else and he'd have got promotion like a shot. That's the only way to get on in this place. Make your presence felt.'

'He seems to have done that now,' said Braintree. 'The Principal is already blaming him for throwing the building programme off schedule and if we don't get the Joint Honours degree past the CNAA, Henry's going to be made the scapegoat. It's too bad. Eva should have had more sense than to walk out on him like that.'

Mr Morris took a more sombre view. 'She'd have shown a damned sight more sense if she'd walked out on him before the sod took it into his head to beat her to death and dump her down that bloody shaft. Now who the hell can I get to take Gasfitters One tomorrow?'

10

At 34 Parkview Avenue Wilt sat in the kitchen with Clem while the detectives ransacked the house. 'You're not going to find anything incriminating here,' he told Inspector Flint.

'Never you mind what we're going to find. We're just having a look.'

He sent one detective upstairs to examine Mrs Wilt's clothes or what remained of them.

'If she went away she'd have taken half her wardrobe,' he said. 'I know women. On the other hand if she's pushing up twenty tons of premix she wouldn't need more than what she's got on.'

Eva's wardrobe was found to be well stocked. Even Wilt had to admit that she hadn't taken much with her.

'What was she wearing when you last saw her?' the Inspector asked.

'Lemon loungers,' said Wilt.

'Lemon what?'

'Pyjamas,' said Wilt, adding to the list of incriminating evidence against him. The Inspector made a note of the fact in his pocketbook.

'In bed, was she?'

'No,' said Wilt. 'Round at the Pringsheims.'

'The Pringsheims? And who might they be?'

'The Americans I told you about who live in Rossiter Grove.'

'You haven't mentioned any Americans to me,' said the Inspector.

'I'm sorry. I thought I had. I'm getting muddled. She went away with them.'

'Oh did she? And I suppose we'll find they're missing too?'

'Almost certainly,' said Wilt. 'I mean if she was going away with them they must have gone too and if she isn't with them I can't imagine where she has got to.'

'I can,' said the Inspector looking with distasteful interest at a stain on a sheet one of the detectives had found in the dirty linen basket. By the time they left the house the incriminating evidence consisted of the sheet, an old dressing-gown cord that had found its way mysteriously into the attic, a chopper that Wilt had once used to open a tin of red lead, and a hypodermic syringe which Eva had got from the vet for watering cacti very precisely during her Indoor Plant phase. There was also a bottle of tablets with no label on it.

'How the hell would I know what they are?' Wilt asked when confronted with the bottle. 'Probably aspirins. And anyway it's full.'

'Put it with the other exhibits,' said the Inspector. Wilt looked at the box.

'For God's sake, what do you think I did with her? Poisoned her, strangled her, hacked her to bits with a chopper and injected her with Biofood?'

'What's Biofood?' asked Inspector Flint with sudden interest.

'It's stuff you feed plants with,' said Wilt. 'The bottle's on the windowsill.'

The Inspector added the bottle of Biofood to the box. 'We

know what you did with her, Mr Wilt,' he said. 'It's how that interests us now.'

They went out to the police car and drove round to the Pringsheims' house in Rossiter Grove. 'You just sit in the car with the constable here while I go and see if they're in,' said Inspector Flint and went to the front door. Wilt sat and watched while he rang the bell. He rang again. He hammered on the doorknocker and finally he walked round through the gate marked Tradesman's Entrance to the kitchen door. A minute later he was back and fumbling with the car radio.

'You've hit the nail on the head all right, Wilt,' he snapped. 'They've gone away. The place is a bloody shambles. Looks like they've had an orgy. Take him out.'

The two detectives bundled Wilt, no longer Mr Wilt but plain Wilt and conscious of the fact, out of the car while the Inspector called Fenland Constabulary and spoke with sinister urgency about warrants and sending something that sounded like the D brigade up. Wilt stood in the driveway of 12 Rossiter Grove and wondered what the hell was happening to him. The order of things on which he had come to depend was disintegrating around him.

'We're going in the back way,' said the Inspector. 'This doesn't look good.'

They went down the path to the kitchen door and round to the back garden. Wilt could see what the Inspector had meant by a shambles. The garden didn't look at all good. Paper plates lay about the lawn or, blown by the wind, had wheeled across the garden into honeysuckle or climbing rose while paper cups, some squashed and some still filled with Pringsheim punch and rainwater, littered the ground. But it was the beefburgers that gave the place its air of macabre filth. They were all over the lawn, stained with coleslaw so that Wilt was put in mind of Clem.

'The dog returns to his vomit,' said Inspector Flint evidently reading his mind. They crossed the terrace to the lounge windows and peered through. If the garden was bad the interior was awful.

'Smash a pane in the kitchen window and let us in,' said the

Inspector to the taller of the two detectives. A moment later the lounge window slid back and they went inside.

'No need for forcible entry,' said the detective. 'The back door was unlocked and so was this window. They must have cleared out in a hell of a hurry.'

The Inspector looked round the room and wrinkled his nose. The smell of stale pot, sour punch and candle smoke still hung heavily in the house.

'If they went away,' he said ominously and glanced at Wilt.

'They must have gone away,' said Wilt who felt called upon to make some comment on the scene, 'no one would live in all this mess for a whole weekend without ...'

'Live? You did say "live" didn't you?' said Flint stepping on a piece of burnt beefburger.

'What I meant ...'

'Never mind what you meant, Wilt. Let's see what's happened here.'

They went into the kitchen where the same chaos reigned and then into another room. Everywhere it was the same. Dead cigarette ends doused in cups of coffee or ground out on the carpet. Pieces of broken record behind the sofa marked the end of Beethoven's Fifth. Cushions lay crumpled against the wall. Burnt-out candles hung limply post-coital from bottles. To add a final touch to the squalor someone had drawn a portrait of Princess Anne on the wall with a red felt pen. She was surrounded by helmeted policemen and underneath was written. THE FUZZ AROUND OUR ANNY THE ROYAL FAMLYS FANNY THE PRICK IS DEAD LONG LIVE THE CUNT. Sentiments that were doubtless perfectly acceptable in Women's Lib circles but were hardly calculated to establish the Pringsheims very highly in Inspector Flint's regard.

'You've got some nice friends, Wilt,' he said.

'No friends of mine,' said Wilt, with feeling. 'The sods can't even spell.'

They went upstairs and looked in the big bedroom. The bed was unmade, clothes, mostly underclothes, were all over the floor or hung out of drawers and an unstoppered bottle of Joy lay on its side on the dressing-table. The room stank of perfume.

'Jesus wept,' said the Inspector, eyeing a pair of jockstraps belligerently. 'All that's missing is some blood.'

They found it in the bathroom. Dr Scheimacher's cut hand had rained bloodstains in the bath and splattered the tiles with dark blotches. The bathroom door with its broken frame was hanging from the bottom hinge and there were spots of blood on the paintwork.

'I knew it,' said the Inspector, studying their message and that written in lipstick on the mirror above the washbasin. Wilt looked at it too. It seemed unduly personal.

WHERE WILT FAGGED AND EVA RAN WHO WAS THEN THE MALE CHAUVINIST PIG?

'Charming,' said Inspector Flint. He turned to look at Wilt whose face was now the colour of the tiles. 'I don't suppose you'd know anything about that. Not your handiwork?'

'Certainly not,' said Wilt.

'Nor this?' said the Inspector, pointing to the bloodstains in the bath. Wilt shook his head. 'And I suppose this has nothing to do with you either?' He indicated a diaphragm that had been nailed to the wall above the lavatory seat. WHERE THE B SUCKS THERE SUCK I UNDERNEATH A DUTCH CAP NICE AND DRY. Wilt stared at the thing in utter disgust.

'I don't know what to say,' he muttered. 'It's all so awful.'

'You can say that again,' the Inspector agreed, and turned to more practical matters. 'Well, she didn't die in here.'

'How can you tell?' asked the younger of the two detectives.

'Not enough blood.' The Inspector looked round uncertainly. 'On the other hand one hard bash ...' They followed the bloodstains down the passage to the room where Wilt had been dollknotted.

'For God's sake don't touch anything,' said the Inspector, easing the door open with his sleeve, 'the fingerprint boys are going to have a field day here.' He looked inside at the toys.

'I suppose you butchered the children too,' he said grimly.

'Children?' said Wilt, 'I didn't know they had any.'

'Well if you didn't,' said the Inspector, who was a family man, 'the poor little buggers have got something to be thankful for. Not much by the look of things but something.'

Wilt poked his head round the door and looked at the

Teddy Bear and the rocking horse. 'Those are Gaskell's,' he said, 'he likes to play with them.'

'I thought you said you didn't know they had any children?'

'They haven't. Gaskell is Dr Pringsheim. He's a biochemist and a case of arrested development according to his wife.' The Inspector studied him thoughtfully. The question of arrest had become one that needed careful consideration.

'I don't suppose you're prepared to make a full confession now?' he asked without much hope.

'No I am not,' said Wilt.

'I didn't think you would be, Wilt,' said the Inspector. 'All right, take him down to the Station. I'll be along later.'

The detectives took Wilt by the arms. It was the last straw.

'Leave me alone,' he yelled. 'You've got no right to do this. You've got——'

'Wilt,' shouted Inspector Flint, 'I'm going to give you one last chance. If you don't go quietly I'm going to charge you here and now with the murder of your wife.'

Wilt went quietly. There was nothing else to do.

'The screw?' said Sally. 'But you said it was the con rod.'

'So I was wrong,' said Gaskell. 'She cranks over.'

'It, G, it. It cranks over.'

'OK. It cranks over so it can't be a con rod. It could be something that got tangled with the propshaft.'

'Like what?'

'Like weeds.'

'Why don't you go down and have a look yourself?'

'With these glasses?' said Gaskell. 'I wouldn't be able to see anything.'

'You know I can't swim,' said Sally. 'I have this leg.'

'I can swim,' said Eva.

'We'll tie a rope round you. That way you won't drown,' said Gaskell, 'all you've got to do is go under and feel if there's anything down there.'

'We know what's down there,' said Sally. 'Mud is.'

'Round the propshaft,' said Gaskell. 'Then if there is you can take it off.'

Eva went into the cabin and put on the bikini.

'Honestly, Gaskell, sometimes I think you're doing this on purpose. First it's the con rod and now it's the screw.'

'Well, we've got to try everything. We can't just sit here,' said Gaskell, 'I'm supposed to be back in the lab tomorrow.'

'You should have thought of that before,' said Sally. 'Now all we need is a goddam Albatross.'

'If you ask me we've got one,' said Gaskell, as Eva came out of the cabin and put on a bathing cap.

'Now where's the rope?' she asked. Gaskell looked in a locker and found some. He tied it round her waist and Eva clambered over the side into the water.

'It's ever so cold,' she giggled.

'That's because of the Gulf Stream,' said Gaskell, 'it doesn't come this far round.'

Eva swam out and put her feet down.

'It's terribly shallow and full of mud.'

She waded round hanging on to the rope and groped under the stern of the cruiser.

'I can't feel anything,' she called.

'It will be further under,' said Gaskell, peering down at her. Eva put her head under the water and felt the rudder.

'That's the rudder,' said Gaskell.

'Of course it is,' said Eva, 'I know that, silly. I'm not stupid.'

She disappeared under the boat. This time she found the propeller but there was nothing wrapped round it.

'It's just muddy, that's all,' she said, when she resurfaced. 'There's mud all along the bottom.'

'Well there would be wouldn't there,' said Gaskell. Eva waded round to the side. 'We just happen to be stuck on a mudbank.'

Eva went down again but the propshaft was clear too. 'I told you so,' said Sally, as they hauled Eva back on board. 'You just made her do it so you could see her in her plastic kini all covered with mud. Come, Botticelli baby, let Sally wash you off.'

'Oh Jesus,' said Gaskell. 'Penis arising from the waves.' He went back to the engine and looked at it uncertainly. Perhaps there was a blockage in the fuel line. It didn't seem very likely but he had to try something. They couldn't stay stuck on the mudbank forever.

On the foredeck Sally was sponging Eva down.

'Now the bottom half, darling,' she said untying the string.

'Oh, Sally. No, Sally.'

'Labia babia.'

'Oh, Sally, you are awful.'

Gaskell struggled with the adjustable wrench. All this Touch Therapy was getting to him. And the plastic.

At the County Hall the Principal was doing his best to pacify the members of the Education Committee who were demanding a full enquiry into the recruitment policy of the Liberal Studies Department.

'Let me explain,' he said patiently, looking round at the Committee, which was a nice balance of business interests and social commitment. 'The 1944 Education Act laid down that all apprentices should be released from their places of employment to attend Day Release Classes at Technical Colleges ...'

'We know all that,' said a building contractor, 'and we all know it's a bloody waste of time and public money. This country would be a sight better off if they were left to get on with their jobs.'

'The courses they attend,' continued the Principal before anyone with a social conscience could intervene, 'are craft-oriented with the exception of one hour, one obligatory hour of Liberal Studies. Now the difficulty with Liberal Studies is that no one knows what it means.'

'Liberal Studies means,' said Mrs Chatterway, who prided herself on being an advocate of progressive education, in which role she had made a substantial contribution to the illiteracy rate in several previously good primary schools, 'providing socially deprived adolescents with a firm grounding in liberal attitudes and culturally extending topics ...'

'It means teaching them to read and write,' said a company director. 'It's no good having workers who can't read instructions.'

'It means whatever anyone chooses it to mean,' said the Principal hastily. 'Now if you are faced with the problem of having to find lecturers who are prepared to spend their lives going into classrooms filled with Gasfitters or Plasterers or Printers who see no good reason for being there, and keeping them occupied with a subject that does not, strictly speaking, exist, you cannot afford to pick and choose the sort of staff you employ. That is the crux of the problem.'

The Committee looked at him doubtfully.

'Am I to understand that you are suggesting that Liberal Studies teachers are not devoted and truly creative individuals imbued with a strong sense of vocation?' asked Mrs Chatterway belligerently.

'No,' said the Principal, 'I am not saying that at all. I am merely trying to make the point that Liberal Studies lecturers are not as other men are. They either start out odd or they end up odd. It's in the nature of their occupation.'

'But they are all highly qualified,' said Mrs Chatterway, 'they all have degrees.'

'Quite. As you say they all hold degrees. They are all qualified teachers but the stresses to which they are subject leave their mark. Let me put it this way. If you were to take a heart transplant surgeon and ask him to spend his working life docking dogs' tails you would hardly expect him to emerge unscathed after ten years' work. The analogy is exact, believe me, exact.'

'Well, all I can say,' protested the building contractor, 'is that not all Liberal Studies lecturers end up burying their murdered wives at the bottom of pile shafts.'

'And all I can say,' said the Principal, 'is that I am extremely surprised more don't.'

The meeting broke up undecided.

11

As dawn broke glaucously over East Anglia Wilt sat in the Interview Room at the central Police Station isolated from the natural world and in a wholly artificial environment that included a table, four chairs, a detective sergeant and a fluorescent light on the ceiling that buzzed slightly. There were no windows, just pale green walls and a door through which people came and went occasionally and Wilt went twice to relieve himself in the company of a constable. Inspector Flint had gone to bed at midnight and his place had been taken by Detective Sergeant Yates who had started again at the beginning.

'What beginning?' said Wilt.

'At the very beginning.'

'God made heaven and earth and all ...'

'Forget the wisecracks,' said Sergeant Yates.

'Now that,' said Wilt, appreciatively, 'is a more orthodox use of wise.'

'What is?'

'Wisecrack. It's slang but it's good slang wisewise if you get my meaning.'

Detective Sergeant Yates studied him closely. 'This is a soundproof room,' he said finally.

'So I've noticed,' said Wilt.

'A man could scream his guts out in here and no one outside would be any the wiser.'

'Wiser?' said Wilt doubtfully. 'Wisdom and knowledge are not the same thing. Someone outside might not be aware that ...'

'Shut up,' said Sergeant Yates.

Wilt sighed. 'If you would just let me get some sleep ...'

'You'll get some sleep when you tell us why you murdered your wife, where you murdered her and how you murdered her.'

'I don't suppose it will do any good if I tell you I didn't murder her.'

Sergeant Yates shook his head.

'No,' he said. 'We know you did. You know you did. We know where she is. We're going to get her out. We know you put her there. You've at least admitted that much.'

'I keep telling you I put an inflatable ...'

'Was Mrs Wilt inflatable?'

'Was she fuck,' said Wilt.

'Right, so we'll forget the inflatable doll crap ...'

'I wish to God I could,' said Wilt. 'I'll be only too glad when you get down there and dig it out. It will have burst of course with all that concrete on it but it will still be recognizably an inflatable plastic doll.'

Sergeant Yates leant across the table. 'Let me tell you something. When we do get Mrs Wilt out of there, don't imagine she'll be unrecognizable.' He stopped and stared intently at Wilt. 'Not unless you've disfigured her.'

'Disfigured her?' said Wilt with a hollow laugh. 'She didn't need disfiguring the last time I saw her. She was looking bloody awful. She had on these lemon pyjamas and her face was all covered with ...' He hesitated. There was a curious expression on the Sergeant's face.

'Blood?' he suggested. 'Were you going to say "blood"?'

'No,' said Wilt, 'I most certainly wasn't. I was going to say powder. White powder and scarlet lipstick. I told her she looked fucking awful.'

'You must have had a very happy relationship with her,' said the Sergeant. 'I don't make a habit of telling my wife she looks fucking awful.'

'You probably don't have a fucking awful-looking wife,' said Wilt making an attempt to conciliate the man.

'What I have or don't have by way of a wife is my business. She lies outside the domain of this discussion.'

'Lucky old her,' said Wilt, 'I wish to God mine did.' By two o'clock they had left Mrs Wilt's appearance and got on to teeth and the question of identifying dead bodies by dental chart.

'Look,' said Wilt wearily, 'I daresay teeth fascinate you but at this time of night I can do without them.'

'You wear dentures or something?'

'No. No, I don't,' said Wilt, rejecting the plural.

'Did Mrs Wilt?'

'No,' said Wilt, 'she was always very ...'

'I thank you,' said Sergeant Yates, 'I knew it would come out in the end.'

'What would?' said Wilt, his mind still on teeth.

'That "was". The past tense. That's the giveaway. Right, so you admit she's dead. Let's go on from there.'

'I didn't say anything of the sort. You said "Did she wear dentures?" and I said she didn't ...'

'You said "she was". It's that "was" that interests me. If you had said "is" it would have been different.'

'It might have sounded different,' said Wilt, rallying his defences, 'but it wouldn't have made the slightest difference to the facts.'

'Which are?'

'That my wife is probably still around somewhere alive and kicking ...'

'You don't half give yourself away, Wilt,' said the Sergeant. 'Now it's "probably" and as for "kicking" I just hope for your sake we don't find she was still alive when they poured that concrete down on top of her. The Court wouldn't take kindly to that.'

'I doubt if anyone would,' said Wilt. 'Now when I said "probably" what I meant was that if you had been held in custody for a day and half the night being questioned on the trot by detectives you'd begin to wonder what had happened to your wife. It might even cross your mind that, all evidence to the contrary, she might not be alive. You want to try sitting on this side of the table before you start criticizing me for using terms like "probable". Anything more improbable than being accused of murdering your wife when you know for a fact that you haven't you can't imagine.'

'Listen, Wilt,' said the Sergeant, 'I'm not criticizing you for your language. Believe me I'm not. I'm merely trying as patiently as I can to establish the facts.'

'The facts are these,' said Wilt. 'Like a complete idiot I

116

made the mistake of dumping an inflatable doll down the bottom of a pile shaft and someone poured concrete in and my wife is away from home and ...'

'I'll tell you one thing,' Sergeant Yates told Inspector Flint when he came on duty at seven in the morning. 'This one is a hard nut to crack. If you hadn't told me he hadn't a record I'd have sworn he was an old hand and a good one at that. Are you sure Central Records have got nothing on him?' Inspector Flint shook his head.

'He hasn't started squealing for a lawyer yet?'

'Not a whimper. I tell you he's either as nutty as a fruit cake or he's been through this lot before.'

And Wilt had. Day after day, year in year out. With Gasfitters One and Printers Three, with Day Release Motor Mechanics and Meat Two. For ten years he had sat in front of classes answering irrelevant questions, discussing why Piggy's rational approach to life was preferable to Jack's brutishness, why Pangloss' optimism was so unsatisfactory, why Orwell hadn't wanted to shoot that blasted elephant or hang that man, and all the time fending off verbal attempts to rattle him and reduce him to the state poor old Pinkerton was in when he gassed himself. By comparison with Bricklayers Four, Sergeant Yates and Inspector Flint were child's play. If only they would let him get some sleep he would go on running inconsequential rings round them.

'I thought I had him once,' the Sergeant told Flint as they conferred in the corridor. 'I had got him on to teeth.'

'Teeth?' said the Inspector.

'I was just explaining we can always identify bodies from their dental charts and he almost admitted she was dead. Then he got away again.'

'Teeth, eh? That's interesting. I'll have to pursue that line of questioning. It may be his weak link.'

'Good luck on you,' said the Sergeant. 'I'm off to bed.'

'Teeth?' said Wilt. 'We're not going through that again are we? I thought we'd exhausted that topic. The last bloke wanted to know if Eva had them in the past tense. I told him she did and ...'

'Wilt,' said Inspector Flint, 'I am not interested in whether or not Mrs Wilt had teeth. I presume she must have done. What I want to know is if she still has them. Present tense.'

'I imagine she must have,' said Wilt patiently. 'You'd better ask her when you find her.'

'And when we find her will she be in a position to tell us?'

'How the hell should I know? All I can say is that if for some quite inexplicable reason she's lost all her teeth there'll be the devil to pay. I'll never hear the end of it. She's got a mania for cleaning the things and sticking bits of dental floss down the loo. You've got no idea the number of times I've thought I'd got worms.'

Inspector Flint sighed. Whatever success Sergeant Yates had had with teeth, it was certainly eluding him. He switched to other matters.

'Let's go over what happened at the Pringsheims' party again,' he said.

'Let's not,' said Wilt who had so far managed to avoid mentioning his contretemps with the doll in the bathroom. 'I've told you five times already and it's wearing a bit thin. Besides it was a filthy party. A lot of trendy intellectuals boosting their paltry egos.'

'Would you say you were an introverted sort of man, Wilt? A solitary type of person?'

Wilt considered the question seriously. It was certainly more to the point than teeth.

'I wouldn't go that far,' he said finally. 'I'm fairly quiet but I'm gregarious too. You have to be to cope with the classes I teach.'

'But you don't like parties?'

'I don't like parties like the Pringsheims', no.'

'Their sexual behaviour outrages you? Fills you with disgust?'

'Their sexual behaviour? I don't know why you pick on that. Everything about them disgusts me. All that crap about Women's Lib for one thing when all it means to someone like

Mrs Pringsheim is that she can go around behaving like a bitch on heat while her husband spends the day slaving over a hot test tube and comes home to cook supper, wash up and is lucky if he's got enough energy to wank himself off before going to sleep. Now if we're talking about real Women's Lib that's another matter. I've got nothing against ...'

'Let's just hold it there,' said the Inspector. 'Now two things you said interest me. One, wives behaving like bitches on heat. Two, this business of you wanking yourself off.'

'Me?' said Wilt indignantly. 'I wasn't talking about myself.'

'Weren't you?'

'No, I wasn't.'

'So you don't masturbate?'

'Now look here, Inspector. You're prying into areas of my private life which don't concern you. If you want to know about masturbation read the Kinsey Report. Don't ask me.'

Inspector Flint restrained himself with difficulty. He tried another tack. 'So when Mrs Pringsheim lay on the bed and asked you to have intercourse with her ...'

'Fuck is what she said,' Wilt corrected him.

'You said no?'

'Precisely,' said Wilt.

'Isn't that a bit odd?'

'What, her lying there or me saying no?'

'You saying no.'

Wilt looked at him incredulously.

'Odd?' he said. 'Odd? A woman comes in here and throws herself flat on her back on this table, pulls up her skirt and says "Fuck me, honey, prick me to the quick." Are you going to leap on to her with a "Whoopee, let's roll baby"? Is that what you mean by not odd?'

'Jesus wept, Wilt,' snarled the Inspector, 'you're walking a fucking tightrope with my patience.'

'You could have fooled me,' said Wilt. 'All I do know is that your notion of what is odd behaviour and what isn't doesn't begin to make sense with me.'

Inspector Flint got up and left the room. 'I'll murder the bastard, so help me God I'll murder him,' he shouted at the

Duty Sergeant. Behind him in the Interview Room Wilt put his head on the table and fell asleep.

At the Tech Wilt's absence was making itself felt in more ways than one. Mr Morris had had to take Gasfitters One at nine o'clock and had come out an hour later feeling that he had gained fresh insight into Wilt's sudden excursion into homicide. The Vice-Principal was fighting off waves of crime reporters anxious to find out more about the man who was helping the police with their enquiries into a particularly macabre and newsworthy crime. And the Principal had begun to regret his criticisms of Liberal Studies to the Education Committee. Mrs Chatterway had phoned to say that she had found his remarks in the worst of taste and had hinted that she might well ask for an enquiry into the running of the Liberal Studies Department. But it was at the meeting of the Course Board that there was most alarm.

'The visitation of the Council for National Academic Awards takes place on Friday,' Dr Mayfield, Head of Sociology, told the committee. 'They are hardly likely to approve the Joint Honours degree in the present circumstances.'

'If they had any sense they wouldn't approve it in any circumstances,' said Dr Board. 'Urban Studies and Medieval Poetry indeed. I know academic eclecticism is the vogue these days but Helen Waddell and Lewis Mumford aren't even remotely natural bedfellows. Besides the degree lacks academic content.'

Dr Mayfield bristled. Academic content was his strong point. 'I don't see how you can say that,' he said. 'The course has been structured to meet the needs of students looking for a thematic approach.'

'The poor benighted creatures we manage to lure away from universities to take this course wouldn't know a thematic approach if they saw one,' said Dr Board. 'Come to think of it I wouldn't either.'

'We all have our limitations,' said Dr Mayfield suavely.

'Precisely,' said Dr Board, 'and in the circumstances we should recognize them instead of concocting Joint Honours degrees which don't make sense for students who, if their

A-level results are anything to go by, haven't any in the first place. Heaven knows I'm all for educational opportunity but—'

'The point is,' interjected Dr Cox, Head of Science, 'that it is not the degree course as such that is the purpose of the visitation. As I understand it they have given their approval to the degree in principle. They are coming to look at the facilities the College provides and they are hardly likely to be impressed by the presence of so many murder squad detectives. That blue caravan is most off-putting.'

'In any case with the late Mrs Wilt structured into the foundations . . .' began Dr Board.

'I am doing my best to get the police to remove her from . . .'

'The syllabus?' asked Dr Board.

'The premises,' said Dr Mayfield. 'Unfortunately they seem to have hit a snag.'

'A snag?'

'They have hit bedrock at eleven feet.'

Dr Board smiled. 'One wonders why there was any need for thirty-foot piles in the first instance if there is bedrock at eleven,' he murmured.

'I can only tell you what the police have told me,' said Dr Mayfield. 'However they have promised to do all they can to be off the site by Friday. Now I would just like to run over the arrangements again with you. The Visitation will start at eleven with an inspection of the library. We will then break up into groups to discuss Faculty libraries and teaching facilities with particular reference to our ability to provide individual tuition . . .'

'I shouldn't have thought that was a point that needed emphasizing,' said Dr Board. 'With the few students we're likely to get we're almost certain to have the highest teacher to student radio in the country.'

'If we adopt that approach the Committee will gain the impression that we are not committed to the degree. We must provide a united front,' said Dr Mayfield, 'we can't afford at this stage to have divisions among ourselves. This degree could mean our getting Polytechnic status.'

•

There were divisions too among the men boring down on the building site. The foreman was still at home under sedation suffering nervous exhaustion brought on by his part in the cementation of a murdered woman and it was left to Barney to superintend operations. 'There was this hand, see . . .' he told the Sergeant in charge.

'On which side?'

'On the right,' said Barney.

'Then we'll go down on the left. That way if the hand is sticking out we won't cut it off.'

They went down on the left and cut off the main electricity cable to the canteen.

'Forget that bleeding hand,' said the Sergeant, 'we go down on the right and trust to luck. Just so long as we don't cut the bitch in half.'

They went down on the right and hit bedrock at eleven feet.

'This is going to slow us up no end,' said Barney. 'Who would have thought there'd be rock down there.'

'Who would have thought some nut would incorporate his missus in the foundation of a college of further education where he worked,' said the Sergeant.

'Gruesome,' said Barney.

In the meantime the staff had as usual divided into factions. Peter Braintree led those who thought Wilt was innocent and was joined by the New Left on the grounds that anyone in conflict with the fuzz must be in the right. Major Millfield reacted accordingly and led the Right against Wilt on the automatic assumption that anyone who incurred the support of the Left must be in the wrong and that anyway the police knew what they were doing. The issue was raised at the meeting of the Union called to discuss the annual pay demand. Major Millfield proposed a motion calling on the union to support the campaign for the reintroduction of capital punishment. Bill Trent countered with a motion expressing solidarity with Brother Wilt. Peter Braintree proposed that a fund be set up to help Wilt with his legal fees. Dr Lomax, Head of Commerce, argued against this and pointed out that Wilt had, by dismembering his wife, brought the profession into disrepute. Braintree said Wilt hadn't dismembered anyone and that even the police hadn't suggested he had, and there was such a thing as a law against slander. Dr Lomax withdrew his remark. Major Millfield insisted that there were good grounds for thinking Wilt had murdered his wife and that anyway Habeas Corpus didn't exist in Russia. Bill Trent said that capital punishment didn't either. Major Millfield said, 'Bosh.' In the end, after prolonged argument, Major Millfield's motion on hanging was passed by a block vote of the Catering Department while Braintree's proposal and the motion of the New Left were defeated, and the meeting went on to discuss a pay increase of forty-five per cent to keep Teachers in Technical Institutes in line with comparably qualified professions. Afterwards Peter Braintree went down to the Police Station to see if there was anything Henry wanted.

'I wonder if I might see him,' he asked the Sergeant at the desk.

'I'm afraid not, sir,' said the Sergeant, 'Mr Wilt is still helping us with our enquiries.'

'But isn't there anything I can get him? Doesn't he need anything?'

'Mr Wilt is well provided for,' said the Sergeant, with the private reservation that what Wilt needed was his head read.

'But shouldn't he have a solicitor?'

'When Mr Wilt asks for a solicitor he will be allowed to see one,' said the Sergeant. 'I can assure you that so far he hasn't asked.'

And Wilt hadn't. Having finally been allowed three hours sleep he had emerged from his cell at twelve o'clock and had eaten a hearty breakfast in the police canteen. He returned to the Interview Room, haggard and unshaven, and with his sense of the improbable markedly increased.

'Now then, Henry,' said Inspector Flint, dropping an official octave nomenclaturewise in the hope that Wilt would respond, 'about this blood.'

'What blood?' said Wilt, looking round the aseptic room.

'The blood on the walls of the bathroom at the Pringsheims' house. The blood on the landing. Have you any idea how it got there? Any idea at all?'

'None,' said Wilt, 'I can only assume that someone was bleeding.'

'Right,' said the Inspector, 'who?'

'Search me,' said Wilt.

'Quite, and you know what we've found?'

Wilt shook his head.

'No idea?'

'None,' said Wilt.

'Bloodspots on a pair of grey trousers in your wardrobe,' said the Inspector. 'Bloodspots, Henry, bloodspots.'

'Hardly surprising,' said Wilt. 'I mean if you looked hard enough you'd be bound to find some bloodspots in anyone's wardrobe. The thing is I wasn't wearing grey trousers at that party. I was wearing blue jeans.'

'You were wearing blue jeans? You're quite sure about that?'

'Yes.'

'So the bloodspots on the bathroom wall and the bloodspots on your grey trousers have nothing to do with one another?'

'Inspector,' said Wilt, 'far be it from me to teach you your own business but you have a technical branch that specializes in matching bloodstains. Now may I suggest that you make use of their skills to establish ...'

'Wilt,' said the Inspector, 'Wilt, when I need your advice on how to conduct a murder investigation I'll not only ask for it but I'll resign from the force.'

'Well?' said Wilt.

'Well what?'

'Do they match? Do the bloodstains match?'

The Inspector studied him grimly. 'If I told you they did?' he asked.

Wilt shrugged. 'I'm not in any position to argue,' he said. 'If you say they do, I take it they do.'

'They don't,' said Inspector Flint, 'but that proves nothing,' he continued before Wilt could savour his satisfaction. 'Nothing at all. We've got three people missing. There's Mrs Wilt at the bottom of that shaft ... No, don't say it, Wilt, don't say it. There's Dr Pringsheim and there's Mrs Fucking Pringsheim.'

'I like it,' said Wilt appreciatively, 'I definitely like it.'

'Like what?'

'Mrs Fucking Pringsheim. It's apposite.'

'One of these days, Wilt,' said the Inspector softly, 'you'll go too far.'

'Patiencewise? To use a filthy expression,' asked Wilt.

The Inspector nodded and lit a cigarette.

'You know something, Inspector,' said Wilt, beginning to feel on top of the situation, 'you smoke too much. Those things are bad for you. You should try ...'

'Wilt,' said the Inspector, 'in twenty-five years in the service I have never once resorted to physical violence while interrogating a suspect but there comes a time, a time and a place and a suspect when with the best will in the world ...' He got up and went out. Wilt sat back in his chair and looked up at the fluorescent light. He wished it would stop buzzing. It was getting on his nerves.

12

On Eel Stretch – Gaskell's map-reading had misled him and they were nowhere near Frogwater Reach or Fen Broad – the situation was getting on everyone's nerves. Gaskell's attempts to mend the engine had had the opposite effect. The cockpit was flooded with fuel oil and it was difficult to walk on deck without slipping.

'Jesus, G, anyone would think to look at you that this was a goddam oil rig,' said Sally.

'It was that fucking fuel line,' said Gaskell, 'I couldn't get it back on.'

'So why try starting the motor with it off?'

'To see if it was blocked.'

'So now you know. What you going to do about it? Sit here

till the food runs out? You've gotta think of something.'

'Why me? Why don't you come up with something?'

'If you were any sort of a man . . .'

'Shit,' said Gaskell. 'The voice of the liberated woman. Comes the crunch and all of a sudden I've got to be a man. What's up with you, man-woman? You want us off here, you do it. Don't ask me to be a man, uppercase M, in an emergency. I've forgotten how.'

'There must be some way of getting help,' said Sally.

'Oh sure. You just go up top and take a crowsnest at the scenery. All you'll get is a beanfeast of bullrushes.' Sally climbed on top of the cabin and scanned the horizon. It was thirty feet away and consisted of an expanse of reeds.

'There's something over there looks like a church tower,' she said. Gaskell climbed up beside her.

'It is a church tower. So what?'

'So if we flashed a light or something someone might see it.'

'Brilliant. A highly populated place like the top of a church tower there's bound to be people just waiting for us to flash a light.'

'Couldn't we burn something?' said Sally. 'Somebody would see the smoke and . . .'

'You crazy? You start burning anything with all that fuel oil floating around they'll see something all right. Like an exploding cruiser with bodies.'

'We could fill a can with oil and put it over the side and float it away before lighting it.'

'And set the reedbeds on fire? What the hell do you want? A fucking holocaust?'

'G baby, you're just being unhelpful.'

'I'm using my brains is all,' said Gaskell. 'You keep coming up with bright ideas like that you're going to land us in a worse mess than we're in already.'

'I don't see why,' said Sally.

'I'll tell you why,' said Gaskell, 'because you went and stole this fucking *Hesperus*. That's why.'

'I didn't steal it. I . . .'

'You tell the fuzz that. Just tell them. You start setting fire to reedbeds and they'll be all over us asking questions. Like whose boat this is and how come you're sailing someone else's cruiser ... So we got to get out of here without publicity.'

It started to rain.

'That's all we need. Rain,' said Gaskell. Sally went down into the cabin where Eva was tidying up after lunch. 'God, G's hopeless. First he lands us on a mudbank in the middle of nowhere, then he gefucks the motor but good and now he says he doesn't know what to do.'

'Why doesn't he go and get help?' asked Eva.

'How? Swimming? G couldn't swim that far to save his life.'

'He could take the airbed and paddle down to the open water,' said Eva. 'He wouldn't have to swim.'

'Airbed? Did I hear you say airbed? What airbed?'

'The one in the locker with the lifejackets. All you've got to do is blow it up and ...'

'Honey you're the practicallest,' said Sally, and rushed outside. 'G, Eva's found a way for you to go and get help. There's an airbed in the locker with the lifejackets.' She rummaged in the locker and took out the airbed.

'You think I'm going anywhere on that damned thing you've got another think coming,' said Gaskell.

'What's wrong with it?'

'In this weather? You ever tried to steer one of those things? It's bad enough on a sunny day with no wind. Right now I'd end up in the reeds and anyhow the rain's getting on my glasses.'

'All right, so we wait till the storm blows over. At least we know how to get off here.'

She went back into the cabin and shut the door. Outside Gaskell squatted by the engine and toyed with the wrench. If only he could get the thing to go again.

'Men,' said Sally contemptuously, 'claim to be the stronger sex but when the chips are down it's us women who have to bail them out.'

'Henry's impractical too,' said Eva. 'It's all he can do to mend a fuse. I do hope he isn't worried about me.'

'He's having himself a ball,' said Sally.

'Not Henry. He wouldn't know how.'

'He's probably having it off with Judy.'

Eva shook her head. 'He was just drunk, that's all. He's never done anything like that before.'

'How would you know?'

'Well he is my husband.'

'Husband hell. He just uses you to wash the dishes and cook and clean up for him. What does he give you? Just tell me that.'

Eva struggled with her thoughts inarticulately. Henry didn't give her anything very much. Not anything she could put into words. 'He needs me,' she said finally.

'So he needs you. Who needs needing? That's the rhetoric of female feudalism. So you save someone's life, you've got to be grateful to them for letting you? Forget Henry. He's a jerk.'

Eva bristled. Henry might not be very much but she didn't like him insulted.

'Gaskell's nothing much to write home about,' she said and went into the kitchen. Behind her Sally lay back on the bunk and opened the centre spread of *Playboy*. 'Gaskell's got bread,' she said.

'Bread?'

'Money, honey. Greenstuff. The stuff that makes the world go round Cabaretwise. You think I married him for his looks? Oh no. I can smell a cool million when it comes by me and I do mean buy me.'

'I could never marry a man for his money,' said Eva primly. 'I'd have to be in love with him. I really would.'

'So you've seen too many movies. Do you really think Gaskell was in love with me?'

'I don't know. I suppose he must have been.'

Sally laughed. 'Eva baby you are naïve. Let me tell you about G. G's a plastic freak. He'd fuck a goddam chimpanzee if you dressed it up in plastic.'

'Oh honestly. He wouldn't,' said Eva. 'I don't believe it.'

'You think I put you on the Pill for nothing? You go around

in that bikini and Gaskell's drooling over you all the time —
if I wasn't here he'd have raped you.'

'He'd have a hard time,' said Eva, 'I took Judo classes.'

'Well he'd try. Anything in plastic drives him crazy. Why do
you think he had that doll?'

'I wondered about that.'

'Right. You can stop wondering,' said Sally.

'I still don't see what that has to do with you marrying him,'
said Eva.

'Then let me tell you a little secret. Gaskell was referred to
me . . .'

'Referred?'

'By Dr Freeborn. Gaskell had this little problem and he
consulted Dr Freeborn and Dr Freeborn sent him to me.'

Eva looked puzzled. 'But what were you supposed to do?'

'I was a surrogate,' said Sally.

'A surrogate?'

'Like a sex counsellor,' said Sally. 'Dr Freeborn used to
send me clients and I would help them.'

'I wouldn't like that sort of job,' said Eva, 'I couldn't bear
to talk to men about sex. Weren't you embarrassed?'

'You get used to it and there are worse ways of earning a
living. So G comes along with his little problem and I
straightened him out but literally and we got married. A
business arrangement. Cash on the tail.'

'You mean you . . .'

'I mean I have Gaskell and Gaskell has plastic. It's an elastic
relationship. The marriage with the two-way stretch.'

Eva digested this information with difficulty. It didn't seem
right somehow. 'Didn't his parents have anything to say about
it?' she asked. 'I mean did he tell them about you helping him
and all that?'

'Say? What could they say? G told them he'd met me at
summer school and Pringsy's greedy little eyes popped out of
his greasy little head. Baby, did that fat little man have penis
projection. Sell? He could sell anything. The Rockefeller
Centre to Rockefeller. So he accepted me. Old Ma Pringsheim
didn't. She huffed and she puffed and she blew but this little

piggy stayed right where the bank was. G and me went back to California and G graduated in plastic and we've been biodegradable ever since.'

'I'm glad Henry isn't like that,' said Eva. 'I couldn't live with a man who was queer.'

'G's not queer, honey. Like I said he's a plastic freak.'

'If that's not queer I don't know what is,' said Eva.

Sally lit a cigarillo.

'All men get turned on by something,' she said. 'They're manipulable. All you've got to do is find the kink. I should know.'

'Henry's not like that. I'd know if he was.'

'So he makes with the doll. That's how much you know about Henry. You telling me he's the great lover?'

'We've been married twelve years. It's only natural we don't do it as often as we used to. We're so busy.'

'Busy lizzie. And while you're housebound what's Henry doing?'

'He's taking classes at the Tech. He's there all day and he comes home tired.'

'Takes classes takes asses. You'll be telling me next he's not a sidewinder.'

'I don't know what you mean,' said Eva.

'He has his piece on the side. His secretary knees up on the desk.'

'He doesn't have a secretary.'

'Then students prudence. Screws their grades up. I know. I've seen it. I've been around colleges too long to be fooled.'

'I'm sure Henry would never . . .'

'That's what they all say and then bingo, it's divorce and bobbysex and all you're left to look forward to is menopause and peeking through the blinds at the man next door and waiting for the Fuller Brush man.'

'You make it all sound so awful,' said Eva. 'You really do.'

'It is, Eva teats. It is. You've got to do something about it before it's too late. You've got to liberate yourself from Henry. Make the break and share the cake. Otherwise it's male domination doomside.'

Eve sat on the bunk and thought about the future. It didn't seem to hold much for her. They would never have any children now and they wouldn't ever have much money. They would go on living in Parkview Avenue and paying off the mortgage and maybe Henry would find someone else and then what would she do? And even if he didn't, life was passing her by.

'I wish I knew what to do,' she said presently. Sally sat up and put her arm round her.

'Why don't you come to the States with us in November?' she said. 'We could have such fun.'

'Oh I couldn't do that,' said Eva. 'It wouldn't be fair to Henry.'

No such qualms bothered Inspector Flint. Wilt's intransigence under intense questioning merely indicated that he was harder than he looked.

'We've had him under interrogation for thirty-six hours now,' he told the conference of the Murder Squad in the briefing room at the Police Station, 'and we've got nothing out of him. So this is going to be a long hard job and quite frankly I have my doubts about breaking him.'

'I told you he was going to be a hard nut to crack,' said Sergeant Yates.

'Nut being the operative word,' said Flint. 'So it's got to be concrete evidence.'

There was a snigger which died away quickly. Inspector Flint was not in a humorous mood.

'Evidence, hard evidence is the only thing that is going to break him. Evidence is the only thing that is going to bring him to trial.'

'But we've got that,' said Yates. 'It's at the bott ...'

'I know exactly where it is, thank you Sergeant. What I am talking about is evidence of multiple murder. Mrs Wilt is accounted for. Dr and Mrs Pringsheim aren't. Now my guess is that he murdered all three and that the other two bodies are ...' He stopped and opened the file in front of him and hunted through it for Notes on Violence and the Break-Up of

Family Life. He studied them for a moment and shook his head. 'No,' he muttered, 'it's not possible.'

'What isn't, sir?' asked Sergeant Yates. 'Anything is possible with this bastard.'

But Inspector Flint was not to be drawn. The notion was too awful.

'As I was saying,' he continued, 'what we need now is hard evidence. What we have got is purely circumstantial. I want more evidence on the Pringsheims. I want to know what happened at that party, who was there and why it happened and at the rate we're going with Wilt we aren't going to get anything out of him. Snell, you go down to the Department of Biochemistry at the University and get what you can on Dr Pringsheim. Find out if any of his colleagues were at that party. Interview them. Get a list of his friends, his hobbies, his girl friends if he had any. Find out if there is any link between him and Mrs Wilt that would suggest a motive. Jackson, you go up to Rossiter Grove and see what you can get on Mrs Pringsheim...'

By the time the conference broke up detectives had been despatched all over town to build up a dossier on the Pringsheims. Even the American Embassy had been contacted to find out what was known about the couple in the States. The murder investigation had begun in earnest.

Inspector Flint walked back to his office with Sergeant Yates and shut the door. 'Yates,' he said, 'this is confidential. I wasn't going to mention it in there but I've a nasty feeling I know why that sod is so bloody cocky. Have you ever known a murderer sit through thirty-six hours of questioning as cool as a cucumber when he knows we've got the body of his victim pinpointed to the nearest inch?'

Sergeant Yates shook his head. 'I've known some pretty cool customers in my time and particularly since they stopped hanging but this one takes the biscuit. If you ask me he's a raving psychopath.'

Flint dismissed the idea. 'Psychopaths crack easy,' he said. 'They confess to murders they haven't committed or they confess to murders they have committed, but they confess.

This Wilt doesn't. He sits there and tells me how to run the investigation. Now take a look at this.' He opened the file and took out Wilt's notes. 'Notice anything peculiar?'

Sergeant Yates read the notes through twice.

'Well, he doesn't seem to think much of our methods,' he said finally. 'And I don't much like this bit about low level of intelligence of average policeman.'

'What about Point Two D?' said the Inspector. 'Increasing use of sophisticated methods such as diversionary tactics by criminals. Diversionary tactics. Doesn't that suggest anything to you?'

'You mean he's trying to divert our attention away from the real crime to something else?'

Inspector Flint nodded. 'What I mean is this. I wouldn't mind betting that when we do get down to the bottom of that fucking pile we're going to find an inflatable doll dressed up in Mrs Wilt's clothes and with a vagina. That's what I think.'

'But that's insane.'

'Insane? It's fucking diabolical,' said the Inspector. 'He's sitting in there like a goddam dummy giving as good as he gets because he knows he's got us chasing a red herring.'

Sergeant Yates sat down mystified. 'But why? Why draw attention to the murder in the first place? Why didn't he just lie low and act normally?'

'What, and report Mrs Wilt missing? You're forgetting the Pringsheims. A wife goes missing, so what? Two of her friends go missing and leave their house in a hell of a mess and covered with bloodstains. That needs explaining, that does. So he puts out a false trail ...'

'But that still doesn't help him,' objected the Sergeant. 'We dig up a plastic doll. Doesn't mean we're going to halt the investigation.'

'Maybe not but it gives him a week while the other bodies disintegrate.'

'You think he used an acid bath like Haigh?' asked the Sergeant. 'That's horrible.'

'Of course it's horrible. You think murder's nice or something? Anyway the only reason they got Haigh was that stupid bugger told them where to look for the sludge. If he'd kept his trap shut for another week they wouldn't have found anything. The whole lot would have been washed away. Besides I don't know what Wilt's used. All I do know is he's an intellectual, a clever sod and he thinks he's got it wrapped up. First we take him in for questioning, maybe even get him remanded and when we've done that, we go and dig up a plastic inflatable doll. We're going to look right Charlies going into court with a plastic doll as evidence of murder. We'll be the laughing stock of the world. So the case gets thrown out of court and what happens when we pick him up a second time for questioning on the real murders? We'd have the Civil Liberties brigade sinking their teeth into our throats like bleeding vampire bats.'

'I suppose that explains why he doesn't start shouting for a lawyer,' said Yates.

'Of course it does. What does he want with a lawyer now? But pull him in a second time and he'll have lawyers falling over themselves to help him. They'll be squawking about police brutality and victimization. You won't be able to hear yourself speak. His bloody lawyers will have a field day. First plastic dolls and then no bodies at all. He'll get clean away.'

'Anyone who can think that little lot up must be a madman,' said the Sergeant.

'Or a fucking genius,' said Flint bitterly. 'Christ what a case.' He stubbed out a cigarette resentfully.

'What do you want me to do? Have another go at him?'

'No, I'll do that. You go up to the Tech and chivvy his boss there into saying what he really thinks of Wilt. Get any little bit of dirt on the blighter you can. There's got to be something in his past we can use.'

He went down the corridor and into the Interview Room. Wilt was sitting at the table making notes on the back of a statement form. Now that he was beginning to feel, if not at home in the Police Station, at least more at ease with his surroundings, his mind had turned to the problem of Eva's disappearance. He had to admit that he had been worried by the bloodstains in the Pringsheims' bathroom. To while away the time he had tried to formulate his thoughts on paper and he was still at it when Inspector Flint came into the room and banged the door.

'Right, so you're a clever fellow, Wilt,' he said, sitting down and pulling the paper towards him. 'You can read and write and you've got a nice logical and inventive mind so let's just see what you've written here. Who's Ethel?'

'Eva's sister,' said Wilt. 'She's married to a market gardener in Luton. Eva sometimes goes over there for a week.'

'And "Blood in the bath"?'

'Just wondering how it got there.'

'And "Evidence of hurried departure"?'

'I was simply putting down my thoughts about the state of the Pringsheims' house,' said Wilt.

'You're trying to be helpful?'

'I'm here helping you with your enquiries. That's the official term isn't it?'

'It may be the official term, Wilt, but in this case it doesn't correspond with the facts.'

'I don't suppose it does very often,' said Wilt. 'It's one of those expressions that covers a multitude of sins.'

'And crimes.'

'It also happens to ruin a man's reputation,' said Wilt. 'I hope you realize what you're doing to mine by holding me here like this. It's bad enough knowing I'm going to spend the rest of my life being pointed out as the man who dressed a plastic doll with a cunt up in his wife's clothes and dropped it down a pile hole without everyone thinking I'm a bloody murderer as well.'

'Where you're going to spend the rest of your life nobody is going to care what you did with that plastic doll,' said the Inspector.

Wilt seized on the admission.

'Ah, so you've found it at last,' he said eagerly. 'That's fine. So now I'm free to go.'

'Sit down and shut up,' snarled the Inspector. 'You're not going anywhere and when you do it will be in a large black van. I haven't finished with you yet. In fact I'm only just beginning.'

'Here we go again,' said Wilt. 'I just knew you'd want to

start at the beginning again. You fellows have primary causes on the brain. Cause and effect, cause and effect. Which came first, the chicken or the egg, protoplasm or demiurge? I suppose this time it's going to be what Eva said when we were dressing to go to the party.'

'This time,' said the Inspector, 'I want you to tell me precisely why you stuck that damned doll down that hole.'

'Now that is an interesting question,' said Wilt, and stopped. It didn't seem a good idea to try to explain to Inspector Flint in the present circumstances just what he had had in mind when he dropped the doll down the shaft. The Inspector didn't look the sort of person who would understand at all readily that a husband could have fantasies of murdering his wife without actually putting them into effect. It would be better to wait for Eva to put in an appearance in the flesh before venturing into that uncharted territory of the wholly irrational. With Eva present Flint might sympathize with him. Without her he most certainly wouldn't.

'Let's just say I wanted to get rid of the beastly thing,' he said.

'Let's not say anything of the sort,' said Flint. 'Let's just say you had an ulterior motive for putting it there.'

Wilt nodded. 'I'll go along with that,' he said.

Inspector Flint nodded encouragingly. 'I thought you might. Well, what was it?'

Wilt considered his words carefully. He was getting into deep waters.

'Let's just say it was by way of being a rehearsal.'

'A rehearsal? What sort of rehearsal?'

Wilt thought for a moment.

'Interesting word "rehearsal",' he said. 'It comes from the old French, *rehercer*, meaning . . .'

'To hell with where it comes from,' said the Inspector, 'I want to know where it ends up.'

'Sounds a bit like a funeral too when you come to think of it,' said Wilt, continuing his campaign of semantic attrition.

Inspector Flint hurled himself into the trap. 'Funeral? Whose funeral?'

'Anyone's,' said Wilt blithely. 'Hearse, rehearse. You could say that's what happens when you exhume a body. You rehearse it though I don't suppose you fellows use hearses.'

'For God's sake,' shouted the Inspector. 'Can't you ever stick to the point? You said you were rehearsing something and I want to know what that something was.'

'An idea, a mere idea,' said Wilt, 'one of those ephemera of mental fancy that flit like butterflies across the summer landscape of the mind blown by the breezes of association that come like sudden showers ... I rather like that.'

'I don't,' said the Inspector, looking at him bitterly. 'What I want to know is what you were rehearsing. That's what I'd like to know.'

'I've told you. An idea.'

'What sort of idea?'

'Just an idea,' said Wilt. 'A mere ...'

'So help me God, Wilt,' shouted the Inspector, 'if you start on these fucking butterflies again I'll break the unbroken habit of a lifetime and wring your bloody neck.'

'I wasn't going to mention butterflies this time,' said Wilt reproachfully, 'I was going to say that I had this idea for a book ...'

'A book?' snarled Inspector Flint. 'What sort of book? A book of poetry or a crime story?'

'A crime story,' said Wilt, grateful for the suggestion.

'I see,' said the Inspector. 'So you were going to write a thriller. Well now, just let me guess the outline of the plot. There's this lecturer at the Tech and he has this wife he hates and he decides to murder her ...'

'Go on,' said Wilt, 'you're doing very well so far.'

'I thought I might be,' said Flint delightedly. 'Well, this lecturerer thinks he's a clever fellow who can hoodwink the police. He doesn't think much of the police. So he dumps a plastic doll down a hole that's going to be filled with concrete in the hope that the police will waste their time digging it out and in the meantime he's buried his wife somewhere else. By the way, where did you bury Mrs Wilt, Henry? Let's get this over once and for all. Where did you put her? Just tell me that. You'll feel better when it's out.'

'I didn't put her anywhere. If I've told you that once I've

137

told you a thousand times. How many more times have I got to tell you I don't know where she is.'

'I'll say this for you, Wilt,' said the Inspector, when he could bring himself to speak. 'I've known some cool customers in my time but I have to take my hat off to you. You're the coolest bastard it's ever been my unfortunate experience to come across.'

Wilt shook his head. 'You know,' he said, 'I feel sorry for you, Inspector, I really do. You can't recognize the truth when it's staring you in the face.'

Inspector Flint got up and left the room. 'You there,' he said to the first detective he could find. 'Go into that Interview Room and ask that bastard questions and don't stop till I tell you.'

'What sort of questions?'

'Any sort. Just any. Keep asking him why he stuffed an inflatable plastic doll down a pile hole. That's all. Just ask it over and over again. I'm going to break that sod.'

He went down to his office and slumped into his chair and tried to think.

13

At the Tech Sergeant Yates sat in Mr Morris's office. 'I'm sorry to disturb you again,' he said, 'but we need some more details on this fellow Wilt.'

The Head of Liberal Studies looked up with a haggard expression from the timetable. He had been having a desperate struggle trying to find someone to take Bricklayers Four. Price wouldn't do because he had Mechanics Two and Williams wouldn't anyway. He had already gone home the day before with a nervous stomach and was threatening to repeat the performance if anyone so much as mentioned Bricklayers Four to him again. That left Mr Morris himself and he was prepared to be disturbed by Sergeant Yates for as long as he liked if it meant he didn't have to take those bloody brick-layers.

'Anything to help,' he said, with an affability that was in curious contrast to the haunted look in his eyes. 'What details would you like to know?'

'Just a general impression of the man, sir,' said the Sergeant. 'Was there anything unusual about him?'

'Unusual?' Mr Morris thought for a moment. Apart from a preparedness to teach the most awful Day Release Classes year in and year out without complaint he could think of nothing unusual about Wilt. 'I suppose you could call what amounted to a phobic reaction to *The Lord of the Flies* a bit unusual but then I've never much cared for ...'

'If you'd just wait a moment, sir,' said the Sergeant busying himself with his notebook. 'You did say "phobic reaction" didn't you?'

'Well what I meant was ...'

'To flies, sir?'

'To *The Lord of the Flies*. It's a book,' said Mr Morris, now uncertain that he had been wise to mention the fact. Police-men were not noticeably sensitive to those niceties of literary taste that constituted his own definition of intelligence. 'I do hope I haven't said the wrong thing.'

'Not at all, sir. It's these little details that help us to build up a picture of the criminal's mind.'

Mr Morris sighed. 'I'm sure I never thought when Mr Wilt came to us from the University that he would turn out like this.'

'Quite so, sir. Now did Mr Wilt ever say anything disparaging about his wife?'

'Disparaging? Dear me no. Mind you he didn't have to. Eva spoke for herself.' He looked miserably out of the window at the pile-boring machine.

'Then in your opinion Mrs Wilt was not a very likeable woman?'

Mr Morris shook his head. 'She was a ghastly woman,' he said.

Sergeant Yates licked the end of his ballpen.

'You did say "ghastly" sir?'

'I'm afraid so. I once had her in an Evening Class for Elementary Drama.'

'Elementary?' said the Sergeant, and wrote it down.

'Yes, though elemental would have been more appropriate in Mrs Wilt's case. She threw herself into the parts rather too vigorously to be wholly convincing. Her Desdemona to my Othello is something I am never likely to forget.'

'An impetuous woman, would you say?'

'Let me put it this way,' said Mr Morris, 'had Shakespeare written the play as Mrs Wilt interpreted it, Othello would have been the one to be strangled.'

'I see, sir,' said the Sergeant. 'Then I take it she didn't like black men.'

'I have no idea what she thought about the racial issue,' said Mr Morris, 'I am talking of her physical strength.'

'A powerful woman, sir?'

'Very,' said Mr Morris with feelings.

Sergeant Yates looked puzzled. 'It seems strange a woman like that allowing herself to be murdered by Mr Wilt without putting up more of a struggle,' he said thoughtfully.

'It seems incredible to me,' Mr Morris agreed, 'and what is more it indicates a degree of fanatical courage in Henry that his behaviour in this department never led me to suspect. I can only suppose he was insane at the time.'

Sergeant Yates seized on the point. 'Then it is your considered opinion that he was not in his right mind when he killed his wife?'

'Right mind? I can think of nothing rightminded about killing your wife and dumping her body ...'

'I meant sir,' said the Sergeant, 'that you think Mr Wilt is a lunatic.'

Mr Morris hesitated. There were a good many members of his department whom he would have classified as mentally unbalanced but he hardly liked to advertise the fact. On the other hand it might help poor Wilt.

'Yes, I suppose so,' he said finally for at heart he was a kindly man. 'Quite mad. Between ourselves, Sergeant, anyone who is prepared to teach the sort of bloodyminded young thugs we get can't be entirely sane. And only last week Wilt got into an altercation with one of the Printers and was punched in the face. I think that may have had something to do with his subsequent behaviour. I trust you will treat what I say in the strictest confidence. I wouldn't want ...'

'Quite so, sir,' said Sergeant Yates. 'Well, I needn't detain you any longer.'

He returned to the Police Station and reported his findings to Inspector Flint.

'Nutty as a fruitcake,' he announced. 'That's his opinion. He's quite positive about it.'

'In that case he had no right to employ the sod,' said Flint. 'He should have sacked the brute.'

'Sacked him? From the Tech? You know they can't sack teachers. You've got to do something really drastic before they give you the boot.'

'Like murdering three people, I suppose. Well as far as I'm concerned they can have the little bastard back.'

'You mean he's still holding out?'

'Holding out? He's counterattacking. He's reduced me to a nervous wreck and now Bolton says he wants to be relieved. Can't stand the strain any longer.'

Sergeant Yates scratched his head. 'Beats me how he does it,' he said. 'Anyone would think he was innocent. I wonder when he'll start asking for a lawyer.'

'Never,' said Flint. 'What does he need a lawyer for? If I had a lawyer in there handing out advice I'd have got the truth out of Wilt hours ago.'

As night fell over Eel Creek the wind increased to Gale Force Eight. Rain hammered on the cabin roof, waves slapped against the hull and the cabin cruiser, listing to starboard, settled more firmly into the mud. Inside the cabin the air was thick with smoke and bad feelings. Gaskell had opened a bottle of vodka and was getting drunk. To pass the time they played Scrabble.

'My idea of hell,' said Gaskell, 'is to be huis closed with a couple of dykes.'

'What's a dyke?' said Eva.

Gaskell stared at her. 'You don't know?'

'I know the sort they have in Holland . . .'

'Yoga bear,' said Gaskell, 'you are the naïvest. A dyke is—'

'Forget it, G,' said Sally. 'Whose turn to play?'

'It's mine,' said Eva. 'I . . . M . . . P spells Imp.'

'O . . . T . . . E . . . N . . . T spells Gaskell,' said Sally.

Gaskell drank some more vodka. 'What the hell sort of game we supposed to be playing? Scrabble or some sort of Truth group?'

'Your turn,' said Sally.

Gaskell put D . . . I . . . L . . . D on the O. 'Try that for size.'

Eva looked at it critically.

'You can't use proper names,' she said. 'You wouldn't let me use Squezy.'

'Eva teats, dildo is not a proper name. It's an improper thing. A surrogate penis.'

'A what?'

'Never mind what it is,' said Sally. 'Your turn to play.' Eva studied her letters. She didn't like being told what to do so often and besides she still wanted to know what a dyke was. And a surrogate penis. In the end she put L . . . O . . . V on the E.

'Is a many-splendoured thing,' said Gaskell and put D . . . I . . . D on the L and O.

'You can't have two of them,' said Eva. 'You've got one Dildo already.'

'This one's different,' said Gaskell, 'it's got whiskers.'

'What difference does that make?'

'Ask Sally. She's the one with penis envy.'

'You asshole,' said Sally and put F . . . A . . . G . . . G . . . O on the T. 'Meaning you.'

'Like I said. Truth Scrabble,' said Gaskell. 'Trubble for short. So why don't we have an encounter group instead. Let the truth hang out like it is.'

Eva used the F to make Faithful. Gaskell followed with Hooker and Sally went Insane.

'Great,' said Gaskell, 'Alphabetical I Ching.'

'Wunderkind, you slay me,' said Sally.

'Go Zelda yourself,' said Gaskell and slid his hand up Eva's thigh.

'Keep your hands to yourself,' said Eva and pushed him away. She put S and N on the I. Gaskell made Butch with the B.

'And don't tell me it's a proper name.'

'Well it's certainly not a word I've heard,' said Eva.

Gaskell stared at her and then roared with laughter.

'Now I've heard it all,' he said. 'Like cunnilingus is a cough medicine. How dumb can you get?'

'Go look in the mirror,' said Sally.

'Oh sure. So I married a goddam lesbian whore who goes round stealing other people's wives and boats and things. I'm dumb. But boobs here beats me. She's so fucking hypocritical she pretends she's not a dyke ...'

'I don't know what a dyke is,' said Eva.

'Well let me inform you, fatso. A dyke is a lesbian.'

'Are you calling me a lesbian?' said Eva.

'Yes,' said Gaskell.

Eva slapped him across the face hard. Gaskell's glasses came off and he sat down on the floor.

'Now G ...' Sally began but Gaskell had scrambled to his feet.

'Right you fat bitch,' he said. 'You want the truth you're going to get it. First off, you think husband Henry got into that doll off his own bat, well let me tell you ...'

'Gaskell, you just shut up,' shouted Sally.

'Like hell I will. I've had about enough of you and your rotten little ways. I picked you out of a cathouse ...'

'That's not true. It was a clinic,' screamed Sally, 'a clinic for sick perverts like you.'

Eva wasn't listening. She was staring at Gaskell. He had called her a lesbian and had said Henry hadn't got into that doll of his own accord.

'Tell me about Henry,' she shouted. 'How did he get into that doll?'

Gaskell pointed at Sally. 'She put him there. That poor goof wouldn't know ...'

'You put him there?' Eva said to Sally. 'You did?'

'He tried to make me, Eva. He tried to——'

'I don't believe it,' Eva shouted. 'Henry isn't like that.'

'I tell you he did. He . . .'

'And you put him in that doll?' Eva screamed and launched herself across the table at Sally. There was a splintering sound and the table collapsed. Gaskell scudded sideways on to the bunk and Sally shot out of the cabin. Eva got to her feet and moved forward towards the door. She had been tricked, cheated and lied to. And Henry had been humiliated. She was going to kill that bitch Sally. She stepped out into the cockpit. On the far side Sally was a dark shadow. Eva went round the engine and lunged at her. The next moment she had slipped on the oily deck and Sally had darted across the cockpit and through the door into the cabin. She slammed the door behind her and locked it. Eva Wilt got to her feet and stood with the rain running down her face and as she stood there the illusions that had sustained her through the week disappeared. She saw herself as a fat, silly woman who had left her husband in pursuit of a glamour that was false and shoddy and founded on brittle talk and money. And Gaskell had said she was a lesbian. The full nausea of knowing what Touch Therapy had meant dawned on Eva. She staggered to the side of the boat and sat down on a locker.

And slowly her self-disgust turned back to anger, and a cold hatred of the Pringsheims. She would get her own back on them. They would be sorry they had ever met her. She got up and opened the locker and took out the lifejackets and threw them over the side. Then she blew up the airbed, dropped it into the water and climbed over herself. She let herself down into the water and lay on the airbed. It rocked alarmingly but Eva was not afraid. She was getting her revenge on the Pringsheims and she no longer cared what happened to her. She paddled off through the little waves pushing the lifejackets in front of her. The wind was behind her and the airbed moved easily. In five minutes she had turned the corner of the reeds and was out of sight of the cruiser. Somewhere in the darkness ahead there was the open water where they had seen the dinghies and beyond it land.

Presently she found herself being blown sideways into the reeds. The rain stopped and Eva lay panting on the airbed. It would be easier if she got rid of the lifejackets. She was far enough from the boat for them to be well hidden. She pushed them into the reeds and then hesitated. Perhaps she should keep one for herself. She disentangled a jacket from the bunch and managed to put it on. Then she lay face down on the airbed again and paddled forward down the widening channel.

Sally leant against the cabin door and looked at Gaskell with loathing.

'You stupid jerk,' she said. 'You had to open your big mouth. So what the hell are you going to do now?'

'Divorce you for a start,' said Gaskell.

'I'll alimony you for all the money you've got.'

'Fat chance. You won't get a red cent,' Gaskell said and drank some more vodka.

'I'll see you dead first,' said Sally.

Gaskell grinned. 'Me dead? Anyone's going to die round here, it's you. Booby baby is out for blood.'

'She'll cool off.'

'You think so? Try opening that door if you're so sure. Go on, unlock it.'

Sally moved away from the door and sat down.

'This time you've really bought yourself some trouble,' said Gaskell. 'You had to pick a goddam prizefighter.'

'You go out and pacify her,' said Sally.

'No way. I'd as soon play blind man's buff with a fucking rhinoceros.' He lay on the bunk and smiled happily. 'You know there's something really ironical about all this. You had to go and liberate a Neanderthal. Women's Lib for paleolithics. She Tarzan, you Jane. You've bought yourself a piece of zoo.'

'Very funny,' said Sally. 'And what's your role?'

'Me Noah. Just be thankful she hasn't got a gun.' He pulled a pillow up under his head and went to sleep.

Sally sat on staring at his back venomously. She was frightened. Eva's reaction had been so violent that it had destroyed her confidence in herself. Gaskell was right. There had been something primeval in Eva Wilt's behaviour. She shuddered at the thought of that dark shape moving towards her in the cockpit. Sally got up and went into the galley and found a long sharp knife. Then she went back into the cabin and checked the lock on the door and lay down on her bunk and tried to sleep. But sleep wouldn't come. There were noises outside. Waves lapped against the side of the boat. The wind blew. God, what a mess it all was! Sally clutched her knife and thought about Gaskell and what he had said about divorce.

Peter Braintree sat in the office of Mr Gosdyke, Solicitor, and discussed the problem. 'He's been in there since Monday and it's Thursday now. Surely they've no right to keep him there so long without his seeing a solicitor.'

'If he doesn't ask for one and if the police want to question him and he is prepared to answer their questions and refuses to demand his legal rights I don't really see that there is anything I can do about it,' said Mr Gosdyke.

'But are you sure that that is the situation?' asked Braintree.

'As far as I can ascertain that is indeed the situation. Mr Wilt has not asked to see me. I spoke to the Inspector in charge, you heard me, and it seems quite clear that Mr Wilt appears, for some extraordinary reason, to be prepared to help the police with their enquiries just as long as they feel his presence at the Police Station is necessary. Now if a man refuses to assert his own legal rights then he has only himself to blame for his predicament.'

'But are you absolutely certain that Henry has refused to see you? I mean the police could be lying to you.'

Mr Gosdyke shook his head. 'I have known Inspector Flint for many years,' he said, 'and he is not the sort of man to deny a suspect his rights. No, I'm sorry, Mr Braintree. I would like to be of more assistance but frankly, in the circumstances, I can do nothing. Mr Wilt's predilection for the company of police officers is quite incomprehensible to me, but it disqualifies me from interfering.'

'You don't think they're giving him third degree or anything of that sort?'

'My dear fellow, third degree? You've been watching too

many old movies on the TV. The police don't use strong-arm methods in this country.'

'They've been pretty brutal with some of our students who have been on demos,' Braintree pointed out.

'Ah, but students are quite another matter and demonstrating students get what they deserve. Political provocation is one thing but domestic murders of the sort your friend Mr Wilt seems to have indulged in come into a different category altogether. I can honestly say that in all my years in the legal profession I have yet to come across a case in which the police did not treat a domestic murderer with great care and not a little sympathy. After all, they are nearly all married men themselves, and in any case Mr Wilt has a degree and that always helps. If you are a professional man, and in spite of what some people may say lecturers in Technical Colleges are members of a profession if only marginally, then you can rest assured that the police will do nothing in the least untoward. Mr Wilt is perfectly safe.'

And Wilt felt safe. He sat in the Interview Room and contemplated Inspector Flint with interest.

'Motivation? Now there's an interesting question,' he said. 'If you had asked me why I married Eva in the first place I'd have some trouble trying to explain myself. I was young at the time and ...'

'Wilt,' said the Inspector, 'I didn't ask you why you married your wife. I asked you why you decided to murder her.'

'I didn't decide to murder her,' said Wilt.

'It was a spontaneous action? A momentary impulse you couldn't resist? An act of madness you now regret?'

'It was none of those things. In the first place it was not an act. It was mere fantasy.'

'But you do admit that the thought crossed your mind?'

'Inspector,' said Wilt, 'if I acted upon every impulse that crossed my mind I would have been convicted of child rape, buggery, burglary, assault with intent to commit grievous bodily harm and mass murder long ago.'

'All those impulses crossed your mind?'

147

'At some time or other, yes,' said Wilt.

'You've got a bloody odd mind.'

'Which is something I share with the vast majority of mankind. I daresay that even you in your odd contemplative moments have ...'

'Wilt,' said the Inspector, 'I don't have odd contemplative moments. Not until I met you anyhow. Now then, you admit you thought of killing your wife ...'

'I said the notion had crossed my mind, particularly when I have to take the dog for a walk. It is a game I play with myself. No more than that.'

'A game? You take the dog for a walk and think of ways and means of killing Mrs Wilt? I don't call that a game. I call it premeditation.'

'Not badly put,' said Wilt with a smile, 'the meditation bit. Eva curls up in the lotus position on the living-room rug and thinks beautiful thoughts. I take the bloody dog for a walk and think dreadful ones while Clem defecates on the grass verge in Grenville Gardens. And in each case the end result is just the same. Eva gets up and cooks supper and washes up and I come home and watch the box or read and go to bed. Nothing has altered one way or another.'

'It has now,' said the Inspector. 'Your wife has disappeared off the face of the earth together with a brilliant young scientist and his wife, and you are sitting here waiting to be charged with their murder.'

'Which I don't happen to have committed,' said Wilt. 'Ah well, these things happen. The moving finger writes and having writ ...'

'Fuck the moving finger. Where are they? Where did you put them? You're going to tell me.'

Wilt sighed. 'I wish I could,' he said, 'I really do. Now you've got that plastic doll ...'

'No we haven't. Not by a long chalk. We're still going down through solid rock. We won't get whatever is down there until tomorrow at the earliest.'

'Something to look forward to,' said Wilt. 'Then I suppose you'll let me go.'

'Like hell I will. I'll have you up for remand on Monday.'

'Without any evidence of murder? Without a body? You can't do that.'

Inspector Flint smiled. 'Wilt,' he said, 'I've got news for you. We don't need a body. We can hold you on suspicion, we can bring you up for trial and we can find you guilty without a body. You may be clever but you don't know your law.'

'Well I must say you fellows have an easy job of it. You mean you can go out in the street and pick up some perfectly innocent passer-by and lug him in here and charge him with murder without any evidence at all?'

'Evidence? We've got evidence all right. We've got a blood-spattered bathroom with a busted-down door. We've got an empty house in a filthy mess and we've got some bloody thing or other down that pile hole and you think we haven't got evidence. You've got it wrong.'

'Makes two of us,' said Wilt.

'And I'll tell you another thing, Wilt. The trouble with bastards like you is that you're too clever by half. You overdo things and you give yourselves away. Now if I'd been in your shoes, I'd have done two things. Know what they are?'

'No,' said Wilt, 'I don't.'

'I'd have washed that bathroom down, number one, and number two I'd have stayed away from that hole. I wouldn't have tried to lay a false trail with notes and making sure the caretaker saw you and turning up at Mr Braintree's house at midnight covered in mud. I'd have sat tight and said nothing.'

'But I didn't know about those bloodstains in the bathroom and if it hadn't been for that filthy doll I wouldn't have dumped the thing down the hole. I'd have gone to bed. Instead of which I got pissed and acted like an idiot.'

'Let me tell you something else, Wilt,' said the Inspector. 'You *are* an idiot, a fucking cunning idiot but an idiot all the same. You need your head read.'

'It would make a change from this lot,' said Wilt.

'What would?'

'Having my head read instead of sitting here and being insulted.'

Inspector Flint studied him thoughtfully. 'You mean that?' he asked.

'Mean what?'

'About having your head read? Would you be prepared to undergo an examination by a qualified psychiatrist?'

'Why not?' said Wilt. 'Anything to help pass the time.'

'Quite voluntarily, you understand. Nobody is forcing you to, but if you want . . .'

'Listen, Inspector, if seeing a psychiatrist will help to convince you that I have not murdered my wife I'll be only too happy to. You can put me on a lie detector. You can pump me full of truth drugs. You can . . .'

'There's no need for any of that other stuff,' said Flint, and stood up. 'A good shrink will do very nicely. And if you think you can get away with guilty but insane, forget it. These blokes know when you're malingering madness.' He went to the door and paused. Then he came back and leant across the table.

'Tell me, Wilt,' he said. 'Tell me just one thing. How come you sit there so coolly? Your wife is missing, we have evidence of murder, we have a replica of her, if you are to be believed, under thirty feet of concrete and you don't turn a hair. How do you do it?'

'Inspector,' said Wilt. 'If you had taught Gasfitters for ten years and been asked as many damnfool questions in that time as I have, you'd know. Besides you haven't met Eva. When you do you'll see why I'm not worried. Eva is perfectly capable of taking care of herself. She may not be bright but she's got a built-in survival kit.'

'Jesus, Wilt, with you around for twelve years she must have had something.'

'Oh she has. You'll like Eva when you meet her. You'll get along like a house on fire. You've both got literal minds and an obsession with trivia. You can take a wormcast and turn it into Mount Everest.'

'Wormcast? Wilt, you sicken me,' said the Inspector, and left the room.

Wilt got up and walked up and down. He was tired of sitting down. On the other hand he was well satisfied with his performance. He had surpassed himself and he took pride in the fact that he was reacting so well to what most people would consider an appalling predicament. But to Wilt it was something else, a challenge, the first real challenge he had had to meet for a long time. Gasfitters and Plasterers had challenged him once but he had learnt to cope with them. You jollied them along. Let them talk, ask questions, divert them, get them going, accept their red herrings and hand out a few of your own, but above all you had to refuse to accept their preconceptions. Whenever they asserted something with absolute conviction as a self-evident truth like all wogs began at Calais, all you had to do was agree and then point out that half the great men in English history had been foreigners like Marconi or Lord Beaverbrook and that even Churchill's mother had been a Yank or talk about the Welsh being the original Englishmen and the Vikings and the Danes and from that lead them off through Indian doctors to the National Health Service and birth control and any other topic under the sun that would keep them quiet and puzzled and desperately trying to think of some ultimate argument that would prove you wrong.

Inspector Flint was no different. He was more obsessive but his tactics were just the same. And besides he had got hold of the wrong end of the stick with a vengeance and it amused Wilt to watch him trying to pin a crime on him he hadn't committed. It made him feel almost important and certainly more of a man than he had done for a long, long time. He was innocent and there was no question about it. In a world where everything else was doubtful and uncertain and open to scepticism the fact of his innocence was sure. For the first time in his adult life Wilt knew himself to be absolutely right, and the knowledge gave him a strength he had never supposed he possessed. And besides there was no question in his mind that Eva would turn up eventually, safe and sound, and more than a little subdued when she realized what her impulsiveness had led to. Serve her right for giving him that disgusting doll. She'd regret that to the end of her days. Yes, if anybody was going to come off badly in this affair it was dear old Eva with her bossiness and her busyness. She'd have a job explaining it to Mavis Mottram and the neighbours. Wilt smiled to himself at the thought. And even the Tech would have to treat him differently in future and with a new respect. Wilt knew the liberal conscience too well not to suppose that he would appear anything less than a martyr when he went back. And a hero. They would bend over backwards to convince themselves that they hadn't thought him as guilty as hell. He'd get promotion too, not for being a good teacher but because they would need to salve their fragile consciences. Talk about killing the fatted calf.

14

At the Tech there was no question of killing the fatted calf, at least not for Henry Wilt. The imminence of the CNAA visitation on Friday, coinciding as it apparently would with the resurrection of the late Mrs Wilt, was causing something approaching panic. The Course Board met in almost continuous session and memoranda circulated so furiously that it was impossible to read one before the next arrived.

'Can't we postpone the visit?' Dr Cox asked. 'I can't have them in my office discussing bibliographies with bits of Mrs Wilt being dug out of the ground outside the window.'

'I have asked the police to make themselves as inconspicuous as possible,' said Dr Mayfield.

'With conspicuous lack of success so far,' said Dr Board. 'They couldn't be more in evidence. There are ten of them peering down that hole at this very moment.'

The Vice-Principal struck a brighter note. 'You'll be glad to hear that we've managed to restore power to the canteen,' he told the meeting, 'so we should be able to lay on a good lunch.'

'I just hope I feel up to eating,' said Dr Cox. 'The shocks of the last few days have done nothing to improve my appetite and when I think of poor Mrs Wilt ...'

'Try not to think of her,' said the Vice-Principal, but Dr Cox shook his head.

'You try not to think of her with a damned great boring machine grinding away outside your office window all day.'

'Talking about shocks,' said Dr Board, 'I still can't understand how the driver of that mechanical corkscrew managed to escape electrocution when they cut through the power cable.'

'Considering the problems we are faced with, I hardly think that's a relevant point just at present,' said Dr Mayfield. 'What we have got to stress to the members of the CNAA committee is that this degree is an integrated course with a fundamental substructure grounded thematically on a concomitance of cultural and sociological factors in no way unsuperficially disparate and with a solid quota of academic content to give students an intellectual and cerebral . . .'

'Haemorrhage?' suggested Dr Board.

Dr Mayfield regarded him balefully. 'I really do think this is no time for flippancy,' he said angrily. 'Either we are committed to the Joint Honours degree or we are not. Furthermore we have only until tomorrow to structure our tactical approach to the visitation committee. Now, which is it to be?'

'Which is what to be?' asked Dr Board. 'What has our commitment or lack of it to do with structuring, for want of several far better words, our so-called tactical approach to a committee which, since it is coming all the way from London to us and not vice versa, is presumably approaching us?'

'Vice-Principal,' said Dr Mayfield, 'I really must protest. Dr Board's attitude at this late stage in the game is quite incomprehensible. If Dr Board . . .'

'Could even begin to understand one tenth of the jargon Dr Mayfield seems to suppose is English he might be in a better position to express his opinion,' interrupted Dr Board. 'As it is, "incomprehensible" applies to Dr Mayfield's syntax, not to my attitude. I have always maintained . . .'

'Gentlemen,' said the Vice-Principal, 'I think it would be best if we avoided inter-departmental wrangles at this point in time and got down to business.'

There was a silence broken finally by Dr Cox. 'Do you think the police could be persuaded to erect a screen round that hole?' he asked.

'I shall certainly suggest that to them,' said Dr Mayfield. They passed on to the matter of entertainment.

'I have arranged for there to be plenty of drinks before lunch,' said the Vice-Principal, 'and in any case lunch will be judiciously delayed to allow them to get into the right mood so the afternoon sessions should be cut short and proceed, hopefully, more smoothly.'

'Just so long as the Catering Department doesn't serve Toad in the Hole,' said Dr Board.

The meeting broke up acrimoniously.

So did Mr Morris's encounter with the Crime Reporter of the *Sunday Post*.

'Of course I didn't tell the police that I employed homicidal maniacs as a matter of policy,' he shouted at the reporter. 'And in any case what I said was, as I understood it, to be treated in the strictest confidence.'

'But you did say you thought Wilt was insane and that quite a number of Liberal Studies lecturers were off their heads?'

Mr Morris looked at the man with loathing. 'To put the record straight, what I said was that some of them were ...'

'Off their rockers?' suggested the reporter.

'No, not off their rockers,' shouted Mr Morris. 'Merely, well, shall we say, slightly unbalanced.'

'That's not what the police say you said. They say quote ...'

'I don't care what the police say I said. I know what I said and what I didn't and if you're implying ...'

'I'm not implying anything. You made a statement that half your staff are nuts and I'm trying to verify it.'

'Verify it?' snarled Mr Morris. 'You put words into my mouth I never said and you call that verifying it?'

'Did you say it or not? That's all I'm asking. I mean if you express an opinion about your staff ...'

'Mr MacArthur, what I think about my staff is my own affair. It has absolutely nothing to do with you or the rag you represent.'

'Three million people will be interested to read your opinion on Sunday morning,' said Mr MacArthur, 'and I wouldn't be at all surprised if this Wilt character didn't sue you if he ever gets out of the copshop.'

'Sue me? What the hell could he sue me for?'

'Calling him a homicidal maniac for a start. Banner headlines HEAD OF LIBERAL STUDIES CALLS LECTURER HOMICIDAL MANIAC should be good for fifty thousand. I'd be surprised if he got less.'

Mr Morris contemplated destitution. 'Even your paper would never print that,' he muttered. 'I mean Wilt would sue you too.'

'Oh we're used to libel actions. They're run-of-the-mill for us. We pay for them out of petty cash. Now if you'd be a bit more cooperative ...' He left the suggestion in mid-air for Mr Morris to digest.

'What do you want to know?' he asked miserably.

'Got any juicy drug scene stories for us?' asked Mr MacArthur. 'You know the sort of thing. LOVE ORGIES IN LECTURES. That always gets the public. Teenyboppers having it off and all that. Give us a good one and we'll let you off the hook about Wilt.'

'Get out of my office!' yelled Mr Morris.

Mr MacArthur got up. 'You're going to regret this,' he said and went downstairs to the students' canteen to dig up some dirt on Mr Morris.

'Not tests,' said Wilt adamantly, 'They're deceptive.'

'You think so?' said Dr Pittman, consultant psychiatrist at the Fenland Hospital and professor of Criminal Psychology at the University. Being plagiocephalic didn't help either.

'I should have thought it was obvious,' said Wilt. 'You show me an ink-blot and I think it looks like my grandmother lying in a pool of blood, do you honestly think I'm going to be fool enough to say so? I'd be daft to do that. So I say a butterfly sitting on a geranium. And every time it's the same. I think what it does look like and then say something completely different. Where does that get you?'

'It is still possible to infer something from that,' said Dr Pittman.

'Well, you don't need a bloody ink-blot to infer, do you?'

said Wilt. Dr Pittman made a note of Wilt's interest in blood. 'You can infer things from just looking at the shape of people's heads.'

Dr Pittman polished his glasses grimly. Heads were not things he liked inferences to be drawn from. 'Mr Wilt,' he said, 'I am here at your request to ascertain your sanity and in particular to give an opinion as to whether or not I consider you capable of murdering your wife and disposing of her body in a singularly revolting and callous fashion. I shall not allow anything you may say to influence my ultimate and objective findings.'

Wilt looked perplexed. 'I must say you're not giving yourself much room for manoeuvre. Since we've dispensed with mechanical aids like tests I should have thought what I had to say would be the only thing you could go on. Unless of course you're going to read the bumps on my head. Isn't that a bit old-fashioned?'

'Mr Wilt,' said Dr Pittman, 'the fact that you clearly have a sadistic streak and take pleasure in drawing attention to other people's physical infirmities in no way disposes me to conclude you are capable of murder ...'

'Very decent of you,' said Wilt, 'though frankly I'd have thought anyone was capable of murder given the right, or to be precise the wrong, circumstances.'

Dr Pittman stifled the impulse to say how right he was. Instead he smiled prognathously. 'Would you say you were a rational man, Henry?' he asked.

Wilt frowned. 'Just stick to Mr Wilt if you don't mind. This may not be a paid consultation but I prefer a little formality.'

Dr Pittman's smile vanished. 'You haven't answered my question.'

'No, I wouldn't say I was a rational man,' said Wilt.

'An irrational one perhaps?'

'Neither the one wholly nor the other wholly. Just a man.'

'And a man is neither one thing nor the other?'

'Dr Pittman, this is your province not mine but in my opinion man is capable of reasoning but not of acting within wholly rational limits. Man is an animal, a developed animal, though come to think of it all animals are developed if we are to believe Darwin. Let's just say man is a domesticated animal with elements of wildness about him ...'

'And what sort of animal are you, Mr Wilt?' said Dr Pittman. 'A domesticated animal or a wild one?'

'Here we go again. These splendidly simple dual categories that seem to obsess the modern mind. Either/Or Kierkegaard as that bitch Sally Pringsheim would say. No, I am not wholly domesticated. Ask my wife. She'll express an opinion on the matter.'

'In what respect are you undomesticated?'

'I fart in bed, Dr Pittman. I like to fart in bed. It is the trumpet call of the anthropoid ape in me asserting its territorial imperative in the only way possible.'

'In the only way possible?'

'You haven't met Eva,' said Wilt. 'When you do you'll see that assertion is her forte not mine.'

'You feel dominated by Mrs Wilt?'

'I *am* dominated by Mrs Wilt.'

'She bullies you? She assumes the dominant role?'

'Eva is, Dr Pittman. She doesn't have to assume anything. She just is.'

'Is what?'

'Now there's the rub,' said Wilt. 'What's today? You lose track of time in this place.'

'Thursday.'

'Well, today being Thursday, Eva is Bernard Leach.'

'Bernard Leach?'

'The potter, Dr Pittman, the famous potter,' said Wilt. 'Now tomorrow she'll be Margot Fonteyn and on Saturday we play bridge with the Mottrams so she'll be Omar Sharif. On Sunday she's Elizabeth Taylor or Edna O'Brien depending on what the Colour Supplements have in store for me and in the afternoon we go for a drive and she's Eva Wilt. It's about the only time in the week I meet her and that's because I'm driving and she's got nothing to do but sit still and nag the pants off me.'

'I begin to see the pattern,' said Dr Pittman. 'Mrs Wilt was ... is given to role-playing. This made for an unstable relationship in which you couldn't establish a distinctive and assertive role as a husband ...'

'Dr Pittman,' said Wilt, 'a gyroscope may, indeed must, spin but in doing so it achieves a stability that is virtually unequalled. Now if you understand the principle of the gyroscope you may begin to understand that our marriage does not lack stability. It may be damned uncomfortable coming home to a centrifugal force but it bloody well isn't unstable.'

'But just now you told me that Mrs Wilt did not assume a dominant role. Now you tell me she is a forceful character.'

'Eva is not forceful. She is a force. There's a difference. And as for character, she has so many and they're so varied it's difficult to keep up with them all. Let's just say she throws herself into whoever she is with an urgency and compulsiveness that is not always appropriate. You remember that series of Garbo pictures they showed on TV some years back? Well, Eva was La Dame Aux Camélias for three days after that and she made dying of TB look like St Vitus' dance. Talk about galloping consumption.'

'I begin to get the picture,' said Dr Pittman making a note that Wilt was a pathological liar with sado-masochistic tendencies.

'I'm glad somebody does,' said Wilt. 'Inspector Flint thinks I murdered her and the Pringsheims in some sort of bloodlust and disposed of their bodies in some extraordinary fashion. He mentioned acid. I mean it's crazy. Where on earth does one get nitric acid in the quantities necessary to dissolve three dead bodies, and one of them overweight at that? I mean it doesn't bear thinking about.'

'It certainly doesn't,' said Dr Pittman.

'In any case do I look like a murderer?' continued Wilt cheerfully. 'Of course I don't. Now if he'd said Eva had slaughtered the brutes, and in my opinion someone should have done years ago, I'd have taken him seriously. God help the poor sods who happen to be around when Eva takes it into her head she's Lizzie Borden.'

Dr Pittman studied him predaciously.

'Are you suggesting that Dr and Mrs Pringsheim were murdered by your wife?' he asked. 'Is that what you're saying?'

'No,' said Wilt, 'I am not. All I'm saying is that when Eva does things she does them wholeheartedly. When she cleans the house she cleans it. Let me tell you about the Harpic. She's got this thing about germs ...'

'Mr Wilt,' said Dr Pittman hastily, 'I am not interested in what Mrs Wilt does with the Harpic. I have come here to understand you. Now then, do you make a habit of copulating with a plastic doll? Is this a regular occurrence?'

'Regular?' said Wilt. 'Do you mean a normal occurrence or a recurring one? Now your notion of what constitutes a normal occurrence may differ from mine ...'

'I mean, do you do it often?' interrupted Dr Pittman.

'Do it?' said Wilt. 'I don't do it at all.'

'But I understood you to have placed particular emphasis on the fact that this doll had a vagina?'

'Emphasis? I didn't have to emphasize the fact. The beastly thing was plainly visible.'

'You find vaginas beastly?' said Dr Pittman stalking his prey into the more familiar territory of sexual aberration.

'Taken out of context, yes,' said Wilt sidestepping, 'and with plastic ones you can leave them in context and I still find them nauseating.'

By the time Dr Pittman had finished the interview he was uncertain what to think. He got up wearily and made for the door.

'You've forgotten your hat, doctor,' said Wilt holding it out to him. 'Pardon my asking but do you have them specially made for you?'

'Well?' said Inspector Flint when Dr Pittman came into his office. 'What's the verdict?'

'Verdict? That man should be put away for life.'

'You mean he's a homicidal maniac?'

'I mean that no matter how he killed her Mrs Wilt must have been thankful to go. Twelve years married to that man ... Good God, it doesn't bear thinking about.'

'Well, that doesn't get us much forrader,' said the Inspector, when the psychiatrist had left having expressed the opinion that while Wilt had the mind of an intellectual jackrabbit he couldn't in all honesty say that he was criminally insane. 'We'll just have to see what turns up tomorrow.'

15

What turned up on Friday was seen not only by Inspector Flint, Sergeant Yates, twelve other policemen, Barney and half a dozen construction workers, but several hundred Tech students standing on the steps of the Science block, most of the staff and by all eight members of the CNAA visitation committee who had a particularly good view from the windows of the mock hotel lounge used by the Catering Department to train waiters and to entertain distinguished guests. Dr Mayfield did his best to distract their attention.

'We have structured the foundation course to maximize student interest,' he told Professor Baxendale, who headed the committee, but the professor was not to be diverted. His interest was maximized by what was being unstructured from the foundations of the new Admin block.

'How absolutely appalling,' he muttered as Judy protruded from the hole. Contrary to Wilt's hopes and expectations she had not burst. The liquid concrete had sealed her in too well for that and if in life she had resembled in many particulars a real live woman, in death she had all the attributes of a real dead one. As the corpse of a murdered woman she was entirely convincing. Her wig was matted and secured to her head at an awful angle by the concrete. Her clothes clung to her and cement to them while her legs had evidently been contorted to the point of mutilation and her outstretched arm had, as Barney had foretold, a desperate appeal about it that was most affecting. It also made it exceedingly difficult to extricate her from the hole. The legs didn't help, added to which the concrete had given her a substance and stature approximate to that of Eva Wilt.

'I suppose that's what they mean by rigor mortice,' said Dr Board, as Dr Mayfield desperately tried to steer the conversation back to the Joint Honours degree.

'Dear Lord,' muttered Professor Baxendale. Judy had eluded the efforts of Barney and his men and had slumped back down the hole. 'To think what she must have suffered. Did you see that damned hand?'

Dr Mayfield had. He shuddered. Behind him Dr Board sniggered. 'There's a divinity that shapes our ends, rough-hew them how we will,' he said gaily. 'At least Wilt has saved himself the cost of a gravestone. All they'll have to do is prop her up with Here Stands Eva Wilt, Born So and So, Murdered last Saturday carved across her chest. In life monumental, in death a monument.'

'I must say, Board,' said Dr Mayfield, 'I find your sense of humour singularly ill-timed.'

'Well they'll never be able to cremate her, that's for certain,' continued Dr Board. 'And the undertaker who can fit that little lot into a coffin will be nothing short of a genius. I suppose they could always take a sledgehammer to her.'

In the corner Dr Cox fainted.

'I think I'll have another whisky if you don't mind,' said Professor Baxendale weakly. Dr Mayfield poured him a double. When he turned back to the window Judy was protruding once more from the hole.

'The thing about embalming,' said Dr Board, 'is that it costs so much. Now I'm not saying that thing out there is a perfect likeness of Eva Wilt as I remember her . . .'

'For heaven's sake, do you have to go on about it?' snarled Dr Mayfield, but Dr Board was not to be stopped. 'Quite apart from the legs there seems to be something odd about the breasts. I know Mrs Wilt's were large but they do seem to have inflated. Probably due to the gases. They putrefy, you know, which would account for it.'

By the time the committee went into lunch they had lost all appetite for food and most of them were drunk.

Inspector Flint was less fortunate. He didn't like being present at exhumations at the best of times and particularly when the corpse on whose behalf he was acting showed such a marked inclination to go back where she came from. Besides he was in two minds whether it was a corpse or not. It looked like a corpse and it certainly behaved like a corpse, albeit a very heavy one, but there was something about the knees that suggested that all was not anatomically as it should have been with whatever it was they had dug up. There was a double jointedness and a certain lack of substance where the legs stuck forwards at right angles that seemed to indicate that Mrs Wilt had lost not only her life but both kneecaps as well. It was this mangled quality that made Barney's job so difficult and exceedingly distasteful. After the body had dropped down the hole for the fourth time Barney went down himself to assist from below.

'If you sods drop her,' he shouted from the depths, 'you'll have two dead bodies down here so hang on to that rope whatever happens. I'm going to tie it round her neck.'

Inspector Flint peered down the shaft. 'You'll do no such thing,' he shouted, 'we don't want her decapitated. We need her all in one piece.'

'She is all in one bloody piece,' came Barney's muffled reply, 'that's one thing you don't have to worry about.'

'Can't you tie the rope around something else?'

'Well I could,' Barney conceded, 'but I'm not going to. A leg is more likely to come off than her head and I'm not going to be underneath her when it goes.'

'All right,' said the Inspector, 'I just hope you know what you're doing, that's all.'

'I'll tell you one thing. The sod who put her down here knew what he was doing and no mistake.'

But this fifth attempt failed, like the previous four, and Judy was lowered into the depths where she rested heavily on Barney's foot.

'Go and get that bloody crane,' he shouted. 'I can't stand much more of this.'

'Nor can I,' muttered the Inspector, who still couldn't make up his mind what it was he was supposed to be disinterring; a doll dressed up to look like Mrs Wilt or Mrs Wilt dressed up to look like something some demented sculptor forgot to finish. What few doubts he had had about Wilt's sanity had been entirely dispelled by what he was presently witnessing. Any man who could go to the awful lengths Wilt had gone to render, and the word was entirely apposite which-ever way you took it, either his wife or a plastic doll with a vagina, both inaccessible and horribly mutilated, must be in-sane.

Sergeant Yates put his thoughts into words. 'You're not going to tell me now that the bastard isn't off his rocker,' he said, as the crane was moved into position and the rope lowered and attached to Judy's neck.

'All right, now take her away,' shouted Barney.

In the dining-room only Dr Board was enjoying his lunch. The eight members of the CNAA committee weren't. Their eyes were glued to the scene below.

'I suppose it could be said she was *in statue pupillari*,' said Dr Board, helping himself to some more Lemon Meringue, 'in which case we stand *in loco parentis*. Not a pleasant thought, gentlemen. Not that she was ever a very bright student. I once had her for an Evening Class in French literature. I don't know what she got out of *Fleurs du Mal* but I do remember thinking that Baudelaire ...'

'Dr Board,' said Dr Mayfield drunkenly, 'for a so-called cultured man you are entirely without feeling.'

'Something I share with the late Mrs Wilt, by the look of things,' said Dr Board, glancing out of the window, 'and while we are still on the subject, things seem to be coming to a head. They do indeed.'

Even Dr Cox, recently revived and coaxed into having some mutton, looked out of the window. As the crane slowly winched Judy into view the Course Board and the Committee rose and went to watch. It was an unedifying sight. Near the top of the shaft Judy's left leg caught in a crevice while her outstretched arm embedded itself in the clay.

'Hold it,' shouted Barney indistinctly, but it was too late.

163

Unnerved by the nature of his load or in the mistaken belief that he had been told to lift harder, the crane driver hoisted away. There was a ghastly cracking sound as the noose tightened and the next moment Judy's concrete head, capped by Eva Wilt's wig, looked as if it was about to fulfil Inspector Flint's prediction that she would be decapitated. In the event he need not have worried. Judy was made of sterner stuff than might have been expected. As the head continued to rise and the body to remain firmly embedded in the shaft Judy's neck rose to the occasion. It stretched.

'Dear God,' said Professor Baxendale frantically, 'will it never end?'

Dr Board studied the phenomenon with increasing interest. 'It doesn't look like it,' he said. 'Mind you we do make a point of stretching our students, eh Mayfield?'

But Dr Mayfield made no response. As Judy took on the configuration of an ostrich that had absentmindedly buried its head in a pail of cement he knew that the Joint Honours degree was doomed.

'I'll say this for Mrs Wilt,' said Dr Board, 'she do hold on. No one could call her stiff-necked. Attenuated possibly. One begins to see what Modigliani was getting at.'

'For God's sake stop,' yelled Dr Cox hysterically. 'I think I'm going off my head.'

'Which is more than can be said for Mrs Wilt,' said Dr Board callously.

He was interrupted by another awful crack as Judy's body finally gave up the struggle with the shaft. With a shower of clay it careered upwards to resume a closer relationship with the head and hung naked, pink and, now that the clothes and the concrete had been removed, remarkably lifelike at the end of the rope some twenty feet above the ground.

'I must say,' said Dr Board, studying the vulva with relish, 'I've never had much sympathy with necrophilia before but I do begin to see its attractions now. Of course it's only of historical interest but in Elizabethan times it was one of the perks of an executioner ...'

'Board,' screamed Dr Mayfield, 'I've known some fucking swine in my time ...'

Dr Board helped himself to some more coffee. 'I believe the slang term for it is liking your meat cold.'

Underneath the crane Inspector Flint wiped the mud from his face and peered up at the awful object swinging above him. He could see now that it was only a doll. He could also see why Wilt had wanted to bury the beastly thing.

'Get it down. For God's sake get it down,' he bawled, as the press photographers circled round him. But the crane driver had lost his nerve. He shut his eyes, pulled the wrong lever and Judy began a further ascent.

'Stop it, stop it, that's fucking evidence,' screamed the Inspector, but it was already too late. As the rope wound through the final pulley Judy followed. The concrete cap disintegrated, her head slid between the rollers and her body began to swell. Her legs were the first to be affected.

'I've often wondered what elephantiasis looked like,' said Dr Board. 'Shelley had a phobia about it, I believe.'

Dr Cox certainly had. He was gibbering in a corner and the Vice-Principal was urging him to pull himself together.

'An apt expression,' observed Dr Board, above the gasps of horror as Judy, now clearly twelve months pregnant, continued her transformation. 'Early Minoan, wouldn't you say, Mayfield?'

But Dr Mayfield was past speech. He was staring dementedly at a rapidly expanding vagina some fourteen inches long and eight wide. There was a pop and the thing became a penis, an enormous penis that swelled and swelled. He was going mad. He knew he was.

'Now that,' said Dr Board, 'takes some beating. I've heard about sex-change operations for men but ...'

'Beating?' screamed Dr Mayfield, 'Beating? You can stand there cold-bloodedly and talk about ...'

There was a loud bang. Judy had come to the end of her tether. So had Dr Mayfield. The penis was the first thing to go. Dr Mayfield the second. As Judy deflated he hurled himself at Dr Board only to sink to the ground gibbering.

Dr Board ignored his colleague. 'Who would have thought the old bag had so much wind in her?' he murmured, and finished his coffee. As Dr Mayfield was led out by the Vice-Principal, Dr Board turned to Professor Baxendale.

'I must apologize for Mayfield,' he said, 'I'm afraid this Joint Honours degree has been too much for him and to tell the truth I have always found him to be fundamentally unsound. A case of dementia post Cox I daresay.'

Inspector Flint drove back to the Police Station in a state bordering on lunacy.

'We've been made to look idiots,' he snarled at Sergeant Yates. 'You saw them laughing. You heard the bastards.' He was particularly incensed by the press photographers who had asked him to pose with the limp remnants of the plastic doll. 'We've been held up to public ridicule. Well, my God, some-body's going to pay.'

He hurled himself out of the car and lunged down the pass-age to the Interview Room. 'Right, Wilt,' he shouted, 'you've had your little joke and a bloody nasty one it was too. So now we're going to forget the niceties and get to the bottom of this business.'

Wilt studied the torn piece of plastic. 'Looks better like that if you ask me,' he said. 'More natural if you know what I mean.'

'You'll look bloody natural if you don't answer my ques-tions,' yelled the Inspector. 'Where is she?'

'Where is who?' said Wilt.

'Mrs Fucking Wilt. Where did you put her?'

'I've told you. I didn't put her anywhere.'

'And I'm telling you you did. Now either you're going to tell me where she is or I'm going to beat it out of you.'

'You can beat me up if you like,' said Wilt, 'but it won't do you any good.'

'Oh yes it will,' said the Inspector and took off his coat.

'I demand to see a solicitor,' said Wilt hastily.

Inspector Flint put his jacket on again. 'I've been waiting to hear you say that. Henry Wilt, I hereby charge you with . . .'

16

In the reeds Eva greeted the dawn of another day by blowing up
the airbed for the tenth time. It had either sprung a leak or
developed a fault in the valve. Whichever it was it had made
her progress exceedingly slow and had finally forced her to
take refuge in the reeds away from the channel. Here, wedged
between the stems, she had spent a muddy night getting off
the airbed to blow it up and getting back on to try and
wash off the sludge and weeds that had adhered to her when
she got off. In the process she had lost the bottom half of her
lemon loungers and had torn the top half so that by dawn she
resembled less the obsessive housewife of 34 Parkview Avenue
than a finalist in the heavyweight division of the Ladies Mud-
wrestling Championship. In addition she was exceedingly cold
and was glad when the sun came up bringing with it the
promise of a hot summer day. All she had to do now was to
find her way to land or open water and get someone to ... At
this point Eva became aware that her appearance was likely to
cause some embarrassment. The lemon loungers had been
sufficiently outré to make her avoid walking down the street
when she had had them on; with them largely off she certainly didn't want to be seen in public. On the other hand she
couldn't stay in the reeds all day. She plunged on, dragging
the airbed behind her, half swimming but for the most part
trudging through mud and water. At last she came out of the
reeds into open water and found herself looking across a
stretch to a house, a garden that sloped down to the water's
edge, and a church. It seemed a long way across but there was
no boat in sight. She would have to swim across and just hope
that the woman who lived there was sympathetic and better
still large enough to lend her some clothes until she got home.
It was at this point that Eva discovered that she had left her
handbag somewhere in the reeds. She remembered having it
during the night but it must have fallen off the airbed when
she was blowing it up. Well she couldn't go back and look for
it now. She would just have to go on without it and ring Henry

up and tell him to come out in the car and get her. He could bring some clothes too. Yes, that was it. Eva Wilt climbed on to the airbed and began to paddle across. Halfway over the airbed went down for the eleventh time. Eva abandoned it and struggled on in the lifejacket. But that too impeded her progress and she finally decided to take it off. She trod water and tried to undo it and after a struggle managed to get it off. In the process the rest of the lemon loungers disintegrated so that by the time she reached the bank Eva Wilt was exhausted and quite naked. She crawled into the cover of a willow tree and lay panting on the ground. When she had recovered she stood up and looked around. She was at the bottom of the garden and the house was a hundred yards away up the hill. It was a very large house by Eva's standards, and not the sort she would feel at home in at the best of times. For one thing it appeared to have a courtyard with stables at the back and to Eva, whose knowledge of large country houses was confined to what she had seen on TV, there was the suggestion of servants, gentility and a social formality that would make her arrival in the nude rather heavy going. On the other hand the whole place looked decidedly run down. The garden was overgrown and unkempt; ornamental bushes which might once have been trimmed to look like birds and animals had reverted to strange and vaguely monstrous shapes; rusted hoops leant half-hidden in the grass of an untended croquet lawn; a tennis net sagged between posts and an abandoned greenhouse boasted a few panes of lichened glass. Finally there was a dilapidated boathouse and a rowing boat. All in all the domain had a sinister and imposing air to it which wasn't helped by the presence of a small church hidden among trees to the left and a neglected graveyard beyond an old iron fence. Eva peered out from the weeping willow and was about to leave its cover when the French windows opened and a man came out on to the terrace with a pair of binoculars and peered through them in the direction of Eel Stretch. He was wearing a black cassock and a dog collar. Eva went back behind the tree and considered the awkwardness of her situation and lack of attire. It was all extremely embarrassing. Nothing on earth would make her go up to the house,

the Vicarage, with nothing on. Parkview Avenue hadn't prepared her for situations of this sort.

Rossiter Grove hadn't prepared Gaskell for the situation he
found when Sally woke him with 'Noah baby, it's drywise top-
side. Time to fly the coop.'

He opened the cabin door and stepped outside to discover
that Eva had already flown and had taken the airbed and the
lifejackets with her.

'You mean you left her outside all night?' he said. 'Now
we're really up Shit Creek. No paddle, no airbed, no goddam
lifejackets, no nothing.'

'I didn't know she'd do something crazy like take off with
everything,' said Sally.

'You leave her outside in the pouring rain all night she's got
to do something. She's probably frozen to death by now. Or
drowned.'

'She tried to kill me. You think I was going to let her in
when she's tried to do that. Anyhow it's all your fault for
shooting your mouth off about that doll.'

'You tell that to the law when they find her body floating
downstream. You just explain how come she goes off in the
middle of a storm.'

'You're just trying to scare me,' said Sally. 'I didn't make her
go or anything.'

'It's going to look peculiar if something has happened to her
is all I'm saying. And you tell me how we're going to get off
here now. You think I'm going swimming without a lifejacket
you're mistaken. I'm no Spitz.'

'My hero,' said Sally.

Gaskell went into the cabin and looked in the cupboard by
the stove. 'And another thing. We've got a food problem.
And water. There's not much left.'

'You got us into this mess. You think of a way out,' said
Sally.

Gaskell sat down on the bunk and tried to think. There had
to be some way of letting people know they were there and in
trouble. They couldn't be far from land. For all he knew dry
land was just the other side of the reeds. He went out and

climbed on top of the cabin but apart from the church spire in the distance he could see nothing beyond the reeds. Perhaps if they got a piece of cloth and waved it someone would spot it. He went down and fetched a pillow case and spent twenty minutes waving it above his head and shouting. Then he returned to the cabin and got out the chart and pored over it in a vain attempt to discover where they were. He was just folding the map up when he spotted the pieces of Scrabble still lying on the table. Letters. Individual letters. Now if they had something that would float up in the air with letters on it. Like a kite. Gaskell considered ways of making a kite and gave it up. Perhaps the best thing after all was to make smoke signals. He fetched an empty can from the kitchen and filled it with fuel oil from beside the engine and soaked a handkerchief in it and clambered up on the cabin roof. He lit the handkerchief and tried to get the oil to burn but when it did there was very little smoke and the tin got too hot to hold. Gaskell kicked it into the water where it fizzled out.

'Genius baby,' said Sally, 'you're the greatest.'

'Yea, well if you can think of something practical let me know.'

'Try swimming.'

'Try drowning,' said Gaskell.

'You could make a raft or something.'

'I could hack this boat of Scheimacher's up. That's all we need.'

'I saw a movie once where there were these gauchos or Romans or something and they came to a river and wanted to cross and they used pigs' bladders,' said Sally.

'Right now all we don't have is a pig,' said Gaskell.

'You could use the garbage bags in the kitchen,' said Sally. Gaskell fetched a plastic bag and blew it up and tied the end with string. Then he squeezed it. The bag went down.

Gaskell sat down despondently. There had to be some simple way of attracting attention and he certainly didn't want to swim out across that dark water clutching an inflated garbage bag. He fiddled with the pieces of Scrabble and thought once again about kites. Or balloons. Balloons.

'You got those rubbers you use?' he asked suddenly.

'Jesus, at a time like this you get a hard on,' said Sally. 'Forget sex. Think of some way of getting us off here.'

'I have,' said Gaskell, 'I want those skins.'

'You going to float downriver on a pontoon of condoms?'

'Balloons,' said Gaskell. 'We blow them up and paint letters on them and float them in the wind.'

'Genius baby,' said Sally and went into the toilet. She came out with a sponge bag. 'Here they are. For a moment there I thought you wanted me.'

'Days of wine and roses,' said Gaskell, 'are over. Remind me to divorce you.' He tore a packet open and blew a contraceptive up and tied a knot in its end.

'On what grounds?'

'Like you're a lesbian,' said Gaskell and held up the dildo. 'This and kleptomania and the habit you have of putting other men in dolls and knotting them. You name it, I'll use it. Like you're a nymphomaniac.'

'You wouldn't dare. Your family would love it, the scandal.'

'Try me,' said Gaskell and blew up another condom.

'Plastic freak.'

'Bull dyke.'

Sally's eyes narrowed. She was beginning to think he meant what he said about divorce and if Gaskell divorced her in England what sort of alimony would she get? Very little. There were no children and she had the idea that British courts were mean in matters of money. So was Gaskell and there was his family too. Rich and mean. She sat and eyed him.

'Where's your nail varnish?' Gaskell asked when he had finished and twelve contraceptives cluttered the cabin.

'Drop dead,' said Sally and went out on deck to think. She stared down at the dark water and thought about rats and death and being poor again and liberated. The rat paradigm. The world was a rotten place. People were objects to be used and discarded. It was Gaskell's own philosophy and now he was discarding her. And one slip on this oily deck could solve her problems. All that had to happen was for Gaskell to slip and drown and she would be free and rich and no one would ever know. An accident. Natural death. But Gaskell could swim and there had to be no mistakes. Try it once and fail and she wouldn't be able to try again. He would be on his guard. It had to be certain and it had to be natural.

Gaskell came out on deck with the contraceptives. He had tied them together and painted on each one a single letter with nail varnish so that the whole read HELP SOS HELP. He climbed up on the cabin roof and launched them into the air. They floated up for a moment, were caught in the light breeze and sagged sideways down on to the water. Gaskell pulled them in on the string and tried again. Once again they floated down on to the water.

'I'll wait until there's some more wind,' he said, and tied the string to the rail where they bobbed gently. Then he went into the cabin and lay on the bunk.

'What are you going to do now?' Sally asked.

'Sleep. Wake me when there's a wind.'

He took off his glasses and pulled a blanket over him.

Outside Sally sat on a locker and thought about drowning. In bed.

'Mr Gosdyke,' said Inspector Flint, 'you and I have had dealings for a good many years now and I'm prepared to be frank with you. I don't know.'

'But you've charged him with murder,' said Mr Gosdyke.

'He'll come up for remand on Monday. In the meantime I am going on questioning him.'

'But surely the fact that he admits burying a lifesize doll ...'

'Dressed in his wife's clothes, Gosdyke. In his wife's clothes. Don't forget that.'

'It still seems insufficient to me. Can you be absolutely sure that a murder has been committed?'

'Three people disappear off the face of the earth without a trace. They leave behind them two cars, a house littered with unwashed glasses and the leftovers of a party ... you should see that house ... a bathroom and landing covered with blood ...'

'They could have gone in someone else's car.'

'They could have but they didn't. Dr Pringsheim didn't like

being driven by anyone else. We know that from his colleagues at the Department of Biochemistry. He had a rooted objection to British drivers. Don't ask me why but he had.'

'Trains? Buses? Planes?'

'Checked, rechecked and checked again. No one answering to their description used any form of public or private transport out of town. And if you think they went on a bicycle ride, you're wrong again. Dr Pringsheim's bicycle is in the garage. No, you can forget their going anywhere. They died and Mr Smart Alec Wilt knows it.'

'I still don't see how you can be so sure,' said Mr Gosdyke.

Inspector Flint lit a cigarette. 'Let's just look at his actions, his admitted actions and see what they add up to,' he said. 'He gets a lifesize doll ..'

'Where from?'

'He says he was given it by his wife. Where he got it from doesn't matter.'

'He says he first saw the thing at the Pringsheims' house.'

'Perhaps he did. I'm prepared to believe that. Wherever he got it, the fact remains that he dressed it up to look like Mrs Wilt. He puts it down that hole at the Tech, a hole he knows is going to be filled with concrete. He makes certain he is seen by the caretaker when he knows that the Tech is closed. He leaves a bicycle covered with his fingerprints and with a book of his in the basket. He leaves a trail of notes to the hole. He turns up at Mrs Braintree's house at midnight covered with mud and says he's had a puncture when he hasn't. Now you're not going to tell me that he hadn't got something in mind.'

'He says he was merely trying to dispose of that doll.'

'And he tells me he was rehearsing his wife's murder. He's admitted that.'

'Yes, but only in fantasy. His story to me is that he wanted to get rid of that doll,' Mr Gosdyke persisted.

'Then why the clothes, why blow the thing up and why leave it in such a position it was bound to be spotted when the concrete was poured down? Why didn't he cover it with earth if he didn't want it to be found? Why didn't he just burn the bloody thing or leave it by the roadside? It just doesn't make sense unless you see it as a deliberate plan to draw our attention away from the real crime.' The Inspector paused. 'Well now, the way I see it is that something happened at that party we don't know anything about. Perhaps Wilt found his wife in bed with Dr Pringsheim. He killed them both. Mrs Pringsheim puts in an appearance and he kills her too.'

'How?' said Mr Gosdyke. 'You didn't find that much blood.'

'He strangled her. He strangled his own wife. He battered Pringsheim to death. Then he hides the bodies somewhere, goes home and lays the doll trail. On Sunday he disposes of the real bodies ...'

'Where?'

'God alone knows, but I'm going to find out. All I know is that a man who can think up a scheme like this one is bound to have thought of somewhere diabolical to put the real victims. It wouldn't surprise me to learn that he spent Sunday making illegal use of the crematorium. Whatever he did you can be sure he did it thoroughly.'

But Mr Gosdyke remained unconvinced. 'I wish I knew how you could be so certain,' he said.

'Mr Gosdyke,' said the Inspector wearily, 'you have spent two hours with your client. I have spent the best part of the week and if I've learnt one thing from the experience it is this, that sod in there knows what he is doing. Any normal man in his position would have been worried and alarmed and downright frightened. Any innocent man faced with a missing wife and the evidence we've got of murder would have had a nervous breakdown. Not Wilt. Oh no, he sits in there as bold as you please and tells me how to conduct the investigation. Now if anything convinces me that that bastard is as guilty as hell that does. He did it and I know it. And what is more, I'm going to prove it.'

'He seems a bit worried now,' said Mr Gosdyke.

'He's got reason to be,' said the Inspector, 'because by Monday morning I'm going to get the truth out of him even if it kills him and me both.'

'Inspector,' said Mr Gosdyke getting to his feet, 'I must warn you that I have advised my client not to say another word and if he appears in Court with a mark on him ...'

'Mr Gosdyke, you should know me better than that. I'm not a complete fool and if your client has any marks on him on Monday morning they will not have been made by me or any of my men. You have my assurance on that.'

Mr Gosdyke left the Police Station a puzzled man. He had to admit that Wilt's story hadn't been a very convincing one. Mr Gosdyke's experience of murderers was not extensive but he had a shrewd suspicion that men who confessed openly that they had entertained fantasies of murdering their wives ended by admitting that they had done so in fact. Besides his attempt to get Wilt to agree that he'd put the doll down the hole as a practical joke on his colleagues at the Tech had failed hopelessly. Wilt had refused to lie and Mr Gosdyke was not used to clients who insisted on telling the truth.

Inspector Flint went back into the Interview Room and looked at Wilt. Then he pulled up a chair and sat down.

'Henry,' he said with an affability he didn't feel, 'you and I are going to have a little chat.'

'What, another one?' said Wilt. 'Mr Gosdyke has advised me to say nothing.'

'He always does,' said the Inspector sweetly, 'to clients he knows are guilty. Now are you going to talk?'

'I can't see why not. I'm not guilty and it helps to pass the time.'

17

It was Friday and as on every other day in the week the little church at Waterswick was empty. And as on every other day of the week the Vicar, the Reverend St John Froude, was drunk. The two things went together, the lack of a congregation and the Vicar's insobriety. It was an old tradition dating back to the days of smuggling when Brandy for the Parson had been about the only reason the isolated hamlet had a vicar at all. And like so many English traditions it died hard. The Church authorities saw to it that Waterswick got idiosyncratic parsons whose awkward enthusiasms tended to make them unsuitable for more respectable parishes and they, to console themselves for its remoteness and lack of interest in things spiritual, got alcoholic. The Rev St John Froude maintained the tradition. He attended to his duties with the same Anglo-Catholic Fundamentalist fervour that had made him so unpopular in Esher and turned an alcoholic eye on the activities of his few parishioners who, now that brandy was not so much in demand, contented themselves with the occasional boatload of illegal Indian immigrants.

Now as he finished a breakfast of eggnog and Irish coffee and considered the iniquities of his more egregious colleagues as related in the previous Sunday's paper he was startled to see something wobbling above the reeds on Eel Stretch. It looked like balloons, white sausage-shaped balloons that rose briefly and then disappeared. The Rev St John Froude shuddered, shut his eyes, opened them again and thought about the virtues of abstinence. If he was right and he didn't know whether he wanted to be or not, the morning was being profaned by a cluster of contraceptives, inflated contraceptives, wobbling erratically where by the nature of things no contraceptive had ever wobbled before. At least he hoped it was a cluster. He was so used to seeing things in twos when they were in fact ones that he couldn't be sure if what looked like a cluster of inflated contraceptives wasn't just one or better still none at all.

He reeled off to his study to get his binoculars and stepped out on to the terrace to focus them. By that time the manifestation had disappeared. The Rev St John Froude shook his head mournfully. Things and in particular his liver had reached a pretty pickle for him to have hallucinations so early in the morning. He went back into the house and tried to concentrate his attention on a case involving an Archdeacon in Ongar who had undergone a sex-change operation before eloping with his verger. There was matter there for a sermon if only he could think of a suitable text.

*

At the bottom of the garden Eva Wilt watched his retreat and wondered what to do. She had no intention of going up to the house and introducing herself in her present condition. She needed clothes, or at least some sort of covering. She looked around for something temporary and finally decided on some ivy climbing up the graveyard fence. With one eye on the Vicarage she emerged from the willow tree and scampered across to the fence and through the gate into the churchyard. There she ripped some ivy off the trunk of a tree and, carrying it in front of her rather awkwardly, made her way surreptitiously up the overgrown path towards the church. For the most part her progress was masked from the house by the trees but once or twice she had to crouch low and scamper from tombstone to tombstone in full view of the Vicarage. By the time she reached the church porch she was panting and her sense of impropriety had been increased tenfold. If the prospect of presenting herself at the house in the nude offended her on grounds of social decorum, going into a church in the raw was positively sacrilegious. She stood in the porch and tried frantically to steel herself to go in. There were bound to be surplices for the choir in the vestry and dressed in a surplice she could go up to the house. Or could she? Eva wasn't sure about the significance of surplices and the Vicar might be angry. Oh dear it was all so awkward. In the end she opened the church door and went inside. It was cold and damp and empty. Clutching the ivy to her she crossed to the vestry door and tried it. It was locked. Eva stood shivering and tried to think. Finally she went outside and stood in the sunshine trying to get warm.

In the Staff Room at the Tech, Dr Board was holding court. 'All things considered I think we came out of the whole business rather creditably,' he said. 'The Principal has always said he wanted to put the college on the map and with the help of friend Wilt it must be said he has succeeded. The newspaper coverage has been positively prodigious. I shouldn't be surprised if our student intake jumped astonishingly.'

'The committee didn't approve our facilities,' said Mr Morris, 'so you can hardly claim their visit was an unqualified success.'

'Personally I think they got their money's worth,' said Dr Board. 'It's not every day you get the chance to see an exhumation and an execution at the same time. The one usually precedes the other and certainly the experience of seeing what to all intents and purposes was a woman turn in a matter of seconds into a man, an instantaneous sex change, was, to use a modern idiom, a mind-blowing one.'

'Talking of poor Mayfield,' said the Head of Geography, 'I understand he's still at the Mental Hospital.'

'Committed?' asked Dr Board hopefully.

'Depressed. And suffering from exhaustion.'

'Hardly surprising. Anyone who can use language ... abuse language like that is asking for trouble. Structure as a verb, for example.'

'He had set great store by the Joint Honours degree and the fact that it has been turned down ...'

'Quite right too,' said Dr Board. 'The educative value of stuffing second-rate students with fifth-rate ideas on subjects as diverse as Medieval Poetry and Urban Studies escapes me. Far better that they should spend their time watching the police dig up the supposed body of a woman coated in concrete, stretch her neck, rip all her clothes off her, hang her and finally blow her up until she explodes. Now that is what I call a truly educational experience. It combines archaeology with criminology, zoology with physics, anatomy with economic theory, while maintaining the students' undivided attention all the time. If we must have Joint Honours degrees let them be of that vitality. Practical too. I'm thinking of sending away for one of those dolls.'

'It still leaves unresolved the question of Mrs Wilt's disappearance,' said Mr Morris.

'Ah, dear Eva,' said Dr Board wistfully. 'Having seen so much of what I imagined to be her I shall, if I ever have the pleasure of meeting her again, treat her with the utmost courtesy. An amazingly versatile woman and interestingly proportioned. I think I shall christen my doll Eva.'

'But the police still seem to think she is dead.'

'A woman like that can never die,' said Dr Board. 'She may explode but her memory lingers on indelibly.'

In his study the Rev St John Froude shared Dr Board's opinion. The memory of the large and apparently naked lady he had glimpsed emerging from the willow tree at the bottom of his garden like some disgustingly oversized nymph and scuttling through the churchyard was not something he was ever likely to forget. Coming so shortly after the apparition of the inflated contraceptives it lent weight to the suspicion that he had been overdoing things on the alcohol side. Abandoning the sermon he had been preparing on the apostate Archdeacon of Ongar – he had had 'By their fruits ye shall know them' in mind as a text – he got up and peered out of the window in the direction of the church and was wondering if he shouldn't go down and see if there wasn't a large fat naked lady there when his attention was drawn to the reeds across the water. They were there again, those infernal things. This time there could be no doubt about it. He grabbed his binoculars and stared furiously through them. He could see them much more clearly than the first time and much more ominously. The sun was high in the sky and a mist rose over Eel Stretch so that the contraceptives had a luminescent sheen about them, an insubstantiality that was almost spiritual in its implications. Worse still, there appeared to be something written on them. The message was clear if incomprehensible. It read PEESOP. The Rev St John Froude lowered his binoculars and reached for the whisky bottle and considered the significance of PEESOP etched ectoplasmically against the sky. By the time he had finished his third hurried glass and had decided that spiritualism might after all have something to be said for it though why you almost always found yourself in touch with a Red Indian who was acting by proxy for an aunt which might account for the misspelling of Peasoup while removing some of the less attractive ingredients from the stuff, the wind had changed the letters round. This time when he looked the message read EELPOPS. The Vicar shuddered. What eel was popping and how?

'The sins of the spirit,' he said reproachfully to his fourth glass of whisky before consulting the oracle once more. POSH-ELLS was followed by HEPOLP to be succeeded by SHHLPSPO which was even worse. The Rev St John Froude thrust his binoculars and the bottle of whisky aside and went down on his knees to pray for deliverance, or at least for some guidance in interpreting the message. But every time he got up to see if his wish had been granted the combination of letters was as meaningless as ever or downright threatening. What, for instance, did HELLSPO signify? Or SLOSHHEEL? Finally, determined to discover for himself the true nature of the occurrence, he put on his cassock and wove off down the garden path to the boathouse.

'They shall rue the day,' he muttered as he climbed into the rowing boat and took the oars. The Rev St John Froude held firm views on contraception. It was one of the tenets of his Anglo-Catholicism.

In the cabin cruiser Gaskell slept soundly. Around him Sally made her preparations. She undressed and changed into the plastic bikini. She took a silk square from her bag and put it on the table and she fetched a jug from the kitchen and leaning over the side filled it with water. Finally she went into the toilet and made her face up in the mirror. When she emerged she was wearing false eyelashes, her lips were heavily red and pancake make-up obscured her pale complexion. She was carrying a bathing-cap. She crossed the door of the galley and put an arm up and stuck her hip out.

'Gaskell baby,' she called.

Gaskell opened his eyes and looked at her. 'What the hell gives?'

'Like it, baby?'

Gaskell put on his glasses. In spite of himself he did like it. 'You think you're going to wheedle round me, you're wrong ...'

Sally smiled. 'Conserve the verbiage. You turn me on, bio-degradable baby.' She moved forward and sat on the bunk beside him.

'What are you trying to do?'

'Make it up, babykink. You deserve a curve.' She fondled him gently. 'Like the old days. Remember?'

Gaskell remembered and felt weak. Sally leant forward and pressed him down on to the bunk.

'Surrogate Sally,' she said and unbuttoned his shirt.

Gaskell squirmed. 'If you think ...'

'Don't think, kink,' said Sally and undid his jeans. 'Only erect.'

'Oh God,' said Gaskell. The perfume, the plastic, the mask of a face and her hands were awakening ancient fantasies. He lay supine on the bunk staring at her while Sally undressed him. Even when she rolled him over on his face and pulled his hands behind his back he made no resistance.

'Bondage baby,' she said softly and reached for the silk square.

'No, Sally, no,' he said weakly. Sally smiled grimly and tied his hands together, winding the silk between his wrists carefully before tightening it. When she had finished Gaskell whimpered. 'You're hurting me.'

Sally rolled him over. 'You love it,' she said and kissed him. She sat back and stroked him gently. 'Harder, baby, real hard. Lift me lover sky high.'

'Oh Sally.'

'That's my baby and now the waterproof.'

'There's no need. I like it better without.'

'But I do, G. I need it to prove you loved me till death did us part.' She bent over and rolled it down.

Gaskell stared up at her. Something was wrong.

'And now the cap.' She reached over and picked up the bathing-cap.

'The cap?' said Gaskell. 'Why the cap? I don't want that thing on.'

'Oh but you do, sweetheart. It makes you look girlwise.' She fitted the cap over his head. 'Now into Sallia inter alia.' She undid the bikini and lowered herself on to him. Gaskell moaned and stared up at her. She was lovely. It was a long time since she had been so good. But he was still frightened. There was a look in her eyes he hadn't seen before. 'Untie me,' he pleaded, 'you're hurting my arm.'

But Sally merely smiled and gyrated. 'When you've come and gone, G baby. When you've been.' She moved her hips. 'Come, bum, come quick.'

Gaskell shuddered.

'Finished?'

He nodded. 'Finished,' he sighed.

'For good, baby, for good,' said Sally. 'That was it. You're past the last.'

'Past the last?'

'You've come and gone, come and gone. It's Styxside for you now.'

'Stickside?'

'S for Sally, T for Terminal, Y for You and X for Exit. All that's left is this.' She reached over and picked up the jug of muddy water. Gaskell turned his head and looked at it.

'What's that for?'

'For you, baby. Mudders milk.' She moved up his body and sat on his chest. 'Open your mouth.'

Gaskell Pringsheim stared up at her frantically. He began to writhe. 'You're mad. You're crazy.'

'Now just lie quietly and it won't hurt. It will soon be over, lover. Natural death by drowning. In bed. You're making history.'

'You bitch, you murderous bitch . . .'

'Cerberuswise,' said Sally, and poured the water into his mouth. She put the jug down and pulled the cap down over his face.

The Rev St John Froude rowed surprisingly steadily for a man with half a bottle of whisky inside him and a wrath in his heart, and the nearer he got to the contraceptives the greater his wrath became. It wasn't simply that he had been given a quite unnecessary fright about the state of his liver by the sight of the things (he could see now that he was close to them that they were real), it was rather that he adhered to the doctrine of sexual non-intervention. God, in his view, had created a perfect world if the book of Genesis was to be believed and it had been going downhill ever since. And the book of Genesis *was* to be believed or the rest of the Bible made no sense at all. Starting from this fundamentalist premise the Rev St John Froude had progressed erratically by way of Blake, Hawker, Leavis and a number of obscurantist theologians to the conviction that the miracles of modern science were the works of the devil, that salvation lay in eschewing every material advance since the Renaissance, and one or two before, and that nature was infinitely less red in tooth and claw than modern mechanized man. In short he was convinced that the end of the world was at hand in the shape of a nuclear holocaust and that it was his duty as a Christian to announce the fact. His sermons on the subject had been of such a vividly horrendous fervour as to lead to his exile in Waterswick. Now as he rowed up the channel into Eel Stretch he fulminated silently against contraception, abortion and the evils of sexual promiscuity. They were all symptoms and causes and causative symptoms of the moral chaos which life on earth had become. And finally there were trippers. The Rev St John Froude loathed trippers. They fouled the little Eden of his parish with their boats, their transistors, and their unabashed enjoyment of the present. And trippers who desecrated the prospect from his study window with inflated contraceptives and meaningless messages were an abomination. By the time he came in sight of the cabin cruiser he was in no mood to be trifled with. He rowed furiously across to the boat, tied up to the rail and, lifting his cassock over his knees, stepped aboard.

In the cabin Sally stared down at the bathing-cap. It deflated and inflated, expanded and was sucked in against Gaskell's face and Sally squirmed with pleasure. She was the liberatedest woman in the world, but the liberatedest. Gaskell was dying and she would be free to be with a million dollars in the kitty. And no one would ever know. When he was dead she would take the cap off and untie him and push his body over the side into the water. Gaskell Pringsheim would have died a natural death by drowning. And at that moment the cabin door opened and she looked up at the silhouette of the Rev St John Froude in the cabin doorway.

'What the hell ...' she muttered and leapt off Gaskell.

The Rev St John Froude hesitated. He had come to say his piece and say it he would but he had clearly intruded on a very naked woman with a horribly made-up face in the act of making love to a man who as far as a quick glance enabled him to tell had no face at all.

'I ...' he began and stopped. The man on the bunk had rolled on to the floor and was writhing there in the most extraordinary fashion. The Rev St John Froude stared down at him aghast. The man was not only faceless but his hands were tied behind his back.

'My dear fellow,' said the Vicar, appalled at the scene and looked up at the naked woman for some sort of explanation. She was staring at him demonically and holding a large kitchen knife. The Rev St John Froude stumbled back into the cockpit as the woman advanced towards him holding the knife in front of her with both hands. She was clearly quite demented. So was the man on the floor. He rolled about and dragged his head from side to side. The bathing-cap came off but the Rev St John Froude was too busy scrambling over the side into his rowing boat to notice. He cast off as the ghastly woman lunged towards him and began to row away, his original mission entirely forgotten. In the cockpit Sally stood screaming abuse at him and behind her a shape had appeared in the cabin door. The Vicar was grateful to see that the man had a face now, not a nice face, a positively horrible face but a face for all that, and he was coming up behind the woman with some hideous intention. The next moment the intention was carried out. The man hurled himself at her, the knife dropped on to the deck, the woman scrabbled at the side of the boat and then slid forward into the water. The Rev St John Froude waited no longer. He rowed vigorously away. Whatever appalling orgy of sexual perversion he had interrupted he wanted none of it and painted women with knives who called him a motherfucking son of a cuntsucker among other things didn't elicit his sympathy when the object of their obscene passions pushed them into the water. And in any case they were Americans. The Rev St John Froude had no time for Americans. They epitomized everything he found offensive about the modern world. Imbued with a new disgust for the present and an urge to hit the whisky he rowed home and tied up at the bottom of the garden.

Behind him in the cabin cruiser Gaskell ceased shouting. The priest who had saved his life had ignored his hoarse pleas for further help and Sally was standing waist-deep in water beside the boat. Well she could stay there. He went back into the cabin, turned so that he could lock the door with his tied hands and then looked around for something to cut the silk scarf with. He was still very frightened.

'Right,' said Inspector Flint, 'so what did you do then?'
'Got up and read the Sunday papers.'
'After that?'
'I ate a plate of All-Bran and drank some tea.'
'Tea? You sure it was tea? Last time you said coffee.'
'Which time?'
'The last time you told it.'
'I drank tea.'
'What then?'
'I gave Clem his breakfast.'
'What sort?'
'Chappie.'
'Last time you said Bonzo.'
'This time I say Chappie.'
'Make up your mind. Which sort was it?'
'What the fuck does it matter which sort it was?'
'It matters to me.'
'Chappie.'
'And when you had fed the dog.'
'I shaved.'
'Last time you said you had a bath.'
'I had a bath and then I shaved. I was trying to save time.'

'Forget the time, Wilt, we've got all the time in the world.'

'What time is it?'

'Shut up. What did you do then?'

'Oh for God's sake, what does it matter. What's the point of going over and over the same things?'

'Shut up.'

'Right,' said Wilt, 'I will.'

'When you had shaved what did you do?'

Wilt stared at him and said nothing.

'When you had shaved?'

But Wilt remained silent. Finally Inspector Flint left the room and sent for Sergeant Yates.

'He's clammed up,' he said wearily. 'So what do we do now?'

'Try a little physical persuasion?'

Flint shook his head. 'Gosdyke's seen him. If he turns up in Court on Monday with so much as a hair out of place, he'll be all over us for brutality. There's got to be some other way. He must have a weak spot somewhere but I'm damned if I can find it. How does he do it?'

'Do what?'

'Keep talking and saying nothing. Not one bloody useful thing. That sod's got more opinions on every topic under the flaming sun than I've got hair on my head.'

'If we keep him awake for another forty-eight hours he's bound to crack up.'

'He'll take me with him,' said Flint.' We'll both go into court in straitjackets.'

In the Interview Room Wilt put his head on the table. They would be back in a minute with more questions but a moment's sleep was better than none. Sleep. If only they would let him sleep. What had Flint said? 'The moment you sign a confession, you can have all the sleep you want.' Wilt considered the remark and its possibilities. A confession. But it would have to be plausible enough to keep them occupied while he got some rest and at the same time so impossible that it would be rejected by the court. A delaying tactic to give Eva time to come back and prove his innocence. It would be like giving

Gasfitters Two *Shane* to read while he sat and thought about putting Eva down the pile shaft. He should be able to think up something complicated that would keep them frantically active. How he had killed them? Beat them to death in the bathroom? Not enough blood. Even Flint had admitted that much. So how? What was a nice gentle way to go? Poor old Pinkerton had chosen a peaceful death when he stuck a tube up the exhaust pipe of his car ... That was it. But why? There had to be a motive. Eva was having it off with Dr Pringsheim? With that twit? Not in a month of Sundays. Eva wouldn't have looked twice at Gaskell. But Flint wasn't to know that. And what about that bitch Sally? All three having it off together? Well at least it would explain why he killed them all and it would provide the sort of motive Flint would understand. And besides it was right for that kind of party. So he got this pipe ... What pipe? There was no need for a pipe. They were in the garage to get away from everyone else. No, that wouldn't do. It had to be the bathroom. How about Eva and Gaskell doing it in the bath? That was better. He had bust the door down in a fit of jealousy. Much better. Then he had drowned them. And then Sally had come upstairs and he had had to kill her too. That explained the blood. There had been a struggle. He hadn't meant to kill her but she had fallen in the bath. So far so good. But where had he put them? It had to be something good. Flint wasn't going to believe anything like the river. Somewhere that made sense of the doll down the hole. Flint had it firmly fixed in his head that the doll had been a diversionary tactic. That meant that time entered into their disposal.

Wilt got up and asked to go to the toilet. As usual the constable came with him and stood outside the door.

'Do you have to?' said Wilt. 'I'm not going to hang myself with the chain.'

'To see you don't beat your meat,' said the constable coarsely.

Wilt sat down. Beat your meat. What a hell of an expression. It called to mind Meat One. Meat One? It was a moment of inspiration. Wilt got up and flushed the toilet. Meat One would keep them busy for a long time. He went back to the pale green

187

room where the light buzzed. Flint was waiting for him.

'You going to talk now?' he asked.

Wilt shook his head. They would have to drag it out of him if his confession was to be at all convincing. He would have to hesitate, start to say something, stop, start again, appeal to Flint to stop torturing him, plead and start again. This trout needed tickling. Oh well, it would help to keep him awake.

'Are you going to start again at the beginning?' he asked.

Inspector Flint smiled horribly. 'Right at the beginning.'

'All right,' said Wilt, 'have it your own way. Just don't keep asking me if I gave the dog Chappie or Bonzo. I can't stand all that talk about dog food.'

Inspector Flint rose to the bait. 'Why not?'

'It gets on my nerves,' said Wilt, with a shudder.

The Inspector leant forward. 'Dog food gets on your nerves?' he said.

Wilt hesitated pathetically. 'Don't go on about it,' he said. 'Please don't go on.'

'Now then which was it, Bonzo or Chappie?' said the Inspector, scenting blood.

Wilt put his head in his hands. 'I won't say anything. I won't. Why must you keep asking me about food? Leave me alone.' His voice rose hysterically and with it Inspector Flint's hopes. He knew when he had touched the nerve. He was on to a good thing.

18

'Dear God,' said Sergeant Yates, 'but we had pork pies for lunch yesterday. It's too awful.'

Inspector Flint rinsed his mouth out with black coffee and spat into the washbasin. He had vomited twice and felt like vomiting again.

'I knew it would be something like that,' he said with a shudder, 'I just knew it. A man who could pull that doll trick had to have something really filthy up his sleeve.'

'But they may all have been eaten by now,' said the Sergeant. Flint looked at him balefully.

'Why the hell do you think he laid that phoney trail?' he asked. 'To give them plenty of time to be consumed. His expression "consumed", not mine. You know what the shelf life of a pork pie is?'

Yates shook his head.

'Five days. Five days. So they went out on Tuesday which leaves us one day to find them or what remains of them. I want every pork pie in East Anglia picked up. I want every fucking sausage and steak and kidney pie that went out of Sweetbreads Meat Factory this week found and brought in. And every tin of dog food.'

'Dog food?'

'You heard me,' said Inspector Flint staggering out of the washroom. 'And while you're about it you'd better make it cat food too. You never know with Wilt. He's capable of leading us up the garden path in one important detail.'

'But if they went into pork pies what's all this about dog food?'

'Where the hell do you think he put the odds and ends and I do mean ends?' Inspector Flint asked savagely. 'You don't imagine he was going to have people coming in and complaining they'd found a tooth or a toenail in the Sweetbreads pie they had bought that morning. Not Wilt. That swine thinks of everything. He drowns them in their own bath. He puts them in plastic garbage bags and locks the bags in the garage while he goes home and sticks the doll down that fucking hole. Then on Sunday he goes back and picks them up and spends the day at the meat factory all by himself ... Well if you want to know what he did on Sunday you can read all about it in his statement. It's more than my stomach can stand.'

The Inspector went back hurriedly into the washroom. He'd been living off pork pies since Monday. The statistical chances of his having partaken of Mrs Wilt were extremely high.

When Sweetbreads Meat and Canning Factory opened at eight,

Inspector Flint was waiting at the gate. He stormed into the manager's office and demanded to speak to him.

'He's not here yet,' said the secretary. 'Is there anything I can do for you?'

'I want a list of every establishment you supply with pork pies, steak and kidney pies, sausages and dog food,' said the Inspector.

'I couldn't possibly give you that information,' said the secretary. 'It's extremely confidential.'

'Confidential? What the hell do you mean confidential?'

'Well I don't know really. It's just that I couldn't take it on myself to provide you with inside information ...' She stopped. Inspector Flint was staring at her with a quite horrible expression on his face.

'Well, miss,' he said finally, 'while we're on the topic of inside information, it may interest you to know that what has been inside your pork pies is by way of being inside information. Vital information.'

'Vital information? I don't know what you mean. Our pies contain perfectly wholesome ingredients.'

'Wholesome?' shouted the Inspector. 'You call three human bodies wholesome? You call the boiled, bleached, minced and cooked remains of three murdered bodies wholesome?'

'But we only use ...' the secretary began and fell sideways off her chair in a dead faint.

'Oh for God's sake,' shouted the Inspector, 'you'd think a silly bitch who can work in an abattoir wouldn't be squeamish. Find out who the manager is and where he lives and tell him to come down here at the double.'

He sat down in a chair while Sergeant Yates rummaged in the desk. 'Wakey, wakey,' he said, prodding the secretary with his foot. 'If anyone has got a right to lie down on the job, it's me. I've been on my feet for three days and nights and I've been an accessory after the fact of murder.'

'An accessory?' said Yates. 'I don't see how you can say that.'

'Can't you? Well what would you call helping to dispose of parts of a murder victim? Concealing evidence of a crime?'

'I never thought of it that way,' said Yates.

'I did,' said the Inspector, 'I can't think of anything else.'

In his cell Wilt stared up at the ceiling peacefully. He was astonished that it had been so easy. All you had to do was tell people what they wanted to hear and they would believe you no matter how implausible your story might be. And three days and nights without sleep had suspended Inspector Flint's disbelief with a vengeance. Then again Wilt's hesitations had been timed perfectly and his final confession a nice mixture of conceit and matter-of-factness. On the details of the murder he had been coldly precise and in describing their disposal he had been a craftsman taking pride in his work. Every now and then when he got to a difficult spot he would veer away into a manic arrogance at once boastful and cowardly with 'You'll never be able to prove it. They'll have disappeared without trace now.' And the Harpic had come in useful once again, adding a macabre touch of realism about evidence being flushed down thousands of U-bends with Harpic being poured after it like salt from a salt cellar. Eva would enjoy that when he told her about it, which was more than could be said for Inspector Flint. He hadn't even seen the irony of Wilt's remark that while he had been looking for the Pringsheims they had been under his nose all the time. He had been particularly upset by the crack about gut reactions and the advice to stick to health foods in future. Yes, in spite of his tiredness Wilt had enjoyed himself watching the Inspector's bloodshot eyes turn from glee and gloating self-satisfaction to open amazement and finally undisguised nausea. And when finally Wilt had boasted that they would never be able to bring him to trial without the evidence, Flint had responded magnificently.

'Oh yes, we will,' he had shouted hoarsely. 'If there is one single pie left from that batch we'll get it and when we do the Lab boys will ...'

'Find nothing but pork in it,' said Wilt before being dragged off to his cell. At least that was the truth and if Flint didn't believe it that was his own fault. He had asked for a confession and he had got one by courtesy of Meat One, the apprentice butchers who had spent so many hours of Liberal Studies explaining the workings of Sweetbreads Meat Factory to him and had actually taken him down there one afternoon to show him how it all worked. Dear lads. And how he had loathed them at the time. Which only went to show how wrong you could be about people. Wilt was just wondering if he had been wrong about Eva and perhaps she was dead when he fell asleep.

In the churchyard Eva watched the Rev St John Froude walk down to the boathouse and start rowing towards the reeds. As soon as he had disappeared she made her way up the path towards the house. With the Vicar out of the way she was prepared to take the risk of meeting his wife. She stole through the doorway into the courtyard and looked about her. The place had a dilapidated air about it and a pile of empty bottles in one corner, whisky and gin bottles, seemed to indicate that he might well be unmarried. Still clutching her ivy, she went across to the door, evidently the kitchen door, and knocked. There was no answer. She crossed to the window and looked inside. The kitchen was large, distinctly untidy and had all the hallmarks of a bachelor existence about it. She went back to the door and knocked again and she was just wondering what to do now when there was the sound of a vehicle coming down the drive.

Eva hesitated for a second and then tried the door. It was unlocked. She stepped inside and shut the door as a milk van drove into the courtyard. Eva listened while the milkman put down several bottles and then drove away. Then she turned and went down the passage to the front hall. If she could find the phone she could ring Henry and he could come out in the car and fetch her. She would go back to the church and wait for him there. But the hall was empty. She poked her head into several rooms with a good deal of care and found them largely bare of furniture or with dustcovers over chairs and sofas. The place was incredibly untidy too. Definitely the Vicar was a bachelor. Finally she found his study. There was a phone on the desk. Eva went over and lifted the receiver and dialled Ipford 66066. There was no reply. Henry would be at the Tech. She dialled the Tech number and asked for Mr Wilt.

'Wilt?' said the girl on the switchboard. 'Mr Wilt?'

'Yes,' said Eva in a low voice.

'I'm afraid he's not here,' said the girl.

'Not there? But he's got to be there.'

'Well he isn't.'

'But he's got to be. It's desperately important I get in touch with him.'

'I'm sorry, but I can't help you,' said the girl.

'But ...' Eva began and glanced out of the window. The Vicar had returned and was walking up the garden path towards her. 'Oh God,' she muttered and put the phone down hurriedly. She turned and rushed out of the room in a state of panic. Only when she had made her way back along the passage to the kitchen did it occur to her that she had left her ivy behind in the study. There were footsteps in the passage. Eva looked frantically around, decided against the courtyard and went up a flight of stone steps to the first floor. There she stood and listened. Her heart was palpitating. She was naked and alone in a strange house with a clergyman and Henry wasn't at the Tech when he should have been and the girl on the switchboard had sounded most peculiar, almost as though there was something wrong with wanting to speak to Henry. She had no idea what to do.

In the kitchen the Rev St John Froude had a very good idea what he wanted to do: expunge for ever the vision of the inferno to which he had been lured by those vile things with their meaningless messages floating across the water. He dug a fresh bottle of Teachers out of the cupboard and took it back to his study. What he had witnessed had been so grotesque, so evidently evil, so awful, so prescient of hell itself that he was in two minds whether it had been real or simply a waking nightmare. A man without a face, whose hands were tied behind his back, a woman with a painted face and a knife, the language ... The Rev St John Froude opened the bottle and was about to pour a glass when his eye fell on the ivy Eva had left on the chair. He put the bottle down hastily and stared at the leaves.

Here was another mystery to perplex him. How had a clump of ivy got on to the chair in his study? It certainly hadn't been there when he had left the house. He picked it up gingerly and put it on his desk. Then he sat down and contemplated it with a growing sense of unease. Something was happening in his world that he could not understand. And what about the strange figure he had seen flitting about between the tombstones? He had quite forgotten her. The Rev St John Froude got up and went out on to the terrace and down the path to the church.

'On a Sunday?' shouted the manager of Sweetbreads. 'On a Sunday? But we don't work on a Sunday. There's nobody here. The place is shut.'

'It wasn't last Sunday and there was someone here, Mr Kidney,' said the Inspector.

'Kidley, please,' said the manager, 'Kidley with an L.'

The Inspector nodded. 'OK Mr Kidley, now what I'm telling you is that this man Wilt was here last Sunday and he ...'

'How did he get in?'

'He used a ladder against the back wall from the car park.'

'In broad daylight? He'd have been seen.'

'At two o'clock in the morning, Mr Kidney.'

'Kidley, Inspector, Kidley.'

'Look Mr Kidley, if you work in a place like this with a name like that you're asking for it.'

Mr Kidley looked at him belligerently. 'And if you're telling me that some bloody maniac came in here with three dead bodies last Sunday and spent the day using our equipment to convert them into cooked meat edible for human consumption under the Food Regulations Act I'm telling you that that comes under the head of ... Head? What did he do with the heads? Tell me that?'

'What do you do with heads, Mr Kidley?' asked the Inspector.

'That rather depends. Some of them go with the offal into the animal food bins ...'

'Right. So that's what Wilt said he did with them. And you keep those in the No. 2 cold storage room. Am I right?'

Mr Kidley nodded miserably. 'Yes,' he said, 'we do.' He paused and gaped at the Inspector. 'But there's a world of difference between a pig's head and a . . .'

'Quite,' said the Inspector hastily, 'and I daresay you think someone was bound to spot the difference.'

'Of course they would.'

'Now I understand from Mr Wilt that you have an extremely efficient mincing machine . . .'

'No,' shouted Mr Kidley desperately. 'No, I don't believe it. It's not possible. It's . . .'

'Are you saying he couldn't possibly have . . .'

'I'm not saying that. I'm saying he shouldn't have. It's monstrous. It's horrible.'

'Of course it's horrible,' said the Inspector. 'The fact remains that he used that machine.'

'But we keep our equipment meticulously clean.'

'So Wilt says. He was definite on that point. He says he cleaned up carefully afterwards.'

'He must have done,' said Mr Kidley. 'There wasn't a thing out of place on Monday morning. You heard the foreman say so.'

'And I also heard this swine Wilt say that he made a list of where everything came from before he used it so that he could put it back exactly where he'd found it. He thought of everything.'

'And what about our reputation for hygiene? He didn't think of that, did he? For twenty-five years we've been known for the excellence of our products and now this has to happen. We've been at the head of . . .' Mr Kidley stopped suddenly and sat down.

'Now then,' said the Inspector, 'what I have to know is who you supply to. We're going to call in every pork pie and sausage . . .'

'Call them in? You can't call them in,' screamed Mr Kidley, 'they've all gone.'

'Gone? What do you mean they've gone?'

'What I say. They've gone. They've either been eaten or destroyed by now.'

'Destroyed? You're not going to tell me that there aren't

195

any left. It's only five days since they went out.'

Mr Kidley drew himself up. 'Inspector, this is an old-fashioned firm and we use traditional methods and a Sweetbreads pork pie is a genuine pork pie. It's not one of your ersatz pies with preservatives that ...'

It was Inspector Flint's turn to slump into a chair. 'Am I to understand that your fucking pies don't keep?' he asked.

Mr Kidley nodded. 'They are for immediate consumption,' he said proudly. 'Here today, gone tomorrow. That's our motto. You've seen our advertisements of course.'

Inspector Flint hadn't.

'Today's pie with yesterday's flavour, the traditional pie with the family filling.'

'You can say that again,' said Inspector Flint.

Mr Gosdyke regarded Wilt sceptically and shook his head. 'You should have listened to me,' he said, 'I told you not to talk.'

'I had to say something,' said Wilt. 'They wouldn't let me sleep and they kept asking me the same stupid questions over and over again. You've no idea what that does to you. It drives you potty.'

'Frankly, Mr Wilt, in the light of the confession you have made I find it hard to believe there was any need to. A man who can, of his own free will make a statement like this to the police is clearly insane.'

'But it's not true,' said Wilt, 'it's all pure invention.'

'With a wealth of such revolting detail? I must say I find that hard to believe. I do indeed. The bit about hip and thighs ... It makes my stomach turn over.'

'But that's from the Bible,' said Wilt, 'and besides I had to put in the gory bits or they wouldn't have believed me. Take the part where I say I sawed their ...'

'Mr Wilt, for God's sake ...'

'Well, all I can say is you've never taught Meat One. I got it all from them and once you've taught them life can hold few surprises.'

Mr Gosdyke raised an eyebrow. 'Can't it? Well I think I can

disabuse you of that notion,' he said solemnly. 'In the light of this confession you have made against my most earnest advice, and as a result of my firm belief that every word in it is true, I am no longer prepared to act on your behalf.' He collected his papers and stood up. 'You will have to get someone else.'

'But, Mr Gosdyke, you don't really believe all that nonsense about putting Eva in a pork pie, do you?' Wilt asked.

'Believe it? A man who can conceive of such a disgusting thing is capable of anything. Yes I do and what is more so do the police. They are this moment scouring the shops, the pubs and the supermarkets and dustbins of the entire county in search of pork pies.'

'But if they find any it won't do any good.'

'It may also interest you to know that they have impounded five thousand cans of Dogfill, an equal number of Catkin and have begun to dissect a quarter of a ton of Sweetbreads Best Bangers. Somewhere in that little lot they are bound to find some trace of Mrs Wilt, not to mention Dr and Mrs Pringsheim.'

'Well, all I can say is that I wish them luck,' said Wilt.

'And so do I,' said Mr Gosdyke disgustedly and left the room. Behind him Wilt sighed. If only Eva would turn up. Where the hell could she have got to?

At the Police Laboratories Inspector Flint was getting restive. 'Can't you speed things up a bit?' he asked.

The Head of the Forensic Department shook his head. 'It's like looking for a needle in a haystack,' he said, glancing significantly at another batch of sausages that had just been brought in. 'So far not a trace. This could take weeks.'

'I haven't got weeks,' said the Inspector, 'he's due in Court on Monday.'

'Only for remand and in any case you've got his statement.'

But Inspector Flint had his doubts about that. He had been looking at that statement and had noticed a number of discrepancies about it which fatigue, disgust and an overwhelming desire to get the filthy account over and done with before he was sick had tended to obscure at the time. For one thing

Wilt's scrawled signature looked suspiciously like Little Tommy Tucker when examined closely and there was a QNED beside it, which Flint had a shrewd idea meant Quod Non Erat Demonstrandum, and in any case there were rather too many references to pigs for his policeman's fancy and fuzzy pigs at that. Finally the information that Wilt had made a special request for two pork pies for lunch and had specified Sweetbreads in particular suggested an insane cannibalism that might fit in with what he had said he had done but seemed to be carrying things too far. The word 'provocation' sprang to mind and since the episode of the doll Flint had been rather conscious of bad publicity. He read through the statement again and couldn't make up his mind about it. One thing was quite certain. Wilt knew exactly how Sweetbreads factory worked. The wealth of detail he had supplied proved that. On the other hand Mr Kidley's incredulity about the heads and the mincing machine had seemed, on inspection, to be justified. Flint had looked gingerly at the beastly contraption and had found it difficult to believe that even Wilt in a fit of homicidal mania could have ... Flint put the thought out of his mind. He decided to have another little chat with Henry Wilt. Feeling like death warmed up he went back to the Interview Room and sent for Wilt.

'How's it going?' said Wilt when he arrived. 'Had any luck with the frankfurters yet? Of course you could always try your hand at black puddings ...'

'Wilt,' interrupted the Inspector, 'why did you sign that statement Little Tommy Tucker?'

Wilt sat down. 'So you've noticed that at last, have you? Very observant of you I must say.'

'I asked you a question.'

'So you did,' said Wilt. 'Let's just say I thought it was appropriate.'

'Appropriate?'

'I was singing, I think that's the slang term for it isn't it, for my sleep, so naturally ...'

'Are you telling me you made all that up?'

'What the hell do you think I did? You don't seriously think

I would inflict the Pringsheims and Eva on an unsuspecting public in the form of pork pies, do you? I mean there must be some limits to your credulity.'

Inspector Flint glared at him. 'My God, Wilt,' he said, 'if I find you've deliberately fabricated a story . . .'

'You can't do very much more,' said Wilt. 'You've already charged me with murder. What more do you want? You drag me in here, you humiliate me, you shout at me, you keep me awake for days and nights bombarding me with questions about dog food, you announce to the world that I am helping you in your enquiries into a multiple murder thus leading every citizen in the country to suppose that I have slaughtered my wife and a beastly biochemist and . . .'

'Shut up,' shouted Flint, 'I don't care what you think. It's what you've done and what you've said you've done that worries me. You've gone out of your way to mislead me . . .'

'I've done nothing of the sort,' said Wilt. 'Until last night I had told you nothing but the truth and you wouldn't accept it. Last night I handed you, in the absurd shape of a pork pie, a lie you wanted to believe. If you crave crap and use illegal methods like sleep deprivation to get it you can't blame me for serving it up. Don't come in here and bluster. If you're stupid that's your problem. Go and find my wife.'

'Someone stop me from killing the bastard,' yelled Flint, as he hurled himself from the room. He went to his office and sent for Sergeant Yates. 'Cancel the pie hunt. It's a load of bull,' he told him.

'Bull?' said the Sergeant uncertainly.

'Shit,' said Flint. 'He's done it again.'

'You mean . . .'

'I mean that that little turd in there has led us up the garden path again.'

'But how did he know about the factory and all that?'

Flint looked up at him pathetically. 'If you want to know why he's a walking encyclopedia, you go and ask him yourself.'

Sergeant Yates went out and returned five minutes later. 'Meat One,' he announced enigmatically.

'Meet won?'

'A class of butchers he used to teach. They took him round the factory.'

'Jesus,' said Flint, 'is there anybody that little swine hasn't taught?'

'He says they were most instructive.'

'Yates, do me a favour. Just go back and find out all the names of the classes he's taught. That way we'll know what to expect next.'

'Well I have heard him mention Plasterers Two and Gasfitters One ...'

'All of them, Yates, all of them. I don't want to be caught out with some tale about Mrs Wilt being got rid of in the Sewage Works because he once taught Shit Two.' He picked up the evening paper and glanced at the headlines. POLICE PROBE PIES FOR MISSING WIFE.

'Oh my God,' he groaned. 'This is going to do our public image no end of good.'

At the Tech the Principal was expressing the same opinion at a meeting of the Heads of Departments.

'We've been held up to public ridicule,' he said. 'First it is popularly supposed that we make a habit of employing lecturers who bury their unwanted wives in the foundations of the new block. Secondly we have lost all chance of attaining Polytechnic status by having the Joint Honours degree turned down by the CNAA on the grounds that those facilities we do provide are not such as befit an institution of higher learning. Professor Baxendale expressed himself very forcibly on that point and particularly on a remark he heard from one of the senior staff about necrophilia ...'

'I merely said ...' Dr Board began.

'We all know what you said, Dr Board. And it may interest you to know that Dr Cox in his lucid moments is still refusing cold meat. Dr Mayfield has already tendered his resignation. And now to cap it all we have this.'

He held up a newspaper, across the top of whose second page there read SEX LECTURES STUN STUDENTS.

'I hope you have all taken good note of the photograph,' said the Principal bitterly, indicating a large and unfortunately angled picture of Judy hanging from the crane. 'The article goes on ... well never mind. You can read it for yourselves. I would merely like answers to the following questions. Who authorized the purchase of thirty copies of *Last Exit From Brooklyn* for use with Fitters and Turners?'

Mr Morris tried to think who had taken FTs. 'I think that must have been Watkins,' he said. 'He left us last term. He was only a part-time lecturer.'

'Thank God we were spared him full-time,' said the Principal. 'Secondly which lecturer makes a habit of advocating to Nursery Nurses that they wear ... er ... Dutch Caps all the time?'

'Well Mr Sedgwick is very keen on them,' said Mr Morris.

'Nursery Nurses or Dutch Caps?' enquired the Principal.

'Possibly both together?' suggested Dr Board sotto voce.

'He's got this thing against the Pill,' said Mr Morris.

'Well please ask Mr Sedgwick to see me in my office on Monday at ten. I want to explain the terms under which he is employed here. And finally, how many lecturers do you know of who make use of Audio Visual Aid equipment to show blue movies to the Senior Secs?'

Mr Morris shook his head emphatically. 'No one in my department,' he said.

'It says here that blue movies have been shown,' said the Principal, 'in periods properly allocated to Current Affairs.'

'Wentworth did show them *Women in Love*,' said the Head of English.

'Well never mind. There's just one more point I want to mention. We are not going to conduct an Evening Class in First Aid with particular reference to the Treatment of Abdominal Hernia for which it was proposed to purchase an inflatable doll. From now on we are going to have to cut our coats to suit our cloth.'

'On the grounds of inflation?' asked Dr Board.

'On the grounds that the Education Committee has been waiting for years for an opportunity to cut back our budget,' said the Principal. 'That opportunity has now been given them. The fact that we have been providing a public service by keeping, to quote Mr Morris, "a large number of mentally unbalanced and potentially dangerous psychopaths off the streets" unquote seems to have escaped their notice.'

'I presume he was referring to the Day Release Apprentices,' said Dr Board charitably.

'He was not,' said the Principal. 'Correct me if I am wrong, Morris, but hadn't you in mind the members of the Liberal Studies Department?'

The meeting broke up. Later that day Mr Morris sat down to compose his letter of resignation.

19

From the window of an empty bedroom on the first floor of the Vicarage, Eva Wilt watched the Rev St John Froude walk pensively down the path to the church. As soon as he had passed out of sight she went downstairs and into the study. She would phone Henry again. If he wasn't at the Tech he must be at home. She crossed to the desk and was about to pick up the phone when she saw the ivy. Oh dear, she had forgotten all about the ivy and she had left it where he was bound to have seen it. It was all so terribly embarrassing. She dialled 34 Parkview Avenue and waited. There was no reply. She put the phone down and dialled the Tech. And all the time she watched the gate into the churchyard in case the Vicar should return.

'Fenland College of Arts and Technology,' said the girl on the switchboard.

'It's me again,' said Eva, 'I want to speak to Mr Wilt.'

'I'm very sorry but Mr Wilt isn't here.'

'But where is he? I've dialled home and ...'

'He's at the Police Station.'

'He's what?' Eva said.

'He's at the Police Station helping the police with their enquiries ...'

'Enquiries? What enquiries?' Eva shrieked.

'Didn't you know?' said the girl. 'It's been in all the papers. He's been and murdered his wife ...'

Eva took the phone from her ear and stared at it in horror. The girl was still speaking but she was no longer listening. Henry had murdered his wife. But she was his wife. It wasn't possible. She couldn't have been murdered. For one horrible moment Eva Wilt felt sanity slipping from her. Then she put the receiver to her ear again.

'Are you there?' said the girl.

'But I am his wife,' Eva shouted. There was a long silence at the other end and she heard the girl telling someone that there was a crazy woman on the line who said she was Mrs Wilt and what ought she to do.

'I tell you I am Mrs Wilt. Mrs Eva Wilt,' she shouted but the line had gone dead. Eva put the phone down weakly. Henry at the Police Station ... Henry had murdered her ... Oh God. The whole world had gone mad. And here she was naked in a vicarage at ... Eva had no idea where she was. She dialled 999.

'Emergency Services. Which department do you require?' said the operator.

'Police,' said Eva. There was a click and a man's voice came on.

'Police here.'

'This is Mrs Wilt,' said Eva.

'Mrs Wilt?'

'Mrs Eva Wilt. Is it true that my husband has murdered ... I mean has my husband ... oh dear I don't know what to say.'

'You say you're Mrs Wilt, Mrs Eva Wilt?' said the man.

Eva nodded and then said, 'Yes.'

'I see,' said the man dubiously. 'You're quite sure you're Mrs Wilt?'

'Of course I'm sure. That's what I'm ringing about.'

'Might I enquire where you're calling from?'

'I don't know,' said Eva. 'You see I'm in this house and I've got no clothes and ... oh dear.' The Vicar was coming up the path on to the terrace.

'If you could just give us the address.'

'I can't stop now,' said Eva and put the phone down. For a moment she hesitated and then grabbing the ivy from the desk she rushed out of the room.

'I tell you I don't know where she is,' said Wilt. 'I expect you'll find her under missing persons. She has passed from the realm of substantiality into that of abstraction.'

'What the hell do you mean by that?' asked the Inspector, reaching for his cup of coffee. It was eleven o'clock on Saturday morning but he persisted. He had twenty-eight hours to get to the truth.

'I always warned her that Transcendental Meditation carried potential dangers,' said Wilt, himself in a no-man's-land between sleeping and walking. 'But she would do it.'

'Do what?'

'Meditate transcendentally. In the lotus position. Perhaps she has gone too far this time. Possibly she has transmogrified herself.'

'Trans what?' said Inspector Flint suspiciously.

'Changed herself in some magical fashion into something else.'

'Jesus, Wilt, if you start on those pork pies again . . .'

'I was thinking of something more spiritual, Inspector, something beautiful.'

'I doubt it.'

'Ah, but think. Here am I sitting in this room with you as a direct result of going for walks with the dog and thinking dark thoughts about murdering my wife. From those hours of idle fancy I have gained the reputation of being a murderer without committing a murder. Who is to say but that Eva whose thoughts were monotonously beautiful has not earned herself a commensurately beautiful reward? To put it in your terms, Inspector, we get what we ask for.'

'I fervently hope so, Wilt,' said the Inspector.

'Ah,' said Wilt, 'but then where is she? Tell me that. Mere speculation will not do . . .'

'Me tell you?' shouted the Inspector upsetting his cup of

coffee. 'You know which hole in the ground you put her in or which cement mixer or incinerator you used.'

'I was speaking metaphorically ... I mean rhetorically,' said Wilt. 'I was trying to imagine what Eva would be if her thoughts such as they are took on the substance of reality. My secret dream was to become a ruthless man of action, decisive, unhindered by moral doubts or considerations of conscience, a Hamlet transformed into Henry the Fifth without the patriotic fervour that inclines one to think that he would not have approved of the Common Market, a Caesar ...'

Inspector Flint had heard enough. 'Wilt,' he snarled, 'I don't give a damn what you wanted to become. What I want to know is what has become of your wife.'

'I was just coming to that,' said Wilt. 'What we've got to establish first is what I am.'

'I know what you are, Wilt. A bloody word merchant, a verbal contortionist, a fucking logic-chopper, a linguistic Houdini, an encyclopedia of unwanted information ...' Inspector Flint ran out of metaphors.

'Brilliant, Inspector, brilliant. I couldn't have put it better myself. A logic-chopper, but alas not a wife one. If we follow the same line of reasoning Eva in spite of all her beautiful thoughts and meditations has remained as unchanged as I. The ethereal eludes her. Nirvana slips ever from her grasp. Beauty and truth evade her. She pursues the absolute with a fly-swatter and pours Harpic down the drains of Hell itself ...'

'That's the tenth time you have mentioned Harpic,' said the Inspector, suddenly alive to a new dreadful possibility. 'You didn't ...'

Wilt shook his head. 'There you go again. So like poor Eva. The literal mind that seeks to seize the evanescent and clutches fancy by its non-existent throat. That's Eva for you. She will never dance Swan Lake. No management would allow her to fill the stage with water or install a double bed and Eva would insist.'

Inspector Flint got up. 'This is getting us nowhere fast.'

'Precisely,' said Wilt, 'nowhere at all. We are what we are and nothing we can do will alter the fact. The mould that forms our natures remains unbroken. Call it heredity, call it chance . . .'

'Call it a load of codswallop,' said Flint and left the room. He needed his sleep and he intended to get it.

In the passage he met Sergeant Yates.

'There's been an emergency call from a woman claiming to be Mrs Wilt,' the Sergeant said.

'Where from?'

'She wouldn't say where she was,' said Yates. 'She just said she didn't know and that she had no clothes on . . .'

'Oh one of those,' said the Inspector. 'A bloody nutter. What the hell are you wasting my time for? As if we didn't have enough on our hands without that.'

'I just thought you'd want to know. If she calls again we'll try and get a fix on the number.'

'As if I cared,' said Flint and hurried off in search of his lost sleep.

The Rev St John Froude spent an uneasy day. His investigation of the church had revealed nothing untoward and there was no sign that an obscene ritual (a Black Mass had crossed his mind) had been performed there. As he walked back to the Vicarage he was glad to note that the sky over Eel Stretch was empty and that the contraceptives had disappeared. So had the ivy on his desk. He regarded the space where it had been with apprehension and helped himself to whisky. He could have sworn there had been a sprig of ivy there when he had left. By the time he had finished what remained in the bottle his mind was filled with weird fancies. The Vicarage was strangely noisy. There were odd creaks from the staircase and inexplicable sounds from the upper floor as if someone or something was moving stealthily about but when the Vicar went to investigate the noises ceased abruptly. He went upstairs and poked his head into several empty bedrooms. He came down again and stood in the hall listening. Then he returned to his study and tried to concentrate on his sermon, but the feeling that he was not alone persisted. The Rev St John Froude sat at his desk and considered the possibility of ghosts. Something very odd was going on. At one o'clock he went down the hall to the kitchen for lunch and discovered that a pint of milk had disappeared from the pantry and that the remains of an apple pie that Mrs Snape who did his cleaning twice weekly had brought him had also vanished. He made do with baked beans on toast and tottered upstairs for his afternoon nap. It was while he was there that he first heard the voices. Or rather one voice. It seemed to come from his study. The Rev St John Froude sat up in bed. If his ears weren't betraying him and in view of the morning's weird events he was inclined to believe that they were he could have sworn someone had been using his telephone. He got up and put on his shoes. Someone was crying. He went out on to the landing and listened. The sobbing had stopped. He went downstairs and looked in all the rooms on the ground floor but, apart from the fact that a dust cover had been removed from one of the armchairs in the unused sitting-room, there was no sign of anyone. He was just about to go upstairs again when the telephone rang. He went into the study and answered it.

'Waterswick Vicarage,' he mumbled.

'This is Fenland Constabulary,' said a man. 'We've just had a call from your number purporting to come from a Mrs Wilt.'

'Mrs Wilt?' said the Rev St John Froude. 'Mrs Wilt? I'm afraid there must be some mistake. I don't know any Mrs Wilt.'

'The call definitely came from your phone, sir.'

The Rev St John Froude considered the matter. 'This is all very peculiar,' he said, 'I live alone.'

'You are the Vicar?'

'Of course I'm the Vicar. This is the Vicarage and I am the Vicar.'

'I see, sir. And your name is?'

'The Reverend St John Froude. F...R...O...U...D...E.'

'Quite sir, and you definitely don't have a woman in the house.'

'Of course I don't have a woman in the house. I find the suggestion distinctly improper. I am a ...'

'I'm sorry, sir, but we just have to check these things out.

We've had a call from Mrs Wilt, at least a woman claiming to be Mrs Wilt, and it came from your phone ...'

'Who is this Mrs Wilt? I've never heard of a Mrs Wilt.'

'Well sir, Mrs Wilt .. it's a bit difficult really. She's supposed to have been murdered.'

'Murdered?' said the Rev St John Froude. 'Did you say "murdered"?'

'Let's just say she is missing from home in suspicious circumstances. We're holding her husband for questioning.'

The Rev St John Froude shook his head. 'How very unfortunate,' he murmured.

'Thank you for your help, sir,' said the Sergeant. 'Sorry to have disturbed you.'

The Rev St John Froude put the phone down thoughtfully. The notion that he was sharing the house with a disembodied and recently murdered woman was not one that he had wanted to put to his caller. His reputation for eccentricity was already sufficiently widespread without adding to it. On the other hand what he had seen on the boat in Eel Stretch bore, now that he came to think of it, all the hallmarks of murder. Perhaps in some extraordinary way he had been a witness to a tragedy that had already occurred, a sort of post-mortem déja vu if that was the right way of putting it. Certainly if the husband were being held for questioning the murder must have taken place before ... In which case ... The Rev St John Froude stumbled through a series of suppositions in which Time with a capital T, and appeals for help from beyond the grave figured largely. Perhaps it was his duty to inform the police of what he had seen. He was just hesitating and wondering what to do when he heard those sobs again and this time quite distinctly. They came from the next room. He got up, braced himself with another shot of whisky and went next door. Standing in the middle of the room was a large woman whose hair straggled down over her shoulders and whose face was ravaged. She was wearing what appeared to be a shroud. The Rev St John Froude stared at her with a growing sense of horror. Then he sank to his knees.

'Let us pray,' he muttered hoarsely.

The ghastly apparition slumped heavily forward clutching the shroud to its bosom. Together they kneeled in prayer.

'Check it out? What the hell do you mean "check it out"?' said Inspector Flint who objected strongly to being woken in the middle of the afternoon when he had had no sleep for thirty-six hours and was trying to get some. 'You wake me with some damned tomfoolery about a vicar called Sigmund Freud ...'

'St John Froude,' said Yates.

'I don't care what he's called. It's still improbable. If the bloody man says she isn't there, she isn't there. What am I supposed to do about it?'

'I just thought we ought to get a patrol car to check, that's all.'

'What makes you think ...'

'There was definitely a call from a woman claiming to be Mrs Wilt and it came from that number. She's called twice now. We've got a tape of the second call. She gave details of herself and they sound authentic. Date of birth, address, Wilt's occupation, even the right name of their dog and the fact that they have yellow curtains in the lounge.'

'Well, any fool can tell that. All they've got to do is walk past the house.'

'And the name of the dog. It's called Clem. I've checked that and she's right.'

'She didn't happen to say what she'd been doing for the past week did she?'

'She said she'd been on a boat,' said Yates. 'Then she rang off.'

Inspector Flint sat up in bed. 'A boat? What boat?'

'She rang off. Oh and another thing, she said she takes a size ten shoe. She does.'

'Oh shit,' said Flint. 'All right, I'll come down.' He got out of bed and began to dress.

In his cell Wilt stared at the ceiling. After so many hours of interrogation his mind still reverberated with questions. 'How did you kill her? Where did you put her? What did you do with the weapon?' Meaningless questions continually reiterated in the hope they would finally break him. But Wilt hadn't broken. He had triumphed. For once in his life he knew himself to be invincibly right and everyone else totally wrong. Always before he had had doubts. Plasterers Two might after all have been right about there being too many wogs in the country. Perhaps hanging was a deterrent. Wilt didn't think so but he couldn't be absolutely certain. Only time would tell. But in the case of Regina *versus* Wilt *re* the murder of Mrs Wilt there could be no question of his guilt. He could be tried, found guilty and sentenced, it would make no difference. He was innocent of the charge and if he was sentenced to life imprisonment the very enormity of the injustice done to him would compound his knowledge of his own innocence. For the very first time in his life Wilt knew himself to be free. It was as though the original sin of being Henry Wilt, of 34 Parkview Avenue, Ipford, lecturer in Liberal Studies at the Fenland College of Arts and Technology, husband of Eva Wilt and father of none, had been lifted from him. All the encumbrances of possessions, habits, salary and status, all the social conformities, the niceties of estimation of himself and other people which he and Eva had acquired, all these had gone. Locked in his cell Wilt was free to be. And whatever happened he would never again succumb to the siren calls of self-effacement. After the flagrant contempt and fury of Inspector Flint, the abuse and the opprobrium heaped on him for a week, who needed approbation? They could stuff their opinions of him. Wilt would pursue his independent course and put to good use his evident gifts of inconsequence. Give him a life sentence and a progressive prison governor and Wilt would drive the man mad within a month by the sweet reasonableness of his refusal to obey the prison rules. Solitary confinement and a regime of bread and water, if such punishments still existed, would not deter him. Give him his freedom and he would apply his newfound talents at the Tech. He would sit happily on committees and reduce them to dissensions by his untiring adoption of whatever argument was most contrary to the consensus

opinion. The race was not to the swift after all, it was to the in-
defatigably inconsequential and life was random, anarchic and
chaotic. Rules were made to be broken and the man with the
grasshopper mind was one jump ahead of all the others. Having
established this new rule, Wilt turned on his side and tried to
sleep but sleep wouldn't come. He tried his other side with
equal lack of success. Thoughts, questions, irrelevant answers
and imaginary dialogues filled his mind. He tried counting
sheep but found himself thinking of Eva. Dear Eva, damnable
Eva, ebullient Eva and Eva irrepressibly enthusiastic. Like him
she had sought the Absolute, the Eternal Truth which would
save her the bother of ever having to think for herself again.
She had sought it in Pottery, in Transcendental Meditation, in
Judo, on trampolines and most incongruously of all in Oriental
Dance. Finally she had tried to find it in sexual emancipation,
Women's Lib and the Sacrament of the Orgasm in which she
could forever lose herself. Which, come to think of it, was what
she appeared to have done. And taken the bloody Pringsheims
with her. Well she would certainly have some explaining to do
when and if she ever returned. Wilt smiled to himself at the
thought of what she would say when she discovered what her
latest infatuation with the Infinite had led to. He'd see to it
that she had cause to regret it to her dying day.

On the floor of the sitting-room at the Vicarage Eva Wilt
struggled with the growing conviction that her dying day was
already over and done with. Certainly everyone she came into
contact with seemed to think she was dead. The policeman she
had spoken to on the phone had seemed disinclined to believe her assertion that she was alive and at least relatively
well and had demanded proofs of her identity in the most dis-
concerting fashion. Eva had retreated stricken from the encounter with her confidence in her own continuing existence
seriously undermined and it had only needed the reaction of the
Rev St John Froude to her appearance in his house to complete
her misery. His frantic appeals to the Almighty to rescue the
soul of our dear departed, one Eva Wilt, deceased, from its
present shape and unendurable form had affected Eva pro-

foundly. She knelt on the carpet and sobbed while the Vicar stared at her over his glasses, shut his eyes, lifted up a shaky voice in prayer, opened his eyes, shuddered and generally behaved in a manner calculated to cause gloom and despondency in the putative corpse and when, in a last desperate attempt to get Eva Wilt, deceased, to take her proper place in the heavenly choir he cut short a prayer about 'Man that is born of Woman hath but a short time to live and is full of misery' and struck up 'Abide with me' with many a semi-quaver, Eva abandoned all attempt at self-control and wailed 'Fast falls the eventide' most affectingly. By the time they had got to 'I need thy presence every passing hour' the Rev St John Froude was of an entirely contrary opinion. He staggered from the room and took sanctuary in his study. Behind him Eva Wilt, espousing her new role as deceased with all the enthusiasm she had formerly bestowed on trampolines, judo and pottery, demanded to know where death's sting was and where, grave, thy victory. 'As if I bloody knew,' muttered the Vicar and reached for the whisky bottle only to find that it too was empty. He sat down and put his hands over his ears to shut out the dreadful noise. On the whole 'Abide with me' was the last hymn he should have chosen. He'd have been better off with 'There is a green hill far away'. It was less open to misinterpretation.

When at last the hymn ended he sat relishing the silence and was about to investigate the possibility that there was another bottle in the larder when there was a knock on the door and Eva entered.

'Oh Father I have sinned,' she shrieked, doing her level best to wail and gnash her teeth at the same time. The Rev St John Froude gripped the arms of his chair and tried to swallow. It was not easy. Then overcoming the reasonable fear that delirium tremens had come all too suddenly he managed to speak. 'Rise, my child,' he gasped as Eva writhed on the rug before him, 'I will hear your confession.'

20

Inspector Flint switched the tape recorder off and looked at Wilt.

'Well?'

'Well what?' said Wilt.

'Is that her? Is that Mrs Wilt?'

Wilt nodded. 'I'm afraid so.'

'What do you mean you're afraid so? The damned woman is alive. You should be fucking grateful. Instead of that you sit there saying you're afraid so.'

Wilt sighed. 'I was just thinking what an abyss there is between the person as we remember and imagine them and the reality of what they are. I was beginning to have fond memories of her and now . . .'

'You ever been to Waterswick?'

Wilt shook his head. 'Never.'

'Know the Vicar there?'

'Didn't even know there was a vicar there.'

'And you wouldn't know how she got there?'

'You heard her,' said Wilt. 'She said she'd been on a boat.'

'And you wouldn't know anyone with a boat, would you?'

'People in my circle don't have boats, Inspector. Maybe the Pringsheims have a boat.'

Inspector Flint considered the possibility and rejected it. They had checked the boatyards out and the Pringsheims didn't have a boat and hadn't hired one either.

On the other hand the possibility that he had been the victim of some gigantic hoax, a deliberate and involved scheme to make him look an idiot, was beginning to take shape in his mind. At the instigation of this infernal Wilt he had ordered the exhumation of an inflatable doll and had been photographed staring lividly at it at the very moment it changed sex. He had instituted a round-up of pork pies unprecedented in the history of the country. He wouldn't be at all surprised if Sweetbreads instituted legal proceedings for the damage done to their previously unspotted reputation. And finally he had held an apparently innocent man for questioning for a week and would doubtless be held responsible for the delay and additional cost in building the new Administration block at the Tech. There were, in all probability, other appalling consequences to be considered, but that was enough to be going on with. And he had nobody to blame but himself. Or Wilt. He looked at Wilt venomously.

Wilt smiled. 'I know what you're thinking,' he said.

'You don't,' said the Inspector. 'You've no idea.'

'That we are all the creatures of circumstance, that things are never what they seem, that there's more to this than meets ...'

'We'll see about that,' said the Inspector.

Wilt got up. 'I don't suppose you'll want me for anything else,' he said. 'I'll be getting along home.'

'You'll be doing no such thing. You're coming with us to pick up Mrs Wilt.'

They went out into the courtyard and got into a police car. As they drove through the suburbs, past the filling stations and factories and out across the fens Wilt shrank into the back seat of the car and felt the sense of freedom he had enjoyed in the Police Station evaporate. And with every mile it dwindled further and the harsh reality of choice, of having to earn a living, of boredom and the endless petty arguments with Eva, of bridge on Saturday nights with the Mottrams and drives on Sundays with Eva, reasserted itself. Beside him, sunk in sullen silence, Inspector Flint lost his symbolic appeal. No longer the mentor of Wilt's self-confidence, the foil to his inconsequentiality, he had become a fellow sufferer in the business of living, almost a mirror-image of Wilt's own nonentity. And ahead, across this flat bleak landscape with its black earth and cumulus skies, lay Eva and a lifetime of attempted explanations and counter-accusations. For a moment Wilt considered shouting 'Stop the car. I want to get out', but the moment passed. Whatever the future held he would learn to live with it. He had not discovered the paradoxical nature of freedom only to succumb once more to the servitude of Parkview Avenue, the

214

Tech and Eva's trivial enthusiasms. He was Wilt, the man with the grasshopper mind.

Eva was drunk. The Rev St John Froude's automatic reaction to her appalling confession had been to turn from whisky to 150% Polish spirit which he kept for emergencies and Eva, in between agonies of repentance and the outpourings of lurid sins, had wet her whistle with the stuff. Encouraged by its effect, by the petrified benevolence of the Vicar's smile and by the growing conviction that if she was dead eternal life demanded an act of absolute contrition while if she wasn't it allowed her to avoid the embarrassment of explaining what precisely she was doing naked in someone else's house, Eva confessed her sins with an enthusiasm that matched her deepest needs. This was what she had sought in judo and pottery and Oriental dance, an orgiastic expiation of her guilt. She confessed sins she had committed and sins she hadn't, sins that had occurred to her and sins she had forgotten. She had betrayed Henry, she had wished him dead, she had lusted after other men, she was an adulterated woman, she was a lesbian, she was a nymphomaniac. And interspersed with these sins of the flesh there were sins of omission. Eva left nothing out. Henry's cold suppers, his lonely walks with the dog, her lack of appreciation for all he had done for her, her failure to be a good wife, her obsession with Harpic ... everything poured out. In his chair the Rev St John Froude sat nodding incessantly like a toy dog in the back window of a car, raising his head to stare at her when she confessed to being a nymphomaniac and dropping it abruptly at the mention of Harpic, and all the time desperately trying to understand what had brought a fat naked – the shroud kept falling off her – lady, no definitely not lady, woman to his house with all the symptoms of religious mania upon her.

'My child, is that all?' he muttered when Eva finally exhausted her repertoire.

'Yes, Father,' sobbed Eva.

'Thank God,' said the Rev St John Froude fervently and wondered what to do next. If half the things he had heard were true he was in the presence of a sinner so depraved as to make the ex-Archdeacon of Ongar a positive saint. On the other hand there were incongruities about her sins that made him hesitate before granting absolution. A confession full of false-hoods was no sign of true repentance.

'I take it that you are married,' he said doubtfully, 'and that Henry is your lawful wedded husband?'

'Yes,' said Eva. 'Dear Henry.'

Poor sod, thought the Vicar but he was too tactful to say so. 'And you have left him?'

'Yes.'

'For another man?'

Eva shook her head. 'To teach him a lesson,' she said with sudden belligerence.

'A lesson?' said the Vicar, trying frantically to imagine what sort of lesson the wretched Mr Wilt had learnt from her absence. 'You did say a lesson?'

'Yes,' said Eva, 'I wanted him to learn that he couldn't get along without me.'

The Rev St John Froude sipped his drink thoughtfully. If even a quarter of her confession was to be believed her husband must be finding getting along without her quite delightful. 'And now you want to go back to him?'

'Yes,' said Eva.

'But he won't have you?'

'He can't. The police have got him.'

'The police?' said the Vicar. 'And may one ask what the police have got him for?'

'They say he's murdered me,' said Eva.

The Rev St John Froude eyed her with new alarm. He knew now that Mrs Wilt was out of her mind. He glanced round for something to use as a weapon should the need arise and finding nothing better to choose from than a plaster bust of the poet Dante and the bottle of Polish spirit, picked up the latter by its neck. Eva held her glass out.

'Oh you are awful,' she said. 'You're getting me tiddly.'

'Quite,' said the Vicar and put the bottle down again hastily. It was bad enough being alone in the house with a

216

large, drunk, semi-naked woman who imagined that her husband had murdered her and who confessed to sins he had previously only read about without her jumping to the conclusion that he was deliberately trying to make her drunk. The Rev St John Froude had no desire to figure prominently in next Sunday's *News of the World*.

'You were saying that your husband murdered ...' He stopped. That seemed an unprofitable subject to pursue.

'How could he have murdered me?' asked Eva. 'I'm here in the flesh, aren't I?'

'Definitely,' said the Vicar. 'Most definitely.'

'Well then,' said Eva. 'And anyway Henry couldn't murder anyone. He wouldn't know how. He can't even change a fuse in a plug. I have to do everything like that in the house.' She stared at the Vicar balefully. 'Are you married?'

'No,' said the Rev St John Froude, wishing to hell that he was.

'What do you know about life if you aren't married?' asked Eva truculently. The Polish spirit was getting to her now and with it there came a terrible sense of grievance. 'Men. What good are men? They can't even keep a house tidy. Look at this room. I ask you.' She waved her arms to emphasize the point and the dustcover dropped. 'Just look at it.' But the Rev St John Froude had no eyes for the room. What he could see of Eva was enough to convince him that his life was in danger. He bounded from the chair, trod heavily on an occasional table, overturned the wastepaper basket and threw himself through the door into the hall. As he stumbled away in search of sanctuary the front door bell rang. The Rev St John Froude opened it and stared into Inspector Flint's face.

'Thank God, you've come,' he gasped, 'she's in there.'

The Inspector and two uniformed constables went across the hall. Wilt followed uneasily. This was the moment he had been dreading. In the event it was better than he had expected. Not so for Inspector Flint. He entered the study and found himself confronted by a large naked woman.

'Mrs Wilt ...' he began but Eva was staring at the two uniformed constables.

'Where's my Henry?' Eva shouted. 'You've got my Henry.' She hurled herself forward. Unwisely the Inspector attempted to restrain her.

'Mrs Wilt, if you'll just ...' A blow on the side of his head ended the sentence.

'Keep your hands off me,' yelled Eva, and putting her knowledge of Judo to good use hurled him to the floor. She was about to repeat the performance with the constables when Wilt thrust himself forward.

'Here I am, dear,' he said. Eva stopped in her tracks. For a moment she quivered and, seen from Inspector Flint's viewpoint, appeared to be about to melt. 'Oh Henry,' she said, 'what have they been doing to you?'

'Nothing at all, dear,' said Wilt. 'Now get your clothes on. We're going home.' Eva looked down at herself, shuddered and allowed him to lead her out of the room.

Slowly and wearily Inspector Flint got to his feet. He knew now why Wilt had put that bloody doll down the hole and why he had sat so confidently through days and nights of interrogation. After twelve years of marriage to Eva Wilt the urge to commit homicide if only by proxy would be overwhelming. And as for Wilt's ability to stand up to cross-examination ... it was self-evident. But the Inspector knew too that he would never be able to explain it to anyone else. There were mysteries of human relationships that defied analysis. And Wilt had stood there calmly and told her to get her clothes on. With a grudging sense of admiration Flint went out into the hall. The little sod had guts, whatever else you could say about him.

They drove back to Parkview Avenue in silence. In the back seat Eva, wrapped in a blanket, slept with her head lolling on Wilt's shoulder. Beside her Henry Wilt sat proudly. A woman who could silence Inspector Flint with one swift blow to the head was worth her weight in gold and besides that scene in the study had given him the weapon he needed. Naked and drunk in a vicar's study ... There would be no questions now about why he had put that doll down the hole. No accusations, no recriminations. The entire episode would be relegated to the best forgotten. And with it would go all doubts about his virility or his ability to get on in the world. It was checkmate. For a moment Wilt almost lapsed into sentimentality and thought of love before recalling just how dangerous a topic that was. He would be better off sticking to indifference and undisclosed affection. 'Let sleeping dogs lie,' he muttered.

It was an opinion shared by the Pringsheims. As they were helped from the cruiser to a police launch, as they climbed ashore, as they explained to a sceptical Inspector Flint how they had come to be marooned for a week in Eel Stretch in a boat that belonged to someone else, they were strangely uncommunicative. No they didn't know how the door of the bathroom had been bust down. Well maybe there had been an accident. They had been too drunk to remember. A doll? What doll? Grass? You mean marijuana? They had no idea. In their house?

Inspector Flint let them go finally. 'I'll be seeing you again when the charges have been properly formulated,' he said grimly. The Pringsheims left for Rossiter Grove to pack. They flew out of Heathrow next morning.

21

The Principal sat behind his desk and regarded Wilt incredulously. 'Promotion?' he said. 'Did I hear you mention the word "promotion"?'

'You did,' said Wilt. 'And what is more you also heard "Head of Liberal Studies" too.'

'After all you've done? You mean to say you have the nerve to come in here and demand to be made Head of Liberal Studies?'

'Yes,' said Wilt.

The Principal struggled to find words to match his feelings. It wasn't easy. In front of him sat the man who was responsible for the series of disasters that had put an end to his fondest hopes. The Tech would never be a Poly now. The Joint Honours degree's rejection had seen to that. And then there was the adverse publicity, the cut in the budget, his battles with the Education Committee, the humiliation of being heralded as the Principal of Dollfuckers Hall . . .

'You're fired!' he shouted.

Wilt smiled. 'I think not,' he said. 'Here are my terms . . .'

'Your what?'

'Terms,' said Wilt. 'In return for my appointment as Head of Liberal Studies, I shall not institute proceedings against you for unfair dismissal with all the attendant publicity that would entail. I shall withdraw my case against the police for unlawful arrest. The contract I have here with the *Sunday Post* for a series of articles on the true nature of Liberal Studies – I intend to call them Exposure to Barbarism – will remain unsigned. I will cancel the lectures I had promised to give for the Sex Education Centre. I will not appear on *Panorama* next Monday. In short I will abjure the pleasures and rewards of public exposure . . .'

The Principal raised a shaky hand. 'Enough,' he said, 'I'll see what I can do.'

Wilt got to his feet. 'Let me know your answer by lunchtime,' he said. 'I'll be in my office.'

'Your office?' said the Principal.

'It used to belong to Mr Morris,' said Wilt and closed the door. Behind him the Principal picked up the phone. There had been no mistaking the seriousness of Wilt's threats. He would have to hurry.

Wilt strolled down the corridor to the Liberal Studies Department and stood looking at the books on the shelves. There were changes he had in mind. *The Lord of the Flies* would go and with it *Shane, Women in Love,* Orwell's *Essays* and *Catcher in the Rye,* all those symptoms of intellectual condescension, those dangled worms of sensibility. In future Gasfitters One and Meat Two would learn the how of things not why. How to read and write. How to make beer. How to fiddle their income tax returns. How to cope with the police when arrested. How to make an incompatible marriage work. Wilt would give the last two lessons himself. There would be objections from the staff, even threats of resignation, but it would make no difference. He might well accept several resignations from those who persisted in opposing his ideas. After all you didn't require a degree in English literature to teach Gasfitters the how of anything. Come to think of it, they had taught him more than they had learnt from him. Much more. He went into Mr Morris's empty office and sat down at the desk and composed a memorandum to Liberal Studies Staff. It was headed Notes on a System of Self-Teaching for Day Release Classes. He had just written 'non-hierarchical' for the fifth time when the phone rang. It was the Principal.

'Thank you,' said the new Head of Liberal Studies.

Eva Wilt walked gaily up Parkview Avenue from the doctor's office. She had made breakfast for Henry and Hoovered the front room and polished the hall and cleaned the windows and Harpicked the loo and been round to the Harmony Community Centre and helped with Xeroxing an appeal for a new play group and done the shopping and paid the milkman and been to the doctor to ask if there was any point in taking a course of fertility drugs and there was. 'Of course we'll have to do tests,' the doctor had told her, 'but there's no reason to think they'd prove negative. The only danger is that you might have sextuplets.' It wasn't a danger to Eva. It was what she had always wanted, a house full of children. And all at once. Henry would be pleased. And so the sun shone brighter, the sky was bluer, the flowers in the gardens were rosier and even Parkview Avenue itself seemed to have taken on a new and brighter aspect. It was one of Eva Wilt's better days.

About the Author

Tom Sharpe was born in 1928 and educated at Lancing College and Pembroke College, Cambridge. He did his National Service in the Marines before going to South Africa in 1951, where he did social work for the Non-European Affairs Department and taught. He had a photographic studio in Pietermaritzburg from 1957 until 1961, when he was deported. From 1963 to 1972, he was a lecturer in History at the Cambridge College of Arts and Technology. He is married and lives in Dorset. Tom Sharpe's other books include *Riotous Assembly, Indecent Exposure, Porterhouse Blue, Blott on the Landscape, The Great Pursuit, The Throwback, The Wilt Alternative, Ancestral Vices,* and *Vintage Stuff.*